HOW OLD DAN BECAME A TREE

Yang Zhengguang was born in Qian County, Shaanxi, in 1957. After graduating from Shandong University in 1982 with a degree in Chinese literature, he moved to the city of Tianjin to be part of the Chinese People's Political Consultative Conference, an advisory body promoting multi-party cooperation. Four years later, he moved to a small village in northern Shaanxi to write poetry.

He then became a successful scriptwriter, most notably adapting the classic Chinese epic *The Outlaws of the Marsh* to great acclaim. Yang also founded and served as CEO of the Chang'an Film & Television Production Company, and became chairman of the Shenzhen Association of Literature and Art.

This book is part of *Shaanxi Stories*, a series of translated works by acclaimed authors from the Shaanxi province of China, produced by Valley Press in collaboration with Northwest University, Xi'an. The series editors are Hu Zongfeng and Robin Gilbank. Books in the series so far include:

MOUNTAIN STORIES, YE GUANGQIN
HOW OLD DAN BECAME A TREE, YANG ZHENGGUANG
THE EARTHEN GATE, JIA PINGWA

How Old Dan Became a Tree

Yang Zhengguang

Valley Press

First published in 2018 by Valley Press
Woodend, The Crescent, Scarborough, YO11 2PW
www.valleypressuk.com

First edition, first printing (August 2017)

ISBN 978-1-908853-96-7
Cat. no. VP0113

Copyright © Yang Zhengguang 2018

The right of Yang Zhengguang to be identified as the
author of this work has been asserted in accordance with
the Copyright, Designs and Patents Act 1988.

All rights reserved. No part of this publication may be
reproduced, stored in or introduced into a retrieval system,
or transmitted in any form, by any means (electronic,
mechanical, photocopying, recording or otherwise) without
prior written permission from the rights holders.

A CIP record for this book is available from the British Library.

Cover design by Jamie McGarry. Text design by Harriet Clifford.
Cover photograph by The Tenth Dragon.

Printed and bound in Great Britain by
TJ International Ltd, Padstow, Cornwall.

Contents

Blue Fish — 7
How Old Dan Became a Tree — 20
The Red Heat — 82
The Billy Goat Pops In — 90
Buying Wives — 114
The Road from Sandy Terrace Town — 181
Dark Scenery — 188

Notes on the Text — 251
Acknowledgements — 254

Blue Fish

I.

BLUE FISH WAS not a fish but a girl named Fish. A woman of more than thirty, neither beautiful nor ugly, she sliced sweet potatoes in the courtyard. Those sliced pieces of sweet potato oozed out an abundance of juice, which adhered to her fingers like a thick layer of cream. When licked at by the tongue, as Blue Fish did, one could savour a kind of spongy stickiness. From time to time she would extend her tongue and dab at her fingers. She would then retract her tongue and suck her lips, cherishing that sweetness. In this manner, nothing would go to waste. That action also allowed her to take check of her monotonous mood as she performed this chore. After slicing the potatoes, she would boil them in water and eat them.

At that time, folks took this as a staple. Following the movement of 'Smelting Iron to Make Steel' and 'Taking Rations Together Collectively' there came the period of hard famine. For several years there were poor harvests, with folks having only sweet potatoes to eat. A lot of them vomited sour bile and became lean. They grew so pinched that their faces altered and took on a ghostly appearance. Anyhow, Blue Fish was different from the rest. She too coughed up bile, but never grew thin. She was the type of woman who could remain plump even if she were only to subsist on cold water. If you were able to see how Blue Fish licked her fingers and sucked her lips you would not be surprised to know that she might remain plump on cold water alone. She sucked noisily as though she was sucking something lovely. When her saliva combined with the sweet juice and slid down her throat, a naïve and innocent smile would blossom upon her face. She would appear fulfilled. That look of fulfillment was to last her whole life long. You could only witness such fulfillment in a baby which has sucked its mama's teat.

Blue Fish was just this type of woman.

Pup, pup. Blue Fish sucked her fingers twice. This time she didn't proceed to cut the sweet potatoes straightaway. She heard footsteps outside the door. *Tramp, tramp.* She knew that it was her husband Gallant Ren. With his cotton shoes half-on and his crossed hands tucked into his sleeves, Gallant Ren entered through the gate. He leant against the corner of the wall, peering at Blue Fish with something heavy weighing upon his heart. Some hard nut was vexing him.

"Deadly sweet, deadly sweet," Blue Fish said to her man. She was referring to the white juice on her fingers. "If you don't believe me, take a suck." She waved her five digits. Gallant Ren looked at Blue Fish's hand but remained silent. Blue Fish thought that he wanted to suck though felt embarrassed. "If you want it, just suck. There is nobody around to watch," she said. "What would it matter if someone did see? You are sucking my fingers not my titty." A sort of warm feeling arose within Blue Fish's heart. "Come over." She waved her hand to her man. "Come over." Once again she waved her hand while staring fixedly at him. Gallant Ren's brow un-creased itself, a kind of ecstatic hue flashing from his eyes. She was quite familiar with this kind of expression on her man. When he wanted to do something with her, such a hue would become evident in his irises. It was this hue that transfixed her and compelled her to weather a poor, hard life together with him. Much more than that, it suffused this poor life with flavour and colour. Gallant Ren left the corner of the wall and walked towards her. The warm fantasy in Blue Fish's heart was stirred up in an instant. The stirring sensation migrated to her thighs and made the muscles in that region twitch. She thought that he might grab her up and tuck her under his arm, before planting her down on the *kang* inside the room. Silently he would always tuck her under his arm then throw her down on the *kang*. He would then go about tearing off her clothes until she was left stark naked. He would mount her like a horse, and ride her madly there. She adored his style. Gallant Ren walked silently towards her. Looking at him, she felt that her body was becoming as soft as a lump of dough. She had already forgotten about her hands. She had already forgotten that cream-like sweet potato juice was still all over her fingers.

Gallant Ren didn't tuck her under his arm. She soon learned that Gallant Ren had come not for her body, but for her hands. He grabbed her hands, turned them over and over, inspecting them for a long time. He then said, "Blue Fish, I've been sleeping with you on the same *kang* for years now. How could I not notice that you have such delicate hands?" Blue Fish was stunned for a while and then it dawned on her that her man was praising her hands. She withdrew them from her man's palms and turned one over and over, studying it for a while. She said, "Yeah, I'd never realised that until you told me just now." She laid down the cutting knife and raised her other hand to scrutinise.

"Really, they are like a backscratcher," Blue Fish commented.

In this way, both of them came to notice Blue Fish's hands were as neat as the claw of a backscratcher. A stream of burbling sounds came out of Gallant Ren's mouth. He muttered, "There it is, there it is. There's the way to sort out these motherfucking worries." Before Blue Fish was able to open her mouth, Gallant Ren had run out of the gate. *Tramp, tramp.* He only left behind a succession of treading sounds in the courtyard.

Taking merely a single breath, Gallant Ren raced into the office of the Village Committee. At that moment, the Village Head Washout Liu and 'Peering' Zhou, a cadre from the provincial government, were smoking sullenly. For these three months, while the Four Clean Ups Movement had been in operation, the village of Ren Family Fort had been unable to root out even one corrupt person. The community had lost face at both commune and county level. The prime suspect was the granary guard named Wangwang. Washout Liu was so aggravated that he scratched at his ankles. He hoped that he could prize open Wangwang's rangy jaw and thrust his eyeballs down the guy's throat so as to probe his heart. Washout Liu even went to Wangwang's grass-thatched shelter to implore him. He said, "Wangwang, you may more or less confess to something. There are corrupt people in every village all over the world. How could there be no one like that in our village? Is our village a white dung beetle that's fallen from the sky? How could you bear to let our village become so backwards and not march together with other villages in the commune and the county on the road towards socialism? How can you bear this? Don't you feel embarrassed?" Wangwang turned over the whites of his eyes and answered, "If you can't bear it, you should admit to something yourself. You are the Village Head. Don't you feel embarrassed?" Washout Liu's windpipe sounded like it had been choked up with cold water. He raised his head and gagged, spluttering, "Wangwang, you donkey-fucked so-and-so, you've hit on a home truth." Washout Liu told 'Peering' Zhou, "Wangwang's mouth is even tougher than pig's trotters. We should hang him up from a beam." 'Peering' Zhou parried, "No, the CCP is not the KMT. We should not beat and browbeat confessions out of people." "Wangwang is acting up simply because he can see through this," Washout Liu maintained. "Haven't you watched all the ancient operas on the stage? They always show torture being used to resolve legal cases." 'Peering' Zhou said, "I have seen these ancient plays, but once we start to rely on torture, the cases won't be just. That is called 'forced confession through torture.'" 'Peering' Zhou's name was not in actual fact Peering Zhou. He was a member of the government working party sent over to the village to supervise the rooting out of miscreants. Thus the villagers referred to him by that name. 'Peering' Zhou was a conscientious man. He said that if the people thought it over hard enough they would be sure to find a solution to the problem. Consequently, for several days and several nights meetings were convened to pool their collective wisdom. Their smoke-sore eyes started to resemble chicken's arseholes. Still, no solution was found. Wangwang still refused to confess. The Four Clean Ups movement at Ren Family Fort had ground to a halt. None of them thought about Blue Fish, the wife of the militia leader Gallant Ren, and her pair of hands.

"There it is. There it mother-fucking well is," Gallant Ren shouted while entering the office of the Village Committee. His lips quivered with excitement as if they were about to drop off.

Washout Liu and 'Peering' Zhou stretched their necks. Eyes-straightened, they waited for Gallant Ren to spit it out. However, Gallant Ren paused. He picked up a teacup from the stovetop and took a few sips of tea. He drank with extreme care. While drinking, he blew away the leaves that were floating on the surface of the water. Perhaps a small twig had found its way into his mouth, for from time to time he tried to push something as if chewing and sucking the taste from inside that twig. Washout Liu became impatient.

"Have you quite finished?" Washout Liu asked. "If you carry on chewing like that you'll chew the shit out of that tea."

A proud expression floated upon Gallant Ren's face. He began: "Village Head, you may have been drinking tea for years but you are still a novice at it. Haven't you heard, folks who don't know the art of tea call it 'drinking'; those who do call it 'chewing'?" "Put your mug down," Washout Liu ordered. "If you are holding back a fart please let it rip now. I don't want to listen to a little puff." Gallant Ren then spat out the twig he'd chewed in two and started to address the real business.

"My missus has hands like a backscratcher," he said.

Washout Liu and 'Peering' Zhou nearly choked to death.

"Go and fuck your ancestor," Washout Liu cursed. "I thought that you had hit upon some wonderful solution, but you are talking about your pussy's hands." 'Peering' Zhou was an educated man. His words were more literate. "Comrade Gallant Ren," 'Peering' Zhou said. "You've made the Four Clean Ups movement very pornographic."

"Pornographic? I don't get you. I've only heard about coquettishness," replied Gallant Ren.

"Oh, Oh," 'Peering' Zhou exclaimed. "Pornographic and coquettish are almost the same thing. Can't we make the Four Clean Ups movement succeed by being coquettish?"

"Of course, certainly," Gallant Ren said. "We can't beat people and we can't string 'em up, but we can tickle them."

This made Washout Liu and 'Peering' Zhou blink. They did not know what Gallant Ren was driving at.

"Beating people and stringing them up is against the law, but tickling them and making them laugh is not. We can tickle the truth out. People may resist a beating but they can't stand being tickled and forced to laugh, don't you agree? People can hold back their tears, but laughs will always find a way out, don't you agree? If you don't agree with this, I definitely do." As he spoke these words Gallant Ren cast a serious glance at Washout Liu and 'Peering' Zhou.

Washout Liu and 'Peering' Zhou were now bewildered. They gazed at Gallant Ren for a long time. They then turned around and looked at each other. Suddenly, Gallant Ren's meaning had sunk in. They couldn't help but release the laughter from their throats. After that, they opened their mouths and the guffaws were let out in a stream. They must have imagined a particular situation and laughed themselves until they doubled over. Their faces were flushed red, their bellies were worn out, and their intestines knotted up.

"Hahaha. Gallant Ren, you are such a bastard bear," Washout Liu said with tearful eyes.

"Oh, hahaha, Comrade Gallant Ren." 'Peering' Zhou pinched one of the buttons on his sleeve. He was wearing a suit with three buttons on each sleeve.

They looked at Gallant Ren with fresh eyes. Such a thing

would always arise in a great era. That is to say, ordinary people are able to suddenly make others view them with fresh eyes and thereby cause great surprise.

They all thought that this was worth trying. They instantly summoned Blue Fish over. From top to toe Blue Fish seemed to exude the smell of sweet potatoes. She stretched out her hands which were drenched in sweet potato juice and displayed them before the eyes of Washout Liu and 'Peering' Zhou. Gallant Ren was quite right. This was truly a nimble pair of hands. They even felt confused as to how these could belong to a plump woman. Fat women's hands are normally like leavened dough, the fingers and wrists being stumpy and swollen. Fleshy creases encircle the wrists like coils of thread. Blue Fish's wrists and fingers were long and slender like onion shoots. When those five digits were laid out in a row and the knuckles bent a little they really did resemble a couple of backscratchers. No one's hands could be better adapted for tickling than Blue Fish's. One by one, they each shared their ideas with her and then the matter was fixed.

The tickling of Wangwang was scheduled for that evening. After supper, all of the villagers at Ren Family Fort were summoned to the courtyard of the Village Committee. A gas lamp hung from the eaves. Under its strong light were exposed the excited faces of the old and young and the fat and the lean. None of them were willing to skip this chance at finding excitement. Their bellies were full of sweet potato porridge.

Wangwang had been summoned in advance to the Village Committee. He still remained like a dead piece of cow hide. Washout Liu swallowed down a mouthful of sour water that had welled up from his stomach and said, "Wangwang, you still don't want to own up?" Wangwang kept his silence. Washout Liu asked, "Do you know Gallant Ren's wife?" "How can I not know her?" Wangwang replied. "That's good," Washout Liu said. "After a while, we will get her to tickle you." Wangwang felt that this was ridiculous.

"Kidding?" Wangwang asked.

Washout Liu said that there was no kidding. "You see, the courtyard is full of people. Let's go over there."

"I wouldn't be afraid even if we had to go up to the heavens." Wangwang was as stubborn as a bull.

Washout Liu said, "Let's leave talking about whether you are afraid or not until later. We should go out first." He pushed Wangwang out of the gate. In an instant, the courtyard fell silent. Only the sound of breath was audible.

"Blue Fish, Blue Fish." Washout Liu's head waved like a hawker's hand rattle.

Blue Fish strode out from the corner of the wall and stood in the glare of the gas lamp.

Washout Liu said, "Wangwang, you stand firm against the wall."

Wangwang stood firmly against the wall.

Washout Liu said, "Blue Fish, come over and do your business."

At this moment, Wangwang realised that it was real. He widened his eyes, watching Blue Fish as she walked in his direction. Blue Fish stopped. She stretched out her nimble pair of hands and waggled her fingers. Wangwang became frightened and filled with fear.

Wangwang said, "Blue Fish, you are a woman. Aren't you afraid that if you touch a man's body others will gossip about you?"

Blue Fish replied, "I have no other choice."

"You call me 'uncle.' Uncles should not fool around with their nephew's wives."

"Uncle, this isn't fooling around; this is my duty." With these words, Blue Fish's fingers made a move upon Wangwang's body. His body fell prey to a kind of strong itching. Wangwang leapt up with a shriek.

"Ok, ok. You win. Your uncle will kowtow to you. OK?"

Blue Fish's hands once again set about his body. Wangwang contorted his frame and jumped here and there.

"Haha, you win. Hehe, you are great!"

Blue Fish paused. She turned around and said to Washout Liu, "I cannot do it if he wriggles like this."

Washout Liu said, "Two guys should come over and pin him to the edge of the wall." Two young men came out from the group. They pulled Wangwang's arms taut. Wangwang was now erect against the edge of the wall, his tummy and armpits being left prone, with no shelter. Blue Fish's two hands easily went about their task in the manner of a duo of monsters. They pinched and grappled his every sensitive region.

"Heh-heh-heh-heh," Wangwang laughed as though it were necessary for taking in a breath. His neck pulsed into an arc with the rear of his head firmly planted against the wall.

"Oh, yuh, yuh, yuh," Wangwang tried his best to retract his tummy and his thighs trembled.

"Oh, ha ha ha," Wangwang's tummy suddenly stuck out and his broad, dirty teeth were exposed.

Blue Fish's hands continued as though catching a bunny.

In this fashion, Wangwang twisted like a dough stick. He laughed as perspiration covered his head. His eyes and eyebrows were distorted. Every inch of his flesh and every last one of his bones had been rendered soft. Later on, his laughter turned into a howl. "Awoah! Awoah!" He was howling so that the whites of his eyes were now bared. His appearance was far more distressed than if he had been weeping.

At the beginning, people found this spectacle fun. They laughed in unison with Wangwang. Now, they could not bring themselves to laugh out loud. The smiles on their faces were frozen, their eyes gazed straight at Wangwang, and they thought that a further bout or two would be sure to do him in.

The two young men who were pulling his arms released them.

"Oh, ha. I embezzled two skeps of wheat."

Wangwang said this as he was tumbling softly down.

Wangwang was as supple as a heap of mud.

The next day the villagers of Ren Family Fort beat drums and gongs. The first bulletin of glad tidings concerning the Four Clean Ups movement was sent to the commune.

II.

Later, Blue Fish went on to tickle several more people.

She found the act of tickling Washout Liu pretty much unbearable. She saw Washout Liu become withered like a frost-felled beet. He let out a sigh and called out "Blue Fish, my little sister." His words touched her heart.

"Little sister," Washout Liu gasped. "Tickle as much as you like. If I cannot bear it, I'll confess as well."

"You see what you have done. I've no other choice," Blue Fish commented. "If I didn't tickle anyone for a few days my hands would start to itch."

Blue Fish said this with sincerity.

"Yes, yes," Washout Liu gasped. "It's like smoking. Doing it more makes you into an addict."

Blue Fish tickled him. Washout Liu's resistance was gone. He became another victim of the Four Clean Ups movement.

Later on, it was time to tickle Gallant Ren. By that point, the Village Head had been replaced. The other village cadres were also rotated. Only Gallant Ren stayed in post as leader of the militia. Washout Liu wanted to seek revenge and started to whip up bother.

"Taking all these folks out for a stroll will tell us whether they are horses or mules," Washout Liu observed.

The new Village Head thought that his words sounded reasonable and said, "Let's take them out for a stroll."

Blue Fish was now forced to tickle her man, Gallant Ren. The night before, the two of them sat on the *kang* until midnight, their eyebrows knitted together into bundles.

"Tell me. What shall we do?" Blue Fish asked Gallant Ren.

"What is there to do? You are the one who will do the tickling. You tell me what to do," Gallant Ren said.

"Steamed dumplings are hollow, but steamed buns are solid."

"Don't you think that Wangwang and Washout Liu owned up to things they'd actually done? When they couldn't bear it any longer they started to spout crap."

"You shouldn't spout crap."

"If I can't bear it, I'll spout crap too."

"Try your best to hold out."

"That depends on your hands."

"Let's not sleep. I'll tickle you and you try to hold out," Blue Fish said. "Folks are afraid of being tickled because the hands are not familiar. You know these hands, so maybe you can put up with it."

Blue Fish allowed Gallant Ren to lie down on the *kang* and then attempted to tickle him. It was only now that they realised that although those hands were familiar, being caressed and being tickled were two different sensations. As soon as Blue Fish's fingers began to scratch over Gallant's body, he recoiled and bounced like a skittish bug. He laughed himself breathless. They tried and tried until daybreak was at hand and at last they sank into despair. They embraced each other and wept, shedding copious tears.

The tickling torture went ahead as planned. This time Blue Fish felt the best she had done since she started to tickle people. She thought that he would not be able to hold out come what may. In this case, he should have his fill of laughing. Anyhow, she had to tickle so she should have her fill of tickling. In that way, she would not have lived up to her reputation as a tickler. When they have no path to beat retreat, people must step forward fearlessly. Blue Fish did just that. She tickled with passion and force. Gallant Ren laughed until blood sprang out from his nostrils and eyes. The blood fell onto the back of Blue Fish's hands. She thought at first that it was just snivel but then felt that it was different. Snivel was never as warm as this. She raised her head only to discover that Gallant Ren's eyes and nose were bleeding. The substance was red and bright. Blue Fish was stunned. She had never believed that her man could laugh himself into such a state.

That day, the leader of the militia was replaced. Each of the newly-appointed village cadres fashioned a backscratcher for himself. They did not use them to alleviate itching. Every night they would hone their ability to resist ticklishness. They believed that it was possible to build up their stamina. Who knows if some day Blue Fish's hands would descend onto their bodies?

One year later, Blue Fish was again sitting in the courtyard slicing sweet potatoes. From time to time she would lick her fingers and suck her lips, savouring that sweet, spongy stickiness. Her man, Gallant Ren, squatted on the threshold of the door, watching as she cut. He didn't mount her anymore. It was not that he didn't want to. Rather, the moment that he caught sight of her hands he was struck impotent. He had no way to overcome this and just wanted to cry. He lamented, "Blue Fish, you put your hands underneath your body. I can't bear to look at them." Blue Fish also sank into sadness. She put her hands underneath her body then let Gallant Ren climb on top. Gallant Ren seemed capable now and he proceeded to mount. It was at this moment that Blue Fish lost control of her hands. As soon as she felt comfortable, she was seized with the urge to hold Gallant Ren. "Gallant, Gallant, I'm enjoying this to death." She couldn't help but grasp Gallant Ren's buttock. With a shrill scream, Gallant Ren bounded off her body. Panicked and feeling at a loss he glared at Blue Fish's hands. Blue Fish really wanted to chop her own hands off. For this reason, he was no longer able to mount her.

At this moment, Gallant Ren was watching Blue Fish slicing sweet potatoes. After he had watched her for a while, he stood up and walked towards her. He lifted up one of her hands.

"Let me have a look, let me have a look," Gallant Ren said.

Gallant Ren smiled at Blue Fish.

Suddenly, Gallant Ren took hold of the cutting knife and planted it down on Blue Fish's wrist. Blue Fish's body gave a spasm. Gallant Ren took hold of the other hand and hacked once again. He threw the two amputated hands onto the roof of the house. He then hauled up Blue Fish and went to the county hospital for emergency surgery.

In the years which followed, whenever the villagers of Ren Family Fort saw Blue Fish, she would be staring at a distant place somewhere on the road outside the village, her two handless arms dangling by her sides. They all knew how she missed Gallant Ren. He was in prison and people took pity on her even though they could not bring themselves to say hello.

That pair of hands remained on the rooftop.

How Old Dan Became a Tree

I.

OLD DAN WAS sitting under the eaves, his eyes as deep as a couple of black pills. He was watching the rain. The rain took on the appearance of a fine net, carefully and tightly-woven. It fell strand-by-strand from the dusky sky and pattered down onto the courtyard floor. This was no heavy downpour. From time to time, that net would become laddered with some of the cool droplets decking his face. A bright and sleek aura would radiate from that thin wet visage. Had this been in days past, he would not watch the rain so intently. He would have huddled himself beneath the quilt, either clutching his woman or mounting her to generate a succession of joy. On rainy days, masculine libido soars and feminine attraction blooms. That was his reasoning. Again and again, he passed on the wisdom of his experience to the men of Double-Ditch Village. Holding a woman during times of rain gives one the sensation of being submerged and grasping at a slippery fish. Whether others believed this or not, Old Dan did. "Of course," he added. "All these things happened more than fifteen years ago." Fifteen years ago, Old Dan was erecting the main hall of his house. In the course of the building work, a brand new tile happened to slide down from the rooftop and strike his missus on the head. The sharp edge and the pitch-dark hair of the woman were folded together into her skull. She died without making a sound, leaving only a puddle of blood on the ground. In that way, he became a widower.

Puh ... Old Dan spat skyward. His saliva sliced through the long, silken strands of rain and traced an arc in the air. With the sound of a pitter, it slopped down into the pool on the ground and spread into the shape of a radish flower. He spat without care.

His son, Big Dan, was also watching the rain, only with a different mood from his father. He was a thirty-year-old bachelor and bore an ungainly, ginger root-like head upon his stubby neck. He sat in the hall of the main building, his two legs outstretched and his big toes protruding from the tips of his shoes. He was observing the outside world with wonderment, clutching a raw iron coulter in one of his hands and a rough stone in the other.

Puh ... Big Dan spat out too. He gazed straight at the saliva, watching it flying forth, then landing and dispersing, before being drowned in the rainwater. After that, he turned around and looked at his dad. Their phlegm had landed in the same place – not a run of the mill occurrence. He wanted to see his father's reaction. His father was sitting with his side towards him, so that only one of his ears was visible. The old man was motionless and as solemn as a general. Big Dan felt his self-esteem had been greatly wounded. He wanted his father to say something. He had long wanted his father to say something to him.

"I really want to punch this plough-blade," he said abruptly.

Old Dan seemed not to have heard him. Big Dan's self-esteem was again greatly wounded.

Bam! He did in fact now punch the coulter. The coulter let out a short, harsh *pang!* His father was taken by surprise. He swiftly turned around his head. This time Big Dan was able to see his father's face. His pa said nothing and just peered back at him.

Bam! Another knock.

Big Dan met his father's eyes with a provocative expression on his face.

"Can't you stop knocking that?" asked Old Dan, finally opening his mouth.

"No," Big Dan said.

"If you want to knock that thing go out on the street and do it. Don't force me to hear it. I don't want to listen to it."

"I'll knock my plough-head and you can watch your rain. The water from the well doesn't interfere with the water in the river."

"Knock away. Carry on. If it pleases you just do it."

"Yes, it does please me." He knocked once and then again. He did this neither slowly, nor in a hurry. He gave the impression that he might persist in knocking forever. His head was thrust backwards and occasionally he shot a glance at his father from the corner of his eye.

Bam – bam – bam – bam –

At last Old Dan could bear this no longer.

"You are knocking the death knell!" Old Dan exclaimed.

"No, I'm knocking this plough-head!" Big Dan said.

"Is the plough-head meant to be knocked at by people? Is it a gong? Tell me."

"Is a dog a doorkeeper or is it meant to be killed for meat? You tell me."

"Your knocking is pushing me off my rocker."

"If I didn't knock I'd be off my rocker."

"Are you blaming me for not having a wife? How can you test your strength against mine?"

"I'm not testing our strengths. I'm just knocking this plough-head."

Big Dan felt all the muscles in his body suddenly become warm. He stood up, lifting up the coulter, and beat the stone against it rapidly. The coulter let out a series of short, shrill, raw iron sounds.

Bam – bam – bam – bam …

"You donkey-fucked sod, just knock away." Old Dan stood up too. "Can you knock out a wife for yourself?" He shook his sleeves and made ready to leave.

Big Dan became very anxious. He thought that he was knocking the coulter for his father's benefit. If his father went away, it would become tedious to go on knocking alone.

"Freeze!" he roared at his father.

Old Dan paused. He saw that Big Dan's two red eyes were staring at him like a wolf.

"I'm going to the cabbage patch," Old Dan said. "You just keep on with your knocking."

Old Dan departed, not turning around again. Looking at the shadow of his father's back, Big Dan's eyes seemed to ooze blood. He was dying to pinch his father by the neck and claw him back.

"Yes it does please me to knock –" he jumped up and roared in a falsetto voice.

The tone of the raw iron coulter was angry as well.

Old Dan had walked away from the entrance to the village. He saw that the clouds in the east were receding. He thought that when the rain stopped, his two *mu* of cabbage would shoot up like crazy. He didn't expect that he would run into his sworn-enemy, Zhao Zhen. He didn't even expect that all the things which would happen later on would stem from his encounter with Zhao Zhen.

II.

He heard the sound of someone treading through the slush, and then caught sight of Zhao Zhen.

All at once, the sky cleared. The sun resembled a round, red persimmon cake. The mountains stood in the distance, while autumn crops dotted the foreground. Old Dan watched over his two *mu* of cabbage, quiet as a dog. The cabbages were coming on rather well. One-by-one they squeezed their heads out of the soft, damp mud to form a white barrier that faced the high, lofty sky. The sunshine had awoken the energy they accumulated in the course of rainy days. Now and then they creaked as they flexed their bones and veins. Old Dan was fond of this sound. He was an old hand at growing cabbages. He never sowed too many, making do with just two *mu*, and they would always change hands for a decent price.

Pitter patter, pitter patter. Somebody was treading through the slush. The rains had just ceased, leaving water on the road.

It was Zhao Zhen. He was walking over to Old Dan with a girl in tow. She wasn't local. Zhao Zhen was a known human trafficker. Each time he went far away, he would return with a young woman. This time the girl he brought was named Huanhuan. Her home was in some deep corner of the northern mountains. Zhao Zhen stayed in her village for several days before darkening her threshold. He said, "Come with me and I shall find you a man. That way you'll be able to lead a good life." She then followed him. Zhao Zhen said, "In our village, we have food and drink aplenty. We're only in want of women."

She was on the young side, though not beautiful. She must have been not yet twenty. Her face was full of colour, having been tanned by the sun over a long period. When she went out of her door, she purposefully slipped a colourful handkerchief into her trouser pocket so that one corner was left hanging out. Viewing this from afar, it might have been mistaken for the vibrant tail feathers of a bird. She considered this pose was charming and lots of female villagers did likewise. The vibrant tail wagged up and down. Zhao Zhen told her that if someone accosted them on the road she should say that he was her aunt's husband. Huanhuan cooed, "Uncle, let's go." They walked on for two days and two nights. When they had covered half of the journey it began to rain. Huanhuan asked, "Uncle, should we carry on?" Zhao Zhen replied, "Yes, we must continue." As they waded through the slush, mud stuck to their shoes, becoming thicker and thicker. From time to time they had to shake their feet to kick off the mud. Occasionally the shoe would be kicked off together with the mud. They would shout and scream then hop over with bare feet to retrieve it. In this way, the journey was made less tedious. Zhao Zhen would intermittently make comments to Huanhuan along the lines of "Many girls in my village call me 'uncle.'"

"The cabbages are growing pretty well," Zhao Zhen said, smiling and standing behind Old Dan's posterior.

"Bugger off, this is none of your fucking business," was Old Dan's reply.

Old Dan never hid his loathing of Zhao Zhen. He would always tell others "I hate him. I can't stand the guy. You ask me why? There's no reason. Does everything in the world have to have its reason …? Why do people have to eat? You tell me. It is because they are hungry. Why do they become hungry? Can you give a clear explanation for that? No, you can't." Actually, his loathing for Zhao Zhen was longstanding. It began when his wife was struck dead by that tile. Suddenly he had nothing to keep him occupied, especially in the evening. On the spur of the moment, as he was lying on the *kang*, he struck upon the idea that everybody in their life should have an enemy. Otherwise there'd be no damn interest to be had. He thought that this idea was fantastic and was seized with excitement to the point that all of the flesh on his body prickled. For many days afterwards he would ponder over who to choose as his enemy as he lay on the *kang*, his flesh constantly atremble. One-by-one he combed through every last soul in Double-Ditch village in his brain. Following careful consideration, he selected that human trafficker Zhao Zhen. By this means, Zhao Zhen became his personal enemy. He willed that something unfortunate would happen to him; that he might stumble over into a wagon rut and break the odd limb, but not die. Let him drag a lame leg behind him. How should you feel upon glimpsing your personal enemy dragging his lame leg along? Each time, however, Zhao Zhen returned to Double-Ditch village safe and sound and appeared to relish a very good life. Zhao Zhen, as a matter of fact, experienced great luck in everything to which he set himself. What is more, he grew better and better off. Each time he came back with a woman he would garner a tidy profit. Old Dan was never sure when Zhao Zhen would come to be afflicted by bad luck. That uncertainty made him hate him all the more. It may sound strange for a person to hate someone else without any reason, but to Old

Dan it was not strange at all.

"Old Dan, can't you try to be a little friendlier to me?" Zhao Zhen's eyes were upon the back of Old Dan's head. "Haven't seen you in days. Now I'm greeting you in a friendly way. You see. You just told me to 'bugger off.'"

"I've nothing to say to you," Old Dan answered.

Before Old Dan was able to spout more malicious words, he heard the sound of a woman. It was Huanhuan.

"Uncle, let's go," Huanhuan said.

Old Dan turned around. His two pill-like eyes probed her from top to toe. Then his gaze became fixed upon Zhao Zhen's face.

"You donkey-fucked sod! You've brought over fresh goods," he said.

"Her name is Huanhuan," Zhao Zhen told him.

"Huanhuan? This name is weird," Old Dan mused. Somehow his tone was more level.

"What do you think? Should I give her to Big Dan?" Zhao Zhen asked.

Old Dan's eyes straightened. He had never thought that his personal enemy could spit out words like these. He thought of the situation where Big Dan banged the old plough-head and lost himself.

"You donkey-fucked sod! You are kidding me." It took great courage for him to muster up this sentence.

"I'm not joking around. Unlike you, I don't think everyone in this world is black-hearted," Zhao Zhen commented.

Old Dan could not tell from Zhao Zhen's face whether this was true or false.

"Want her? If you don't, I'll talk to others. The bachelors in our village are shooting up one-by-one like new crops," Zhao Zhen said.

"Uncle let's go," Huanhuan begged. She had become a touch embarrassed.

"You think it over. There is just this one woman on offer and you've given her the once over. If you are interested, drop by at my home."

Pitter patter, pitter patter, pitter patter. Zhao Zen led Huanhuan away.

Old Dan stared on until the pair turned into the village. He suddenly raised a fist and pounded his thigh: "You donkey-fucked sod! Why should I not want her?"

He ran wildly towards the village, stumbling over a number of times on the way. When he reached home, his body was covered with mud. He saw that Big Dan was sleeping against the wall. The iron coulter had been smashed into fragments and scattered on the ground in the hallway. He didn't wake Big Dan up. He paced back and forth over the shards of iron. Then he raised his head and bellowed loudly in the direction of Zhao Zhen's home: "You donkey-fucked sod! Why should I not want her?"

Big Dan was roused by his dad's coarse throat. He saw that his body was awash with mud and his face was red all over. The two veins on his neck had swollen up. Although his roar had penetrated the wall, his mouth was still quivering. He thought that his father was cursing him.

"I was asleep. I wasn't doing you any harm," he told his father.

Old Dan said, "Get up and cook." Big Dan replied, "Ok, I'll cook something." But there was nothing good to eat and they had to heat up leftovers." Old Dan agreed that leftovers were fine, so the two made a meal from leftovers and then went to sleep. Old Dan did not tell his son about Zhao Zhen and Huanhuan. He had the inkling that this was not a dead cert. The next day his was woken by the shrill, loud burst of firecrackers.

III.

That night Zhao Zhen returned home. His wife was so elated that she went into premature labour. She rolled about the *kang*, screaming in agony for half the night. Finally she squeezed out vast quantities of amniotic fluid together with a pale, chubby boy. In his life Zhao Zhen lacked nothing save for an heir to inherit his blood. He had tried various means – going to the temple to pray, consuming various herbs and medicines, giving her one during her period, trying alternative lovemaking positions, even staying with his wife on the *kang* for more than a dozen days without rising – but he was frustrated with the lack of any result. His wife's belly never became swollen. He wished that he could pluck out a lump of flesh from his wife's body and fashion a child by himself. Sometimes he would stroke his wife's belly and beg piteously, "Please bear me a son and I'll respect you as much as my own grandpa." Sometimes he would grit his teeth and pinch his wife's thigh, causing her to meow like a cat. He said, "Don't cry out. If you bear me a son I'll wait on you like I wait on my ma." Sometimes he would make his wife as soft as mud. He insisted that he didn't believe himself incapable of producing a son. This struggle went on for years, and at last he had succeeded. He nearly fell faint. He was as excited as a rooster and could find no way to express his joy. He leaned his head against the cupboard and wept loudly: "Grandpa! Oh, my grandpa!" He then bounded out into the courtyard and shouted wildly: "Fetch the yellow wine!" Someone came out to run the errand. "Buy firecrackers! Buy a few lengths of them!" Again someone appeared to run that errand. "Mill some wheat flour! Mill 150 pounds of it! I'll treat all the villagers to spicy meatball soup!" Early the next morning, the human trafficker Zhao Zhen personally warmed the first bowl of yellow wine for his wife. Three lengths of firecrackers were let off simultaneously.

The news of him gaining a son in his fifties spread all over Double-Ditch Village. In the afternoon, the spicy meatball soup was ready. More than one hundred villagers, old and young, male and female, stood in line grasping their bowls and chopsticks in front of the cauldron that had been set up outside his home. By their very nature, Double-Ditch villagers were fond of free meals. Every last one of them took the attitude that a free meal must equal a delicious meal. Furthermore, to eat a person's meal was to show face to the host. Soon all of the streets were filled with the sound of soup being drunk. Zhao Zhen donned new clothes and a skullcap. From time to time, he would walk out of the door, his face flush with pride as if he had been daubed with fresh oil paint. He clenched his hands together before him and intoned to the people, "Enjoy your food. My wife is weak and needs my attention." After that he went inside through the big gate.

Zhao Zhen's mastiff opened its eyes wide and barked at all the people who were eating. Someone said, "You see that dog. He's not happy." Another person said, "Go and bark at your mother's leg. Your host is offering soup. It's none of your business."

Old Dan and Big Dan took turns to have their bowl of soup. They squatted down to eat behind an earthen pump. Zhao Zhen now had a son. This made Old Dan's heart ache again. Even so, he was loath to refuse the food. A free meal can't do any harm. At least this saved him the trouble of having to cook for himself.

"He is as proud as a bear!" Old Dan remarked. He had already polished off one bowl. "Wait for me. I'll go and get another helping. I want to have a word with you. That donkey-fucked bastard should have offered steamed buns as well. They go well with spicy meatball soup." With those words he went after a second bowl. He felt that it was the right time to fill Big Dan in on that business.

"Big Dan, to tell you the truth, Zhao Zhen has brought back another woman."

Big Dan stopped eating and stared at his dad.

"He asked me whether I wanted her for you."

"What did you say?" Big Dan's heart was astir.

"Why wouldn't I want her? But he happens to be my personal enemy," Old Dan went on. "If we accept a favour from our enemy, our ancestors will not rest soundly in their graves."

"He hasn't offended our ancestors," Big Dan reminded him. "He has offended me!"

"I do want her. You've never had the intention of finding me a wife."

"Bollocks!"

"Hmm."

"Let me think it over again. This means making a deal with our enemy."

"I will kowtow to him if he finds me a wife," Big Dan said. "There is nothing to brood over. If you want to brood just carry on."

Big Dan went away, his bowl in hand. On the turning of the street, Big Dan raised his empty bowl high up into the air and threw it down hard. *Pang!* The bowl smashed into smithereens.

Old Dan blinked and his neck was frozen straight for a long while.

This really was a very serious matter. Over the course of just a few days Old Dan became wizened. Big Dan no longer had a coulter to knock. Thus, he propped himself against the wall and hummed and hawed. When he grew tired of this, he would wrap his arms around his head and sleep. He insisted that he didn't want to cook. He'd been cooking for a dozen years and enough was enough. Whoever wanted to cook could get on with it. Cooking is a woman's business. Old Dan maintained that he was his father and he oughtn't to speak to him in such a manner. Big Dan replied that he was his son and should not have his future ruined for him.

Old Dan exclaimed, "You see, you are just like a dead pig now. I really want to give you a kick."

Big Dan retorted, "A dead pig is not afraid of boiling water. Should it be afraid of being kicked? Just kick away."

Later on, Old Dan was at last able to figure it out. The current was streaming by his threshold, so why not ladle some of it up? Zhao Zhen was contented these days, so he might give him a knockdown rate. In this way, he came to figure out the business. That evening, he walked to Zhao Zhen's home, his footsteps pattering along at an inimitable pace that was all too familiar to his fellow villagers.

"Hi," he shouted. "Tie up the dog!"

"Oh, it's Old Dan," Zhao Zhen observed. "Come in, come in. So many folks are coming and going these days, so the dog is always on its leash."

"I won't come in. Does what you said to me in my cabbage patch still ring true?"

Zhao Zhen thought for a while and then said, "Why ever not? It still rings true."

"I've no money to give you. I've only sowed two *mu* of cabbage."

"Then two *mu* of cabbage will have to do."

Old Dan had been clutching his intermittently-trembling hands behind his back. The trembling now ceased. He appeared as if Zhao Zhen was a stranger to him and he looked up and down at the man's face. He had never expected that Zhao Zhen could keep his clarity of mind when in such a state of happiness.

"I thought that given your mood these days, you might be apt to charge me less," Old Dan said.

"How can you say this, this is my livelihood," Zhao Zhen replied.

"Then I've been growing my cabbages for nothing?"

"But you've gotten a big girl in return."

"Oh, oh, let's seal the deal with cabbages. Within two days I'll come over to fetch her."

"My wife is still lying-in after giving birth. I want Huanhuan to take care of her for a couple of days."

"You want to slice the radish from both ends?"

"If you want to fetch her it's OK. She can stay here and look after my wife during the day then go to your house in the evening to sleep. Is that OK?"

"Once I've fetched her over, she is part of my family. You must pay her."

"I will accept fewer cabbages. Will that do? If not, the fucking deal is off."

"Do as you say, you donkey-fucked bastard."

The deal was made. Still, Old Dan felt as though he had swallowed a fly all the way down to his stomach. Anyway, he was uncomfortable. Early the next morning, someone saw him stalking towards the home of the Village Head, clutching his hands behind his back.

IV.

Ma Lin, the Village Head, was setting up a chicken coop for his family. He didn't raise his eyes, though he could tell from the noise that it was Old Dan. He had heard Old Dan standing behind him and was occupied with measuring a rail which would be slotted into a hole in the wall. He had already put a row of them into place, with several holes still left vacant. They were anxiously waiting to be filled. Ma Lin slotted one in and then another. He went about his task conscientiously. He thought that Old Dan was about to tell him something pressing. There, he was wrong. Old Dan craned his neck and fixed his eyes upon the unused holes. It seemed as though he would not open his mouth until Ma Lin had completed the job. Ma Lin felt a touch of surprise followed by a touch of anger. "If you can wait, you donkey-fucked bastard, go ahead and wait. After I've done these rails, I'll put the grass thatch on. After the grass thatch is done, I have to daub on mud, and then fix on the tiles. You donkey-fucked bastard."

Old Dan, with his neck in a craned position, seemed to possess patience in spades.

So began the interminable wait. At last, Ma Lin could stand this no longer.

"Haven't you watched someone build a chicken coop before, you donkey-fucked bastard?"

"No," Old Dan said. "To tell the truth, I've never seen this before in my life." His words were full of sincerity as if he were determined to learn this skill from Ma Lin. "I've never in my life seen a person build a chicken coop the way you do."

"Then keep your eyes peeled and watch me."

"Why should I watch this? It's not like I've got nothing else to do. I haven't kept chickens since my missus died, don't you know? If I had a woman about the house, I'd also need to build a mother-fucking chicken coop! But there's no chance of me having another woman."

"But, when all is said and done, Big Dan needs to get himself hitched," Ma Lin said.

"Of course, that's for sure. When he gets hitched he can make his own chicken coop."

"You donkey-fucked bastard!"

Ma Lin placed the final rail in the final hole. He then patted the dust from his hands and turned around. He looked at Old Dan's nose and said, "What have you come here for?"

"Zhao Zhen has brought another woman back."

"Is that all?" Ma Lin picked up an earthenware teapot from the ground and took a sip from its spout.

"You are the Village Head, you must handle this business."

"I'm only in charge of collecting grain and taxes."

"Zhao Zhen is a human trafficker."

"I know he's a human trafficker. But if I did something about him, who would the bachelors in our village have to turn to? He only handles women. It's good that he only deals with women." With those words, Ma Lin took another sip of tea.

"Zhao Zhen has all the good fortune. He's made a killing from trafficking girls and he's got a son now as well."

"You'd have to go ask Zhao Zhen's wife about that. If she wants to have a baby no one can stop her. Should Zhao Zhen not be allowed an heir? This is not a hole in a wall. You can't plug it with a rail. Giving birth to a kid is her business!"

"I wish that he didn't have an heir. He enjoys all the good fortune. He can cut the radish from both ends."

"Sometimes that's the way it goes. There are those who can

cut radishes from both ends."

"This means you've made up your mind not to do anything about Zhao Zhen?"

"Oh yeah," Ma Lin said. "If you can do something then do it. I am powerless to step in."

"You won't, you won't. This time the girl he's brought back will be Big Dan's. I don't stand to lose anything."

"You donkey-fucked bastard. He's brought back a woman for your household and you still lodge a complaint against him. You are a real donkey-fucked bastard."

Old Dan smiled at Ma Lin. He thought that this was funny indeed.

"Ha, ha-ha. In two day's time, I'll hold a wedding for Big Dan. You must come over to have some cabbage soup. Make sure you do come. I'm off now. You get back to what you were doing."

Old Dan held his hands behind his back. Ma Lin could see that his fingers were paddling gleefully against his rear end.

Two days later, Big Dan and Huanhuan were introduced for the first time. Another two days later, their wedding was held. Huanhuan became Big Dan's woman. According to the agreement, Huanhuan took care of Zhao Zhen's wife during the daytime and went back to Old Dan's house in the evening to sleep. The previous day, Old Dan lifted fifty heads of cabbage from his field. This was also part of the pre-arranged deal. He made vegetable soup and invited over some of the village dignitaries to eat. The day he lifted the cabbages, Old Dan was exasperated. That two *mu* of cabbage now belonged to Zhao Zhen. He couldn't get his head around what was happening.

Tearfully, he bleated to Big Dan, "This is one year's blood and sweat for us."

Big Dan answered, "Oh, yeah."

"Oh, yeah, your dick. The cabbages went to Zhao Zhen so easily. How can you say 'oh, yeah'?"

"Tell me, what else could I say?"

"Just go away. You go first. I'll sit here for a while. I know that your mind isn't on the cabbages now."

Big Dan left carrying the vegetables on his back. Big Dan thought that his dad was correct. Right now, his brain was awash with the image of Huanhuan's body and thighs.

Soon the wind blew Old Dan's moist eyes dry. He sat for a long time in that cabbage field. The sun had already set and the humidity in the field was rising and crawling like caterpillars upon his buttocks. He thought that he could not sit there any longer. If he lingered there, the humidity would inch into his intestines. He hoped that by morning his two *mu* of cabbage would have become rotten, being reduced into a layer of sticky pulp which smelled of shit and piss. This fantasy roused him. Excitedly, he walked into the middle of the cabbage field. He parted the guard leaves and then prodded his fingers into the heart of one cabbage, crushing it vigorously. After this, he returned the guard leaves to their original position. One-by-one, he inflicted the same damage on a dozen heads.

"Rot away. For the sake of Old Dan's honour, rot away." He proclaimed these words to the whole crop.

He stood among the cabbages like a lone wolf. His fingers were tacky with juice.

v.

When the soup-drinkers from the village left, the courtyard was empty. Dozens of white round porcelain bowls were strewn about as if they had sprouted from the ground. Their mouths were gaping open in the direction of the sky. Each of the bowls had a crossed pair of chopsticks balancing upon the rim. Just now, the place had been alive with the sound of slurping, but suddenly only those dozens of vacant bowls remained. Surveying the empty wares, Old Dan was at a loss and sustained a lengthy silence. He felt his courtyard was like a theatre once the performance had drawn to its end. Big Dan's feelings could not have been more different. He thought the empty bowls were the dregs of the past. Something fresher and more practical was now awaiting his involvement. The performance was yet to begin. He said, "Huanhuan, let's go inside the room. Our pa likes to stew over things, let's leave him to it. Let's go indoors." As Huanhuan was about to turn around, Old Dan opened his mouth:

"You're going inside. What about these empty bowls? You expect me to clean them?"

"I saw you looking at them," Big Dan said.

"Am I looking at empty bowls? Is there anything interesting about them? You are wrong!"

Huanhuan didn't say anything. She just rolled up her sleeves and went about cleaning up the crockery. Big Dan stared blankly for a while and then joined in. The clattering of the big porcelain bowls instantly restored the human atmosphere to Big Dan's home. Old Dan stayed motionless. He just watched them cleaning, sensing that Huanhuan knew the rules. It was already dark, by the time the tidying was done. Big Dan and Huanhuan stood in front of Old Dan, wanting to learn what his next injunctions would be.

"I borrowed twenty-eight bowls from other people. Are you expecting me to return them?"

"They can be returned tomorrow," replied Big Dan. "I'll do it."

"That's the done thing."

"Huanhuan, you go inside first. I want to have a word with Old Dan."

Huanhuan went indoors. Big Dan stood erect. For a long time, Old Dan did not open his mouth.

"Just spit it out," Big Dan said.

"I was meaning to say something very important, but somehow whatever it is has slipped my mind. You go in. I'll call you when I remember."

Big Dan really had the urge to go over and slap his father.

"Go, go inside," Old Dan urged.

When Big Dan entered the room, Huanhuan was already beneath the quilt. The hem was pushed up as far as her chin. She stared at Big Dan with her two dark eyes. Big Dan felt the bones within him suddenly become tender. He thought he shouldn't be going soft. If he were soft he could do nothing. With this idea, he felt his bones stiffen again. He latched the door shut and turned around and returned Huanhuan's gaze for a while.

"Come on," Huanhuan seemed to be saying to him. Actually, she had spoken not a single word. She merely blinked and showed off her long eyelashes.

He walked to the *kang* and tugged his feet from his shoes. His eyes never left Huanhuan's face. Later on, he could not recall the exact appearance of Huanhuan's face.

A huge foot pungent with mud stretched out towards Huanhuan's ear. Huanhuan closed her eyes. She could hear that another huge foot was being extended over her face to be planted on the other side. Then there was the sound of *ge-zhang, ge-zhang* as the matt beneath the blanket protested out loud.

"Blow out the lamp," Huanhuan murmured. Her voice was so gentle.

Later Huanhuan was seized with sharp pains. She immediately bounced up from the *kang* and squatted down on the floor, covering her belly with her hands. Big Dan was propelled to the other corner of the *kang*. His two eyes were filled with panic and his lips twitched.

"Huanhuan, what's wrong with you? What did I do to you?" Big Dan asked. He wasn't sure whether he should climb down to assist her up and fetch her back.

Huanhuan shook her head and groaned.

"I'll scoop you up in my arms."

Again Huanhuan shook her head. She got up and crawled underneath the quilt. Big Dan remained motionless.

"You come on," Huanhuan said.

Big Dan still remained motionless. He was afraid that Huanhuan was playing tricks on him.

"Hehe," Huanhuan tittered. "Come on."

Big Dan was relieved. He thought that this time he should be more careful. He shouldn't let her push him away from her body. But as soon as he touched her body, he could not control himself.

"Huanhuan!" he screeched. "Huanhuan!"

Big Dan felt the woman under his body become an extension of his own flesh. He and she were too dear to each other. He wanted to relay to her all the sweet expressions in the world, but couldn't force out a single sentence. He just called "Huanhuan, oh, Huanhuan" time and time again. He wanted to transform himself into water and rinse through the woman's whole body. It seemed that he was doing something laborious yet pleasant. Anxious as he was, he was unsure how to proceed. All of a sudden, he became motionless. A sad and sorrowful tide flooded through his heart. He slowly lowered his face onto Huanhuan's stomach. As he crawled onto her, tears welled up in his eyes. Huanhuan was startled.

"Huanhuan," he sobbed and muttered. "You've left me at a loss. You're even dearer to me than my mother!"

Early the next morning, as per to the local custom, Huanhuan went and greeted her father-in-law and cleansed Old Dan's bedpan. She also lit a pipe for him. She then said to Old Dan:

"Pa, I'm going to my uncle's home!"

"Uncle? Where did this uncle crawl out from?"

"Zhao Zhen asked me to call him 'uncle.'"

"Oh, oh. From now on don't mention Zhao Zhen. He is my personal enemy."

Huanhuan found her father-in-law funny. She chuckled. When she smiled she always let out a growling sound.

"I'm not cheating you. Don't laugh," Old Dan said. With those words, he too chuckled.

At that time, Old Dan was in a good mood. Soon, though, that clear sky clouded over. When Huanhuan walked out of the gate he noticed that the corner of the handkerchief in her trouser pocket was poking out. He immediately felt that there was something bewitching about her. His mood worsened when lunchtime came.

"You've got a woman, but you still have to cook for yourself. What kind of a world is this?" he asked.

"Huanhuan promised she'll come home as soon as Zhao Zhen's wife's confinement is finished," Big Dan explained.

"Confinement, confinement. I don't want her to stay there for even a single day," Old Dan snarled.

"You made a deal with him already. Who else is to blame for this?"

"Listen to me. Your wife cost us two *mu* of cabbages. With that flowery tail of hers in her pocket who was she seducing?"

When he saw that Big Dan made no response he was a little irritated. "Why do you say nothing?"

"What should I say? I can't say a word."

"Of course you've nothing to say. You've got your woman and there's nothing to be said. A knocked about wife is a pliable wife. Just like kneading dough. I tell you, you must make her obedient."

"Why should I do that and how? I haven't the foggiest what you're talking about."

Old Dan thought it over for a bit and could not come up with a new method. He then swallowed his saliva and said, "You must make her obedient, anyhow."

"Zhao Zhen did ask you for the cabbages."

"Yes, it was down to Zhao Zhen. I'm clear about that. Sooner or later, I shall drag him down. I've been wanting to drag him down for ages. I won't let him off the hook."

He had never expected that the chance would come around so soon.

Huanhuan was the trigger.

VI.

It got all around Double-Ditch Village that Old Dan's daughter-in-law was having a tryst with the human trafficker Zhao Zhen. People jabbered garrulously about it behind closed doors, in front of the privy and at the dining table. Old Dan interrogated Huanhuan like a judge. Even Huanhuan herself was unclear about whether it was Zhao Zhen who had seduced her or if she had handed herself over to him.

She went to Zhao Zhen's home every day and waited on his wife with food and water, washing the nappies as well. The courtyard, the parlour, the kitchen and every last jar containing salt, oil, soya bean sauce, and vinegar were all familiar to her. She was also familiar with the various aromas of Zhao Zhen's home. She always tucked herself beneath the same quilt as Zhao Zhen's wife and talked about women's business. Zhao Zhen's wife was a plump woman who had grown even larger after giving birth. Her body emanated a kind of pungent lactose smell. She produced copious amounts of milk. Her massive breasts protruded out of her blouse and wobbled freely. The baby could not polish off all of the milk so she squirted it into a bowl. Huanhuan didn't know what to do with this. Zhao Zhen's wife just told her to leave it and her uncle would have it in the evening. Huanhuan found it novel and peculiar that an adult should bother with an infant's milk. Zhao Zhen's wife said that this stuff was packed with nutrition. Huanhuan could not imagine the scene of him drinking it – a man with a face full of stubble lapping up his wife's milk together with his baby. Wouldn't that be bizarre?

That day, when Huanhuan entered the room, she saw Zhao Zhen's wife survey her with weary eyes. Huanhuan instantly brought to mind the situation of her lying on the *kang* with Big Dan. Actually, on the way here her mind had been occupied with what happened last night. She could not rid herself of the image of how Big Dan looked. Those weary eyes in front of her in the room made her heart beat fast. It appeared that her mistress could read her thoughts and knew what the couple had done. The baby peed itself, so she removed the cloth nappy and hung it on the bamboo by the gate. When she returned to the room Zhao Zhen's wife was still gazing at her. She said, "Auntie, don't stare at me like that. It's making my heart wriggle like a bunny." Zhao Zhen's wife threw back her head and let out a burst of laughter. Huanhuan climbed onto the *kang* beside her. She still continued to laugh. The girl leant her head against the woman's arms and said, "Laugh. Go on laughing. Can your laughing tear the sky in two?" Zhao Zhen's wife insisted, "No more laughing, no more laughing. Laughter makes my tits sore." Huanhuan fetched a bowl from the top of the sideboard and enjoined, "Squeeze it all out and then my uncle has something to drink." Zhao Zhen's wife pressed down on her nipples, one stroke after another. Her milk fired forcefully into the bowl like a water cannon. Soon half a bowlful had been released. Listening to the sound of the whooshing milk, Huanhuan once more recalled Big Dan's expression. She thought that Big Dan's behaviour was amusing. Zhao Zhen's wife pushed back her nipples and gasped, "Such a relief." Huanhuan said nothing as the woman would repeat the same phrase every time they had finished draining her load. The room was filled with the aroma of sticky milk. Zhao Zhen's wife pulled up the quilt and sat side-by-side with Huanhuan up against the wall.

"I have experienced that myself," Zhao Zhen's wife admitted.

Now Huanhuan's heart stopped wriggling and her face was no longer red. She even wanted to ask her mistress something but didn't know how to open her mouth. She pulled the quilt up to her neck and bit it between her teeth.

"Was it fun?" Zhao Zhen's wife asked looking at Huanhuan's face.

"Was what fun?" Huanhuan pretended to know nothing.

"You and Big Dan. Was it fun?"

"He was in a hurry." After those words, she blushed again.

Zhao Zhen's wife threw back her head again and laughed. Huanhuan patted her on the arm.

"You see. When I told you the truth you laughed at me."

"No laughing, no laughing. Let me talk to you about something serious," Zhao Zhen's wife said. "Carry on with your story."

"I've already told you everything," Huanhuan replied.

"Just one sentence? Only one sentence?" Zhao Zhen's wife asked.

Huanhuan blinked as if she was thinking about something.

"Later," Huanhuan went on. "He crawled onto my body and wept and wept."

"Weird. That is weird." Zhao Zhen's wife blinked as well.

"It startled me at first. Then I showed him pity," Huanhuan described. "He had a really pitiful look."

"Oh … oh."

"Do all men and women behave like this?"

"Yes."

"Does everyone do it in a hurry?"

"They do to start with, but not later on."

"How about you and my uncle?"

"Your uncle? He is really an old hand," Zhao Zhen's wife declared with pride.

"The people in my home village call those who are good at labour work 'an old hand.'"

"It's just the same with men's and women's business."

"I don't believe it."

"You'll believe it later on."

"I don't believe."

"Your uncle can't talk to you about this kind of thing. If it were allowed, I'd let him talk it over with you."

"You see, auntie, you are talking nonsense again."

Nobody interrupted them. The pair chattered vehemently. If Zhao Zhen's wife had known how her words would influence Huanhuan, she might not have chosen to speak to her in this way. But how could she know Huanhuan's mind? Human hearts are all made of flesh, but each flesh has its own composition.

Huanhuan started to feel differently towards the human trafficker Zhao Zhen. The man remained the same, but her feeling altered. There was a kind of unspoken quality in him which she now found attractive. She thought that this man was full of fun. When she was washing diapers in the side courtyard she would think of Zhao Zhen and Big Dan too. Big Dan appeared to have boundless energy and inexhaustible vigour. Big Dan always went about it in a hurry and would then crawl onto her and weep. Big Dan whimpered, "For as long as I live I'll always cling to you. I don't know how to be kind to you. I don't have any other choice." Big Dan always spoke like this. What might it be like when Zhao Zhen and his wife stayed together? She lumped the four of them together. For a while, she thought about herself and Big Dan, before switching to Zhao Zhen and his wife. The side courtyard was the place where firewood was stored and domestic animals raised. It was quiet there and Huanhuan could fantasise alone about whatever took her interest. Later, an affair did begin between her and Zhao Zhen.

That day, Huanhuan was again preparing to go to the side courtyard to wash the nappies. Zhao Zhen's wife observed, "You see, my clothes look like they've been rinsed in the milk basin. They pong." Huanhuan responded, "You take them off and I'll put them in with the rest." Zhao Zhen was about to go out and his wife told him to take off his clothes so that Huanhuan could wash them too. Zhao Zhen commented that they really did need doing, so he stripped off. He then said, "I'll help her carry the bundle over and give her a hand drawing a few pails of water. After that, I'll go to the cornfield. The crops should need gathering in before too long." Zhao Zhen didn't walk to the field. Instead, he drew one bucket of water for Huanhuan and tipped it into the wooden laundry basin. He drew another bucket and squatted before Huanhuan, watching her clean the garments. The water was very cold and made her hands turn red. With Zhao Zhen crouched in front of her, Huanhuan's mind was perturbed and she gasped at short intervals. Zhao Zhen observed her for a while and then walked in the direction of the side gate. Huanhuan heaved a long sigh of relief. Suddenly, though, she became tight-chested again. She noticed that he didn't go through the gate. Rather he latched it closed. He came towards her. The way the stubble on his face quivered revealed that he was laughing. Zhao Zhen picked Huanhuan's hands out of the basin and grasped them in his thick palms.

"What have you been talking about with your auntie?" Zhao Zhen asked.

Huanhuan lowered her head. Her hands were gradually warming up in his hold.

"Your auntie told me all about this."

Zhao Zhen scooped Huanhuan up in his arms and took her to the woodshed. Huanhuan felt her body had become airy as cotton. Among the heap of soft kindling Zhao Zhen made her the object of his masculine tenderness. He didn't use barbarian force. He knew how he could convince her of his good intentions. He claimed that he had slept with many girls and all of them called him "uncle."

"All of them were girls you brought here?"

"Yes."

"Does my auntie approve?"

"You daft egg. How could your auntie approve of this?"

Huanhuan remained silent. She untangled the straw from her hair. Only their breathing was to be heard. The sunshine in the courtyard shone brightly.

"When the confinement is finished I must go back to Old Dan's home."

"No hurry. You can stay here longer. I'll have a word with Old Dan. He's sure to agree."

Zhao Zhen really did catch up with Old Dan. He told him that he wanted Huanhuan to help him longer. Old Dan replied that his idea was great, but stank at the same time. It would not do. Zhao Zhen answered that he would relinquish the two *mu* of cabbages. Old Dan gazed at him for a while with his herbal pill-like eyes. He finally agreed to the deal once he was satisfied that Zhao Zhen wasn't playing any tricks.

"This is the way out," Old Dan said.

When Zhao Zhen left, Old Dan went to the cabbage patch straightaway. He hadn't been there for a long time. He never expected that it would be returned to him again. That deal had been struck too easily. Too easily. He stood by the field with his hands behind his back. His heart was practically dancing in his throat. The world was wonderful. The whole world had been fucked by a donkey! Suddenly, he recalled those dozen cabbages he'd sabotaged. He ran into the field and uncovered the hearts. A rank smell irritated his nose. As expected, they had all gone rotten.

"This donkey-fucked world," he growled.

He felt deep regret but then transferred the blame onto Zhao Zhen's account. He thought that some day in the future he was certain to drag Zhao Zhen down. He drew much comfort from that prospect. Later on, when those cabbages sold out at a good price, his comfort was greater still.

It was only after selling the cabbages that he got wind of the alleged tryst between Huanhuan and Zhao Zhen. At that time, Huanhuan had already completed her contracted service at his home and come back.

"Ha!" Old Dan screamed. He didn't believe it. "Ha!" he screamed again. Then he did believe.

"Ha ha!" he screamed twice. His two cheeks became ruddy. This donkey-fucked world! He had been waiting for many years and the chance had come around at last. He wouldn't let that chance slip away. All of the Double-Ditch villagers would now see how he squared off with his personal enemy. He thought he would approach this step-by-step. First, he would inform Big Dan.

VII.

That evening, Huanhuan laid a fire beneath the two *kangs* as usual. She fanned the flames hard for some time and the yellow smoke rapidly permeated the whole room. Old Dan and Big Dan dashed out through the door like rats. They stood in the courtyard breathless, watching the heady smoke spooling out from the chimneys. The sky was cloudy and the smoke didn't travel upwards. It crawled like snakes along the ground. After a while, Huanhuan also dashed out, though she was carrying a fan in her hand. With Old Dan and Big Dan, she waited for the cloud to dissipate. They looked at each other and coughed for a period. When the smoke got to fill the courtyard, the atmosphere inside the house cleared. All of them went inside, lit a lamp and blew it out when they were ready to sleep.

Old Dan didn't light a lamp. He wanted to lie alone in the darkness and brood over what had happened between him and Zhao Zhen. Based on his past behaviour, he wouldn't exercise restraint. He would go straight to Huanhuan, accost her, and pick over the evidence to ascertain whether it was true or not. This matter was too unusual by far and would require some contemplation. He hated Zhao Zhen. He had hated him for so many years. Formerly, that hate had no concrete manifestation, but now things were different. Once an issue has a solid form it becomes easier to deal with. Thinking about this, his heart started to beat against his breastbone, generating an endless excited knocking sound. He sensed the blood coursing through his system like galloping horses. He rolled onto one side to think for a while and then rolled onto the other side to think. At last, he lay still on his back and continued his cogitation. The night was deep and silent. He could overhear the noises Big Dan and Huanhuan were making in the other room. He had been interrupted by this noise for so many nights. By now it was rather familiar. He knew what they were doing and that sound stirred up countless fantasies in his heart. He could not utter a single sentence, and was unable to open his mouth. Big Dan was his son and Huanhuan his daughter-in-law. What was he to say? He could only share that experience vicariously through the sound and even doing that became a kind of sin. Better to not experience it. Better to not listen to the noise. However, in the stillness of the evening, any sound could spread far and wide and clearly. The sound penetrated into his ears. He couldn't sleep with his ears plugged and couldn't sleep until his mind had been uncluttered. Old Dan always comforted himself with this principle. Sometimes he genuinely wished that Big Dan could do something, but what could Big Dan do in the dead of night? Unable to find a way out of this, he had to put up with the situation. It was not until the noise had sunk deep into the night that he could sleep safe and sound. But now, the noise came again from the old place. Everything stayed the same. He could even tell which sound was being made by Big Dan and which by Huanhuan. Right now Old Dan had been given reason enough to interrupt them. He didn't mean to be hard on his son. He didn't mean to interrupt them. Even so, this could not be passed over without discussion. How could Big Dan be kept in the dark over such a monumental thing? While thinking about this, he fidgeted his way off the *kang* and went out through the door.

The door and window of Big Dan's room were both closed so that they seemed like one large and long blank frame next to a small square one. The noise was seeping out through the cracks in those two frames.

He thought, "I really don't want to interrupt them."

"I can't stand outside here and listen," he then thought.

After that, he shouted "Big Dan!"

The noise stopped abruptly. Old Dan instantly brought to mind a couple of frightened bunnies. He pictured them listening to the call from outside with their eyes wide open. He coughed twice and said, "It's me, Big Dan. Come to my room. I want to have a word with you."

"Can't it wait until tomorrow?" Big Dan's voice was very weak.

"It can't" Old Dan answered.

When he heard the sound of Big Dan putting on his clothes he turned and went back to his chamber and lit a lamp. Big Dan came along in his cotton-padded overcoat, his two legs bare. As soon as he entered the door he squeezed his way beneath the warm quilt with his hands under his buttocks.

"A warm quilt is good. People will freeze to death without it. If you have anything to say, say it quickly," Big Dan remarked. His two legs shivered and were ready to pad back to his own room at any moment. Huanhuan was still waiting for him.

"I cannot say it quickly," Old Dan responded.

"If you can't say it quickly, say it slowly then. You obviously can't hold it in until daybreak," said Big Dan.

"Carry on. I'm listening," Big Dan urged.

"You listen to my dick. Your wife is having it off with Zhao Zhen!"

Big Dan reared up his frame and straightened his neck. After a while, it softened. His head dangled on his chest like a knotted root of ginger.

"You didn't know about this?"

"I know."

Old Dan had never expected this reply from Big Dan. His neck straightened too. However, it didn't soften like Big Dan's. His neck remained straight and his eyes blinked at Big Dan. Big Dan knew that his father was staring at him and didn't raise his head.

"You know? You say you know? If you knew why didn't you tell me it? Why not go and ask her about it? You donkey-fucked sod, you donkey-fucked sod. You didn't ask her?" Old Dan ranted.

"I didn't ask. I don't want to ask."

"Ha!"

"I wanted to ask, but I didn't. I've been pretending that I don't know about it. I just try to imagine that nothing has happened."

"Ha!"

"Huanhuan is not bad to me."

"Your wife is sleeping with my personal enemy and you tell me that she isn't bad to you. Ha!"

"As long as Huanhuan doesn't go to Zhao Zhen's home anymore, that will be enough."

"When a bowl of water's been spilt, the ground is wet!"

"When the sun shines it will dry it out."

Old Dan's eyes stopped blinking. He could not come out with any suitable words to argue with him.

"I don't want to think about it. When I don't think about it, it's as good as if nothing has happened."

Old Dan still couldn't come out with any suitable words.

"That's it? Is that all? I'm leaving now."

"You donkey-fucked sod. If you don't ask her, I shall."

"Go ahead."

Big Dan pulled out his two bare legs from under the quilt. His bare feet slid dexterously into his shoes and he left.

"Of course I will ask!" Old Dan shouted so as to be heard outside the door. "Why not ask?"

The next morning after breakfast, when Huanhuan was about to do the washing-up, Old Dan stopped her.

"I have something to ask you," Old Dan said.

Big Dan spat onto the ground and left with a flick of his sleeve. Old Dan took no notice of him. Huanhuan balanced the weight of her body on one leg while stretching the other one out. One of her thumbs was hooked inside her trouser pocket. The other hand was cupped around her chin. She was waiting for Old Dan to ask away.

"Did Zhao Zhen seduce you?" Old Dan plunged in at the deep end.

"I don't know."

"You seduced him? Did you really seduce him?"

"I don't know." The sincerity in Huanhuan's answer was palpable.

"You put that flowery bird's tail of yours back in your pocket."

Huanhuan gave a glance at the exposed corner of her

handkerchief, though stayed motionless.

"Tuck it in."

Reluctantly Huanhuan tucked it inside. She looked at Old Dan and then turned her head to one side.

"Even if you were the one who seduced him, you shouldn't let others know. You should insist that it was he who seduced you. I shall make sure all the folks in Double-Ditch Village know about this."

"I'll top myself if that's what you're driving at."

"I don't care about that. I'll go to see Ma Lin the Village Head at once. You can talk with them."

"I'm your daughter-in-law. Aren't you afraid of losing face?"

"Losing face? Yes. Losing face. I want everyone to know about this simply because I'm bothered about losing face. *If you lock your child away you'll never catch the wolf.* Have you ever heard that saying?"

VIII.

Sweet corn hung from the eaves of Ma Lin's room and from the forks of tree trunks. The kernels of corn were all plump like rows of gold teeth.

There was no farm work in the winter time. Their chicken coop had been built. When he was idle, Ma Lin would fold his arms and tuck his hands into his sleeves, then pace around his courtyard. He raised his head to survey the kernels and cobs. Old Dan came in from the outside and shouted "Village Head!" Ma Lin's eyes were still fixed on the golden corn. Several sparrows skittered here and there, chirping away briskly. Their tails wagged, but their beaks were too small to pluck a whole kernel.

"You see my corn. It gets more and more charming," Ma Lin commented.

"I'm not in the mood. I've plenty of my own at home," Old Dan snapped. "Zhao Zhen's gone and screwed my daughter-in-law."

Ma Lin wanted to laugh out loud. Instead, he wore an expression of consternation.

"Really?"

"Don't put on a show. You knew about it already."

"Look, I really didn't know."

"This time you must handle it."

"It takes two being caught red-handed for it to be called adultery. It's hard to tell which things you overhear are true and which are false. How I am I supposed to handle it?" Ma Lin asked. "Even an upright official finds it hard to settle a family dispute."

"You call all the members of the Village Committee over to my home this evening."

"Is Huanhuan willing to confess? Is she willing to confess to that kind of thing?"

"You are the Village Head. How dare she refuse? Whatever you ask her she will answer you."

What else could be more intriguing than investigating the truth behind an affair? Nothing. The Village Head Ma Lin soon called all the committee members over to Old Dan's home after supper. In the upper parlour there stood a row of low stools. The members sat there side-by-side exhibiting earnest expressions. When Old Dan ordered that water be served, Huanhuan poured a bowl for each of the folks in turn. Big Dan was about to leave.

Ma Lin said, "You shouldn't go. It's no bad thing for you to listen to this."

Big Dan squatted at the corner of the wall with his head lowered between his knees as if he were asleep.

Ma Lin declared, "Let's give Huanhuan the chance to describe what went on."

The others agreed, saying, "Yes, spit it out."

Ma Lin instructed, "Huanhuan, you find a place and sit down to give your side of the story."

Huanhuan insisted, "I won't sit. I'll just stand here. I can stand and talk at the same time."

Ma Lin then added, "Then you can stand there and talk. Old Dan, you take a seat."

Old Dan replied, "I just want to squat here. I like squatting."

He then turned his head towards Huanhuan and said, "Answer truthfully whatever they ask you."

"Oh yes," was her response.

They grilled her in great detail all the while maintaining that they were not the ones who liked to interfere in other's business. It was her father Old Dan who put them up to this. Whether this was good or bad, it fell to the Double-Ditch villagers to sort this out. Even if they couldn't do a thing about it, it was still a positive step for them to hear about the matter.

Old Dan concurred, "Yes, yes. I just want you to listen in. After you've listened to the details it will become clear."

Ma Lin said, "We know that it is awkward to speak about this. When all said and done, it is not a glamorous business."

Huanhuan said, "This isn't awkward at all. Those who want to poke into it are even more shameful than the accused."

Ma Lin was taken aback and cawed, "Huanhuan are you cursing us?"

Huanhuan answered, "I wasn't."

Ma Lin pointed out, "Whether you are cursing us or not, it doesn't bother us. You're far younger than we are. You don't know much about the world. Is that so?"

The other members agreed with him.

Old Dan said, "Let's not beat around the bush. Carry on with the inquiry."

Ma Lin resumed his investigation and Huanhuan started to recount the events of the day as she washed the clothes and nappies.

"My uncle fetched me two buckets of water. The water was very cold. It chilled me to the bones. I thought my uncle was going out of the gate, but he wasn't. He latched the side gate. My heart stirred and pounded."

"What happened then?"

"Then he walked over to me and watched me washing the clothes."

"What was on your mind right then?"

"I had nothing on my mind. I was just washing clothes and the water was cold."

"Carry on. Continue."

"My uncle said that my hands looked so red. I told him that the water was cold. My uncle then hauled up my hands."

"Don't say 'uncle this,' 'uncle that,'" Old Dan scolded.

"Don't interrupt her. Let her carry on. Interrupting her will make her talk nonsense," Ma Lin admonished.

"He lifted me up and carried me to the woodshed."

Ma Lin and others listened on with wide eyes and mouths agog. They were waiting to hear what happened next, but Huanhuan paused.

"Go on," Ma Lin instructed her.

"Later, that thing happened."

"Too simple. You are telling this in too simple a way," Ma Lin said, "I cannot make out who seduced who. Do all of you agree with me?"

"Yeah," the others answered.

"Did he make the first move? For example – clothes. Your clothes. He must have … You see this is hard to tell out loud. First of all, he ought to have stripped off your clothes," Ma Lin suggested. "Did he strip off your clothes?"

Huanhuan nodded. Her eyes were flooded with tears.

Old Dan stood up.

"How about it – did Zhao Zhen seduce her? It is very clear, Huanhuan. Carry on." Old Dan was elated.

"He undid my top two buttons. I undid the rest myself."

Tears cascaded down from her eyes. She could not bear such torture anymore.

"You are too brazen. If you want to listen to the story, I'll tell it all. He pulled off my trousers and screwed me. I was happy to be screwed by him. Now, are you satisfied? *Whah, Oh whah-*" Huanhuan bawled out. She turned and ran into the bedroom, closing the door with a *pang*!

Big Dan shot up as if he had been stung by a bee. He raced over and pounded on the door.

"Huanhuan, open up! Huanhuan, open up!" he shouted.

Nobody had expected that Huanhuan would act like this. They looked at each other with embarrassment. The committee listened intently to the story and chewed over every word spoken by Huanhuan. Huanhuan's narrative caused them to have many fantasies. They all chose a role to play in these fantasies. They even felt that it was not Zhao Zhen who was doing that thing with Huanhuan, but they themselves. Their eyes were wide open and eyeballs motionless, gazing fixedly upon Huanhuan's face ... They listened with a touch of both nervousness and glee. And yet no one could have predicted that Huanhuan would break down. They no longer knew how to bring this to a close.

"Old Dan, you see what's happened?" Ma Lin asked.

"Better grin and bear it," someone piped up.

"Quite right. Better to grin and bear it." Ma Lin thought that these words had been offered up at the perfect time. He stood up and patted Old Dan on the shoulder, saying, "Men can put up with anything. Don't you think so? Then you must put up with this. The less trouble the better."

All the others stood up from the low stools and looked at Old Dan with a detached air and a touch of affection.

"Put up with it," they told him.

"Old Dan. You stay here. We're leaving," Ma Lin said.

They went out of the gate in a column. They had already forgotten their embarrassment, so only a sense of fulfilment was left behind. In the days to come, they would recall what Huanhuan had told them from time-to-time. They might be unable to stop themselves from erupting into laughter. "Donkey-fucked Zhao Zhen" – curse him in this way they might, but there was no hint of malice.

From outside the gate, they heard Old Dan screeching with sobs: "How can I put up with this? You donkey-fucked sods."

Someone said, "Village Head, do you hear how Old Dan is cursing us?"

Ma Lin answered, "Oh, oh. Let him do as he pleases."

All of them peeled off into their own homes. In the darkness, there was the noise of successive doors being latched.

IX.

The equivocal attitude of Ma Lin the Village Head didn't exactly leave Old Dan dejected. Rather it triggered off the passion he had long harboured in his heart. Twenty years seemed to have been shaved off him. His twenty fingers and toes and hair radiated vitality. Early the next morning, he launched an even more painstaking operation. One-by-one, he told all of the households in Double-Ditch Village about how Zhao Zhen the human trafficker had seduced Huanhuan. Almost every member of each family listened to his story with great interest. They showed their concern and pity towards Old Dan. They offered him a seat and poured him water and he would drink and hold forth. Old Dan had never enjoyed such lordly treatment before. He held his bowl of water and drew a long sip of the boiling water. Then he opened his mouth and hawed.

"He – that donkey-fucked sod – had this scheme cooked up a long time ago." He would always begin his discourse with this phrase. "He asked Huanhuan to wash the clothes. Of course, Huanhuan had to do that. But that donkey-fucked sod, he put the latch on the door. He grabbed hold of her hands. How could she resist that? He carried her to the woodshed. What kind of a place is that? It's practically a pigsty, isn't it?" he ranted.

"Even though he carried her to the woodshed he couldn't have been sure of getting what he wanted," someone commented.

"How could he not have? Had he not done that, I – Old Dan – would not be telling you this. No wonder he – the donkey-fucked sod – was eager for Huanhuan to stay there longer. When he came to me to talk about this he pretended that he was a decent man. 'I want Huanhuan to help me for a few more days,' he said to me."

"So Zhao Zhen gave you back the two *mu* of cabbages for free?" one listener asked.

"Yeah, yeah. Could this really be called 'for free'?" Old Dan replied.

When meal-times came around, Old Dan would return home punctually. After the meal, he would move on to another household and rehash his tale. Within a dozen days, all of the folk in Double-Ditch Village could narrate the story of Zhao Zhen and Huanhuan for themselves. The novelty wore off. When they listened to Old Dan's version again they felt it was as bland as pigswill.

"Old Dan, can you give us something fresh?" someone piped up.

Brought up short, Old Dan blinked for a while.

"What are you driving at?"

"After it's been repeated three times those words stink worse than shit."

"Have I told you this three times? Have I really told you this three times?" Old Dan asked. He sensed that these people were not being reasonable.

"You've told us about it eighteen times," they retorted.

It was not until now that Old Dan realised that they hadn't offered him a seat and they hadn't served him water. He was crestfallen and returned home in low spirits. He lay on the *kang* for the whole morning and was struck by the sensation that this was all a daydream. He felt that what he had been relating to the people for the last dozen days was somehow very distant from himself. Maybe it had never in fact happened? The meal was ready. Huanhuan stood outside and called him over to eat. Huanhuan would always cook the meal on time. She was neither angry nor irritated. She cooked the meal, swept the courtyard and loaded the firewood into the *kang* as if all of Old Dan's machinations had nothing to do with her.

"Pa, the meal is ready," Huanhuan called out. "Come and eat."

While he was eating, Old Dan scanned Huanhuan from top to toe. He couldn't detect the slightest trace that Huanhuan had conducted an affair with the human trafficker Zhao Zhen. He was somewhat upset by this. He thought that maybe he was in the midst of a dream. Following the meal, he hurried into the room and closed the door. He slapped himself on the face once and then again. That way he settled his uneasy heart. "How could I be dreaming? If I were dreaming my face wouldn't hurt when I slapped it," he said. Once again he could feel that the blood in his body was like a galloping horse.

He soon found that the people of Double-Ditch Village were shifting their focus onto the rats. During those days, every household in their village found rats in their home. Day and night the vermin munched at the sweet corn which hung on the eaves and the boughs of the trees. Ma Lin called an assembly of the whole village. Soon thereafter, a community-wide rat cull was launched. When they caught a rat, they wouldn't kill it on the spot. They would instead fasten a string to its rear leg and drag it onto the street for show. Every day they would catch one or two of them. Sometimes a phalanx of people would appear on the street wielding dozens of rats for public amusement. The rats chased hither and thither beneath the sunshine. The sun made their eyes sparkle somewhat. Now high-spirited, the folks would all remark on the size of bodies and the length of the tails of those captives. Then they would pick up a few spades and either slice or splat them. At this moment, the street would be filled with their death-shrieks.

Big Dan and Huanhuan also participated in this because they too found visitors in their home. When they caught a specimen they would high-spiritedly take it out onto the street. When they had trapped nothing, they would still go out onto the street to watch.

The human trafficker Zhao Zhen gave everyone a big surprise. That day, he suddenly appeared on the street with eight rodents. He had been to the northern mountains again and brought back another woman. He was going to barter over her with another expectant bachelor.

"Get out of the way, get out of the way, here are the rats from my house." Zhao Zhen had a grand expression as he shouted. The eight rats scurried along behind him. Everybody on the street screamed with mock exaggeration.

Old Dan was the only one who refused to take part in this activity. He was bitterly disappointed by the degenerate behaviour of the villagers. He thought that his neighbours ought to be sickened by the sight of Zhao Zhen. Nonetheless, he was wrong. They took Zhao Zhen and Huanhuan's adultery lightly. Looking on helplessly, he found that his dozen days of maneuvering had been dried out by the wind like a heap of dog shit. Zhao Zhen had so easily won the people's admiration with those eight rats. What was particularly unbearable to him was that when Zhao Zhen passed by his house he appeared to wink at Huanhuan. Unexpectedly, Huanhuan did not blush and indeed seemed to smile back. At that time, Old Dan was standing behind Big Dan and Huanhuan. He was stabbing his personal enemy with his eyes. He thought that he could delay no longer. He must snap into action. Elbowing his way out from behind Big Dan and Huanhuan, he jumped into the middle of the street.

Kechew! He closed his eyes and spat skyward.

"You are playing with that rat!" he bellowed to everyone on the street.

"As a man, how can you behave like this? I've been talking to you for dozens of days and it was all in vain. How can you behave like this?" he went on.

His face was red all over as he paced several steps back and forth. He then extended one of his fingers and tilted it at Zhao Zhen.

"Why don't you spit in his face!" he called out.

All the onlookers burst into laughter. They found Old Dan as amusing as the rats.

"You wait and see! Sooner or later someone will do Zhao Zhen in," he predicted.

The people's laughter grew louder. Ma Lin walked over. He pressed a hand against Old Dan's forehead.

"Old Dan, maybe you're sick," Ma Lin averred.

Old Dan pushed Ma Lin's hand away and said, "That donkey-fucked sod is the sick one." He spat onto the ground with all his gusto.

Several days later, Old Dan had a serious talk with Huanhuan.

"Huanhuan, all of the villagers know about your affair with Zhao Zhen."

Huanhuan wasn't irritated. She had just finished the dishes and was rubbing her hands against her apron.

"I'm talking to you," Old Dan said.

"Oh, yeah," Huanhuan answered. "You've been talking about this from house to house. How couldn't folks know?"

"Was I making this stuff up? You tell me."

"What do you mean to get out of pestering me? They've long forgotten about that."

"They've forgotten about it, but I haven't."

"If you haven't, just keep it in. Let that become the heir in your belly."

"You should hang yourself. Then Zhao Zhen will be guilty of manslaughter."

Huanhuan shot a glance at Old Dan. She really wanted to claw his face.

"I don't want to die," she said.

"I'll make sure all the folks in the village know about this. You told me that 'if you didn't want me to live in this world I would die.' Promises are promises," Old Dan maintained.

"I don't want to die," Huanhuan repeated.

"You can pretend that you've hanged yourself. Make yourself

half-dead. When you've hanged yourself I'll have evidence to accuse Zhao Zhen with."

"You really are shameless. I've never met a person as shameless as you are. If you corner me, I'll go over to Zhao Zhen and sleep with him again. Sleep with him so you can watch."

"Hooray!" Old Dan shouted. "If you dare sleep with him I dare come and catch you red-handed. I was just thinking of how I might catch you! No wonder you smiled back when Zhao Zhen winked at you."

"Just you wait."

"I'll wait."

Big Dan remained silent. He thought that Huanhuan was just stirring up Old Dan. He never thought that she would keep her word.

x.

Huanhuan waylaid Zhao Zhen at the foot of the slope outside the village. Zhao Zhen's wife had diarrhoea and he had just come back from the county town to buy medicinal herbs. He was carrying manifold packages of herbs. As soon as he got down the slope he saw Huanhuan. She was sitting on a rock and it seemed as though she had been waiting there a long time. They hadn't met one-on-one since the end of Huanhuan's contract.

"Uncle." Huanhuan stood up from the rock and called out to Zhao Zhen. Even when it was just the two of them together she still called him "uncle."

"Oh, it's Huanhuan. What are you doing here? The weather is so cold."

"I've been waiting for you."

"Anything up?" Zhao Zhen looked around and there wasn't a single soul nearby. He then to his seat on a rock and said, "Come over. Let's sit and talk."

Huanhuan sat beside Zhao Zhen. Her heart started to stir

and her face suddenly blushed. Zhao Zhen stared at her face. His breath landed on her forehead. It was warm.

"Tell me, Huanhuan."

"When you were in the northern mountains, Old Dan was spreading nonsense all over the village."

"I know. Let him be. His words are just like farts. There's no use."

"Did my aunt curse you?"

"Curse me? No. She said that Old Dan was a wrong-un."

Zhao Zhen wasn't telling the truth. When he came back from the northern mountains and got home his wife kicked him in the belly. He crawled onto the edge of the *kang* and wanted to take a look at his son. His wife, who was stretching out her leg, happened to strike him in the stomach. She said, "Go out on the street and have a listen. All of the people are talking about your scene with Huanhuan. I really want to take my scissors and snip off your thing. You are just like a dog that can't kick the habit of eating shit."

Zhao Zhen parried, "If you have pent up anger, let it out later. Let me have a look at our son first." Zhao Zhen parted the small cotton quilt and kissed the tender face of the baby. Zhao Zhen's gesture made his wife less angry.

His wife observed, "You see how the baby resembles you more and more." Zhao Zhen replied, "This is thanks to your effort." His words not only drove away her anger but made her feel sweet.

Zhao Zhen perched on the edge of the *kang* and cried, "Don't go believing Old Dan's words. Don't you know what kind of guy he is?"

"Huanhuan's not a good girl either. You go ahead and screw her. If you screwed her broken that would help me vent my spleen."

"Ok, I'll screw her broken. If I screw all the women in the world until they break you'd be the only dear one left for me."

His wife was so amused she couldn't help laughing and chortled, "You are always talking crap."

How could Zhao Zhen tell Huanhuan about all of this?

"Old Dan encouraged me to hang myself so that you would be accused of causing my death," Huanhuan explained.

"He's really dark-hearted."

"I told him that if he kept on pestering me I'd go and sleep with him again."

"Who is the 'him'?" Zhao Zhen asked while knowing the answer. He felt his body was gradually warming up.

"Who else could that 'him' be?" Huanhuan shot a short glance at Zhao Zhen.

Zhao Zhen searched all over the immediate area with his eyes. There was a grass-thatched hut not far away.

"Ok, let's go to the hut to talk," Zhao Zhen suggested and winked at Huanhuan.

"I just want to make Old Dan angry," Huanhuan replied. Her heart was astir again.

"Let's go. Here we can easily be spotted by others. If others spot us, they'll gossip about it again," Zhao Zhen proposed.

As soon as they entered the hut, Zhao Zhen pounced upon Huanhuan. Huanhuan's heart was not pounding anymore. A passion she had never experienced before surged through her body. Before, when she stayed with Zhao Zhen she felt a tinge of shame, but not now. She even longed for Zhao Zhen to violate her. The more ferocious Zhao Zhen was, the deeper her revenge on Old Dan would be. She uttered in her heart, "Now you'll have something to blab about. Don't blame me, Big Dan – it's all your pa's fault. He wanted me to hang myself. Old Dan I'll make you so angry you want to die. Why not come over and watch!"

The brightness that had been at the entrance of the hut was all at once blocked out. Zhao Zhen and Huanhuan were startled.

It was Old Dan. He had half a broken brick in his hand.

"Shoot," Zhao Zhen thought.

Huanhuan lifted her eyes up in the direction of Old Dan's gruesome expression. She didn't know what to do. She thought that Old Dan's brick could very easily end up socking her in the face.

"Ha!" Old Dan shouted.

After Huanhuan had gone out of the door, he had been keeping tabs on her. These days he had been monitoring her closely. He believed that she might very well seek out Zhao Zhen. He watched until Zhao Zhen and Huanhuan entered the hut and he sensed the time was ripe. As he approached the hut, he picked up a brick and caught them red-handed in there.

"What do you intend to do?" Zhao Zhen asked. Pressing down on top of Huanhuan's body he was afraid to move an inch. He too feared the brick in Old Dan's hand.

"I'll fetch all the villagers over to watch. You two don't move. Whoever dares move will feel this brick on their head."

"You go and fetch the people, then. Let us put on our clothes," Zhao Zhen said.

"Don't move or I'll brain you. If you put on your clothes, it won't be amusing anymore. There's sure to be someone passing by. I'll ask them to invite the others over."

"Old Dan, you are really dark-hearted," Zhao Zhen remarked.

Huanhuan covered her face and sobbed.

"How can you have the shame to cry right now? Wait until all the villagers are here and cry as much as you like then," Old Dan advised.

In a flash, Zhao Zhen hopped over Huanhuan's head like a toad and grappled hold of Old Dan's leg. Old Dan hadn't thought he would do this. He raised the brick and struck Zhao Zhen. The brick caught him on the back. Zhao Zhen let out a grunt but wouldn't loosen his grip.

"Huanhuan, hurry. Get hold of him," Zhao Zhen instructed.

Huanhuan got up and grabbed Old Dan. The pair tackled Old Dan to the ground. Old Dan shouted desperately, "Somebody help! Someone's going to get killed!"

Zhao Zhen and Huanhuan took turns to dress, and then Zhao Zhen rode on Old Dan's body, covering his face.

"Huanhuan, get away! Quick!" Huanhuan dashed out of the hut, vanishing like a puff of smoke.

Old Dan tried to bite Zhao Zhen's fingers but couldn't manage to. His throat gurgled.

"You feel comfortable now?" Zhao Zhen taunted. "Your daughter-in-law offered herself to me. *The current's streaming by the threshold. Why not ladle some up?* That's your motto, isn't it? Today it's me who's saying this to you. Do you feel comfortable now?"

"Aw, aw." Old Dan wanted to free his mouth from Zhao Zhen's hands.

Zhao Zhen released Old Dan's mouth.

"My motto comes from ancient times," Old Dan said. "Let me get up."

Zhao Zhen let go of Old Dan and he crawled to his feet and patted the dust from his body.

"Now you can feel free to shout. Call the villagers to come over now."

Old Dan gave off a *yah* and butted his head towards Zhao Zhen. It turned out that he was no match whatsoever for Zhao Zhen. Using his fists and feet Zhao Zhen hit and kicked Old Dan on his buttocks, thighs and shoulders. Old Dan cowered, thinking how different things would have been if he still had that half brick in his hands. He regretted not clutching onto it more tightly. Zhao Zhen raised his foot again. This time he targeted his coccyx. A sharp pain coursed through Old Dan's backbone, reaching up to his neck. Old Dan groaned and toppled to the floor. When he came to, Zhao Zhen was already out of sight. The places where he had been hit and kicked now smarted. He thought that he really had been marmalised by Zhao Zhen. What is more, he had been dealt a proper hiding. Zhao Zhen could deliver a skilful beating. He just aimed for people's blind spots and fleshy zones. Anger burned inside Old Dan, though he soon found an outlet for it. First of all, he covered his face with his hand, then slowly drew the five fingers apart, and scratched downwards forcefully. In an instant, five finger-marks glowed on his thin face. They turned from white to red and at last oozed blood. He didn't stop at this. He then balled his fist and thumped himself on the nose. Trails of spicy and sour tears ran out from his eyes. His nose streamed with blood. He rubbed his face messily so he now wore a ghoulish countenance.

"Someone wants me dead!"

With that shout, he rushed out of the hut.

XI.

Old Dan lay on the *kang* for three whole days. He refused to wash his face.

"It hurts," he wailed.

Before every meal, Big Dan would bring a basin of hot water for his pa and ask him to wash his face. Old Dan always repeated the same words: "It hurts."

"I can eat the food, but can't wash my face," he complained.

Big Dan felt he'd had a raw deal. The news of Old Dan going after the wool but coming back shaved soon went around the village and created a buzz. Once again, folks started to talk about Zhao Zhen and Huanhuan. What is more, there was now new wine in old bottles. Old Dan was rather satisfied with this. Nevertheless, Big Dan had the feeling of some worms infesting his heart. He was at a loss as to what he should do. Zhao Zhen had stolen his wife and beaten his father. As a husband and a son, he had well and truly lost face. He didn't know what to do. He beat Huanhuan, but she neither wept nor put up any resistance. Huanhuan said, "Big Dan, you can beat me and I won't blame you." The next morning, Huanhuan cooked the food and swept the courtyard as usual. She was just that type of woman. He thought that when all was said and done he couldn't throttle her to death.

"Pa, clean your face. People will laugh at you when they see it," Big Dan said.

"It's ugly, don't you think?" Old Dan observed.

Old Dan's face really did not look good. The mess of nasal

blood had dried. Those finger-marks had come up as bruises, which made the face look like a mask.

"I have already given Huanhuan a pasting," Big Dan reported. "She's now as docile as a kitten."

"What's the dicking use of beating her?"

"Should I strangle her then?"

"I want to strangle Zhao Zhen. Why don't you two fight to the death?"

"I'm no match for him."

"Tomorrow, I'll go out on the street. Let all the villagers see the state of my face."

"You are forcing my hand! You want to embarrass me further."

"Why should you be embarrassed? Zhao Zhen didn't beat you up. Your face is not broken. What have you to be embarrassed about?"

Big Dan could not imagine what it would be like when his father went out on the street. If his father went onto the street he would have no face to go on living in this world.

"Let me think about it," Big Dan said.

"You carry on thinking in your way and I'll go out on the street in my way."

Big Dan didn't sleep at all that night.

Early the next morning, he barred his father's way out of the room. His face was livid green.

During the first half of the night, he touched Huanhuan's belly and his heart was full of a kind of sorrowful emotion. Kittenishly Huanhuan sidled up to his thigh. Now and then she opened her eyes and peeped at him. Later, she fell asleep. Her sleeping posture was also similar to that of a feline or the spirit of a feline. Big Dan let out a sigh and then started to think about Zhao Zhen's dog. In his mind, the dog was staring at him ferociously yet in silence. This chilled him to the bones – a barking hound never bites. This thought occupied him for the whole of the second half of the night.

"I shall kill Zhao Zhen for you," he announced.

Old Dan scanned his son.

"Give me the money you got from selling the cabbages. I'll go and buy some dogs."

Old Dan was confused.

"Zhao Zhen has a dog. I shall teach myself how to kill dogs first."

Old Dan now understood. He got out a bundle of cash from the cupboard and tossed it at Big Dan.

"Buy a pig-killing knife too," his father told him.

Big Dan laid his hands on a dozen dogs with great ease. He looked all around Double-Ditch Village and then selected the grass-thatched hut. The hut was originally erected to keep watch over the watermelons. Now it was winter time, nobody stood guard. To begin with, Big Dan was reluctant to use the place because of the bad associations it brought to mind. Later on, he thought that those associations might make it even more suitable. They would intensify his loathing of Zhao Zhen. If Zhao Zhen could smuggle Huanhuan and beat people there, he could kill dogs there as well. He led the dogs into the hut and ground some corn to feed them. After this, he began his test kill. He brought them out one-by-one, luring them with some cornbread. He coaxed them to leap up and bite from different directions and then used the pig-killing knife to stab the hounds in their vital regions. One dog died leaping backwards, two died leaping to the side, and three died leaping forwards, so he had spent more *kung-fu* and money on finding out how to kill the dogs who leapt forwards. He stabbed only one dog per day. He was determined that they shouldn't have an easy death. He would let them expend their power. Every dog would die having demonstrated a different position for leaping and biting. Several of the dogs whose vital regions he didn't target, ran away with blood streaming from their wounds. They howled mournfully in their throes. Big Dan regretted that he didn't catch up with them and finish them off. Every evening he would return home with a knife drenched in canine blood.

"This is snowballing in a big way," the villagers surmised.

"Someone is about to die," they commented.

Old Dan went to visit the hut a number of times. He was very excited.

"Big Dan, this is not only about learning the skill of killing dogs. It's also a means of exercising your guts and innards," he said.

"Kill, kill that donkey-fucked sod!" he cried.

He felt that Zhao Zhen's death was not far away. He was willing Zhao Zhen to be one of the dogs being stabbed.

"Big Dan, I'll go together with you when the time is ripe. When Zhao Zhen has been killed, I'll wash my face straightaway."

"I haven't finished killing the dogs yet," Big Dan pointed out.

"Why do you insist of finishing off all the dogs? You just regard Zhao Zhen as one of them. Long nights produce more dreams. I think we can fix the date as 8th December. Zhao Zhen is sure to be at home then. It's better not to stab him to death. Stab him so that he's left disabled."

"Maybe I shall stab him to death. When the chance comes around, people are in a hurry and the knife has no eyes," Big Dan said.

"Stabbing him to death is letting him off lightly. If you stab him to death you have to pay for that with your own life," Old Dan explained.

"In that case, you can pay with your life."

"I'll do it. If you do happen to stab him to death I'll pay for it with my life."

On 8th December, the folk of Double-Ditch Village drank their eight-treasure porridge in terror. Zhao Zhen did come back to the village. Someone tipped him off.

"Big Dan has been practising killing dogs in the hut," that guy reported.

"Oh yeah," Zhao Zhen said.

"He's got a killer's look on his face," the guy added.

"Oh, yeah."

"You go out and hide somewhere."

"A person can hide for a day but not forever. If somebody wants to kill you, there is no escape," Zhao Zhen judged.

"Yes, what you say is true."

While drinking porridge, Zhao Zhen imagined the situation when the knife punctured his body. He didn't know whether it would get him in the neck or in the belly. Maybe it would be in his side? He felt his teeth turn cold. He put down his porridge bowl and went to the home of Ma Lin, the Village Head. Ma Lin had consumed too much porridge and was stroking his bloated belly.

"Zhao Zhen, you've come. I drank too much porridge and my belly's not comfortable. When you start drinking it you just want more. But when you drink more, you get uncomfortable. People really are wretches," Ma Lin said. "Take a seat."

"I won't sit down. Someone told me that Big Dan plans to kill me. Do you know anything about it?"

Ma Lin answered, "I only know that he's been killing an awful lot of dogs lately. I asked him, and he told me that he was feeling a bad way inside. Killing dogs perhaps brings him relief."

"If he really does want to kill me, what should I do? I've provided a woman for every single guy in Double-Ditch Village. Even if I've not made any other contribution, I've put my heart into doing that."

"Even an upright official finds it hard to settle a family dispute. Big Dan didn't claim out loud that he was going to kill you, so it's difficult for me to get involved."

"I brought back Big Dan's wife for him."

"You cannot help it if people have no conscience."

"If you don't get involved, don't expect me to bring back any more women for this village. Even if I brought them back I wouldn't pass them onto the people."

"Almost all of the bachelors in the village have got their woman now. Only one or two are left and so it doesn't matter.

The family line of the village won't be broken. What is more, you never charged cut-price rates and you made a killing out of bringing women back. Where did the money for you to build a house come from?"

"Your words are like farts."

"My stomach is bloated with porridge. I really want to let out farts."

Zhao Zhen repeated Ma Lin's words to his wife.

His wife responded, "How could Ma Lin become a Village Head? He is just a shit-head."

She then gazed at the paper that covered the window and thought for a while. She continued, "If Big Dan really did kill you, how would your son and I survive?" Before she had finished those words, her face was overrun with tears.

Zhao Zhen remained silent for a long while and then abruptly raised his head and declared, "Big Dan is a shit-head too. Maybe I will kill him first."

He went out of the room and walked a number of circuits around the courtyard. Looking at the halls and side-rooms he had built in recent years, his heart was seized with bitterness. Everybody knew that human traffickers made money, but they didn't know what suffering it brought them. People didn't know how human traffickers risked bleeding to death. There are no good men in the world. Man is no better than a dog. With this idea, he walked to the dog kennel, squatted down and perused the mastiff for a long while.

The mastiff was lying in a heap of warm, fine earth. The earth let off a kind of pungent doggy odour. It penetrated into Zhao Zhen's nose and probed into his heart. The mastiff also gazed back at Zhao Zhen. It then stood up and shook the fine earth from its body. It walked towards him and nudged his knee with its head. Zhao Zhen buried his hands in the long mane of the dog and asked, "Oh doggy, what would you do if somebody wanted to kill me?" The dog said nothing. Of course, it was mute. Zhao Zhen unfastened its chain.

Zhao Zhen didn't love his dog in vain. When Big Dan entered his black door with the pig-killing knife, the mastiff would rip through his Achilles tendon with one bite, not letting out a single bark.

XII.

The assassination of Zhao Zhen commenced at midnight. After supper, Old Dan pushed away his bowl and told Big Dan to sharpen his blade. Big Dan glanced at his father and then went to collect the knife.

"I'll watch you sharpen it," said Old Dan.

Big Dan placed the grindstone in the upper hall. Old Dan carried over a bowl of water. While washing-up in the kitchen Huanhuan peeked at them a few times. Old Dan told her, "Huanhuan carry on with your business. Once you've finished, you can go to bed."

"Begin," Old Dan instructed Big Dan.

Big Dan started to grind the blade. His face was solemn and stirring. The air outside was dry and the breeze gusty. Later the wind would dip down and snowflakes fall from the sky. Big Dan shivered with the cold.

Old Dan glared at Big Dan.

"It's snowing," Big Dan noted.

"Of course, it's winter. There's bound to be snow."

"Cold. I feel cold."

"Are you scared? Look, you've been sharpening that for such a long time. It's already midnight."

"It would be nice to have a bottle of liquor."

"Where could I get some at this hour? Drink water. Hot water can warm you up as well."

"Then I'll make do with water."

Big Dan downed two bowls of hot water in quick succession.

"Go," Old Dan commanded.

"Let's go."

They opened the door and fumbled one-behind-the-other in the direction of Zhao Zhen's home. The snow somehow stopped falling. The wind was still piercing and bore into their necks.

The door of Zhao Zhen's home was shut tightly. They stood there for a while. Big Dan's teeth began to chatter with the cold.

"Even if we find a big pit in front of us we still have to jump over it," Old Dan said.

"Kill the dog first," was Big Dan's idea.

"That's your business," his father replied. "Pry the door open. First, you must pry the door."

Big Dan lunged the knife into the crack in the door, though could not detect the latch. Big Dan's heart suddenly jumped in a crazy fashion.

"The door's not on the latch," Big Dan discerned.

"Then get inside."

Big Dan summoned up his strength, channelling it into the knife-wielding hand. He pushed the door open gently. He placed one foot over the threshold and then the other. His eyes scanned in search of the dog and the upper hall where Zhao Zhen was sleeping. It was dark in the courtyard. The eaves of the upper hall protruded into the dim and empty night.

It was at this moment that Zhao's family mastiff bounded towards Big Dan and bit Big Dan on the heel. *Gatchow!* Big Dan realised that his Achilles tendon had been severed. He didn't feel pain. He only felt the fine hair on his body going *gatchow* and standing on end. Before the dog could open its mouth again he had plunged the knife into its neck. The dog immediately loosened its grip. It teetered for a few steps and then keeled over. Its body was quivering and its throat gurgling. Soon it became motionless. Big Dan studied it firmly in case the creature got up again. He thought that if it were to come bounding over again, he would have no choice but to let it bite him because he hadn't pulled the blade out of its neck.

The dog didn't get up. However, Big Dan's ankle was now unbearably painful. It was at this moment he realised that he had slain a dozen dogs to no end. The bouncing and biting reflex of those dozen dogs bore no resemblance to that of Zhao's mastiff. They bounced and bit because they wanted the cornbread in his hand, whereas this mastiff bounced and bit after his Achilles heel.

As soon as Old Dan came in through the door he caught sight of that mastiff.

"Killed?" Old Dan crouched over Big Dan, his throat shivering with excitement.

"It mangled my leg," Big Dan groaned.

Old Dan stretched out his hand and touched a pool of something warm. He knew that it was Big Dan's blood. A heart-chewing sorrow rose up inside him. He held Big Dan's shoulder and wailed.

"My son, ah, ah, ah."

The lamp in the upper hall was lit. Zhao Zhen came out in a fur overcoat. He looked at Old Dan and Big Dan and then at his mastiff. He squatted in front of the dog and he too touched a pool of something warm. A heart-chewing sorrow rose up inside him as well. He wiped his bloody hand against the dog's fur.

"Oh, my dog!" he shouted. He grasped one of the dog's legs and wailed, "Ah, ah, ah, ah …"

When Zhao Zhen let out a sad cry, Old Dan straightaway wiped off his own tears.

"You donkey-fucked sod. How can you still cry? You feel the neck of this dog. The knife is still stuck in it. That was originally meant for you."

Zhao Zhen wept even more sorrowfully.

Big Dan said, "Let's go back. This pain is making me sweat all over."

Old Dan replied, "Put up with it. I'll carry you home on my back."

He lifted his son onto his back and pulled open the door to

Zhao Zhen's home. He stepped over the threshold.

Zhao Zhen ceased to weep. "Pay me for my dog!"

Old Dan didn't turn around. He strode onto the street carrying Big Dan on his back. He could hear Zhao Zhen's shout running through his ears from behind. This shout spread to the other end of the main street. He realised that that sound could outpace the speed of a walker.

Big Dan applied twenty-seven herbal poultices in succession. New tissue, at last, grew in the wound. Even so, the cut Achilles tendon failed to mend. He would be damaged permanently.

In the course of more than one month's convalescence, Huanhuan waited upon him attentively. She washed his wound and replaced the dressing. Huanhuan's fingers resembled tender cotton balls.

Big Dan commented, "Huanhuan, your hands are very soft."

She responded, "They were even softer in the past."

Big Dan let out an "Oh, oh. You steal men and I still find you kind and pretty. Is that strange?"

"Not strange at all. Let bygones be bygones and never mention this again."

"Oh, oh. Never mother-fucking mention it again."

The day Big Dan was able to get up off the *kang* he ambled one circuit of the courtyard with his crippled leg and then said to Huanhuan, "Huanhuan, you see. From now on, I have to walk like this. If you don't like me, you can find another man to spend the rest of your life with."

Huanhuan replied: "I shall never give you the cold shoulder. I'll live together with you."

"Don't go to Zhao Zhen again."

"Look, just now you said not to mention things from the past."

"Don't mention, don't mention. I regret it."

"What the matter?"

"I'm a silly guy. I couldn't even learn how to grow cabbages from my dad."

"It doesn't matter that you haven't learnt that. Growing cabbages is hardly big business. Your dad has been growing them all his life, but he hasn't had a decent living out of it."

"If we don't grow cabbages, what are we going to do?"

"Let's think about it, Let's think about it. Maybe you can think up a good business to do."

A few days later, someone from the neighbouring village came over with a bitch for Big Dan. Big Dan was walking circuits of the courtyard with his crippled leg. He surveyed the man and then the dog from top to toe and felt at a loss.

"The bitch is in heat," the guy said.

"If she's on heat, why come to our home?" Big Dan asked. He was a trifle angry.

"We can't find a decent sire anywhere around here."

"Oh, oh. Don't we have he-dogs here?" Big Dan wanted to drive that guy away. "You are insulting us."

"Look, Big Dan, how can you say that?" The guy smiled at Big Dan. "You bought up all the decent sires."

"Oh, oh," now Big Dan remembered. "There were two of them I didn't kill, but they might have starved to death."

"Maybe not. Let's go have a look. Without any he-dogs, the villages around here won't have any future generations of hounds. Let's go have a look. We can take this as a chance to build up more good deeds for the next life."

Huanhuan came out of the kitchen and mused, "Maybe they're not dead. The cornbread we prepared for the dog has gone mouldy. I thought it was a waste so tossed it out in the hut. That was a few days after your leg got hurt.

"Go and take a look," the guy from the neighbouring village said.

They went to the grass-thatched hut. The dead bodies of the dogs were scattered around the outside. The two dogs he didn't slay were inside. One was already dead, the other was emaciated. It couldn't even open its eyes.

"You see. It is useless," Big Dan said.

"Maybe you can feed it up," the guy suggested. "After all, we can't make do without a sire."

Big Dan mulled it over for a while and replied, "I see you are a warmhearted chap. I'll have a try. Come over after a few days."

"Are you sure?" The guy didn't believe him.

"Sure," Big Dan insisted. "You can rest assured. The only thing I'm afraid of is that it won't live up to what it's meant to be." Big Dan pointed at the he-dog.

When the guy had left, Big Dan limped back home in a hurry. He said, "We are going to come into money." Huanhuan was confused. She gazed straight at Big Dan. Big Dan said, "One he-dog did survive. We must try our best to feed it up again." Huanhuan still couldn't understand.

"One successful pregnancy can fetch us two yuan."

Huanhuan let out an "Oh" and now understood what was on Big Dan's mind.

"First we should feed him up," Big Dan explained.

"That's not tricky."

Despite his leg being crippled, Big Dan managed to dig a big pit and buried the many canine corpses from around the hut. Every day, Huanhuan would cook corn porridge for that he-dog. Within a few days, it was capable of getting to its feet. More days passed. That dog became a proper, authentic sire. One sight of a bitch and it would leap over enthusiastically. This made both Big Dan and the master of the she-dog very excited. Big Dan said to the guy from outside the village, "I'll charge you one yuan less than the going rate. You just go and spread the news that I'm setting up a breeding station. Folks who have a bitch on heat can come to our home."

In this fashion, Big Dan soon transformed the hut into a dog breeding station. Those who had dogs on heat streamed along. Sometimes a long queue had to be formed. Big Dan said, "Don't line up in a queue. Our he-dog isn't a machine – he can only mount one in a day, two at most."

Big Dan saved a lot of bitches with his he-dog and coined it in.

Huanhuan observed, "All the folks say you are a lump of wood. How come you sprung to life?"

Big Dan rubbed the grease on his neck using his hand and joked, "A watchman's clapper is a piece of wood too but when you knock it, it produces a note."

"In the past, you didn't spring to life simply because you weren't being knocked."

"Right, quite right. It's all thanks to that guy who came over with the bitch on heat. He knocked me, and I came to life. It's incredible. If that damned guy had come a few days later, our he-dog would have been already dead."

Presently, Big Dan came to realize that all of the people from the vicinity of Double-Ditch Village had developed an interest in raising dogs. He had something to do with that. When he was going to kill Zhao Zhen, that mastiff saved his master's life. Many people became giddy at the very mention of this. They said that dogs could not only stand guard but rescue lives as well.

Big Dan asked, "Huanhuan, have you heard what people are talking about?"

Huanhuan answered, "Yes, I have."

"This is mother-fucking strange."

"Yes. I've found it strange too."

By that time, they had moved home. They built an extension onto the grass-thatched hut and were making preparations to construct a bigger house in two years' time. At that point, more and more people were dropping by with their dogs on heat. Big Dan now not only had one breeding hound but two. He purchased another one from outside. He boasted to others that it had been bought in Inner Mongolia. It was a sheepdog that could both run fast and bite hard sparing none of its strength.

Big Dan now had not the slightest interest in his father and Zhao Zhen.

XIII.

Zhao Zhen buried his mastiff with great sorrow. He felt that his dog had died heroically. Old Dan was correct. The knife was lodged in the dog's neck. It was a pig-killing knife, which took a lot of strength to tug out. The dog's blood had already congealed and the entry wound was like a black hole. The animal's eyes were shut tightly and its mouth was opened partially, exposing a few teeth. One could imagine what an ordeal it went through before dying. He pushed the mouth shut and bound a piece of cloth around the wound. By this means, its agonised expression was replaced with one of docility. He carried it to the pit he had dug and completed the burial.

A few days later, he led a group of hooligans from out of the village to Old Dan's home.

"You pay for my dog," he demanded.

Old Dan blinked and scanned the gang Zhao Zhen had brought over.

"It bit Big Dan's Achilles tendon in two. Who should I go to for compensation? Big Dan is now disabled."

"Go up to the roof," Zhao Zhen instructed.

A couple of guys swiftly climbed up to the top of the roof. Two others carried over a pair of long logs and leant them against the eaves.

"Pay or don't pay?"

"Do you dare? Do all of you dare?" Old Dan shouted towards the two guys on the roof.

"Pull off his tiles. Whoever tries to stop us will get a broken leg."

"You robbers!" Old Dan shouted.

"Do it!" Zhao Zhen snarled.

One of the guys on top of the roof kicked all the tiles together into a heap. His accomplice slid them down one-by-one along the long logs. Old Dan's eyes were dark to begin with and then turned red. He felt like there was a cat scratching at his heart, but he had no recourse.

"Daylight robbers!" he shouted and then breezed out of the gate.

He kicked open Ma Lin, the Village Head's door.

"Zhao Zhen is taking the tiles off my roof," he screeched.

"Would he do that without reason?" Ma Lin enquired.

"He asked me to pay for his dog."

"That's it. He wouldn't dare do this without any reason. Has he eaten a leopard's gall bladder and absorbed its courage?"

"He stole a woman from us and he's now throwing down the tiles from my roof."

"You killed his dog."

"But what about him stealing the woman?"

"The woman is safe and sound at home now, but his dog is dead. Those are two different things."

"I can't swallow this."

"Even if you can't swallow this, you shouldn't have killed his dog. You can get your own back! Steal his woman. If you are a real man, you can steal his woman and make him die from anger. You shouldn't kill him and you shouldn't have killed his dog."

When Old Dan returned home, all of the roof-tiles had gone. Zhao Zhen had fetched over a horse-drawn cart and taken them away. The courtyard was in total disarray. Old Dan squatted beneath the eaves. He wanted to cry. He covered his face but didn't cry out loud. He recalled Ma Lin's comments. When he heard them, he initially thought that his words stank worse than shit. Now he realised that there was some reason behind them. He thought that there was no way at all for him to seduce Zhao Zhen's woman. Nevertheless, even if he couldn't seduce his woman, he could still find a way to make him furious.

Soon, he hit on a method. He did something that nobody in Double-Ditch Village had ever done before. One evening, a neighbour witnessed Old Dan leaving the village with a pick and shovel on his shoulder. They wondered what he had in mind going out with those implements at this hour. He had already decided he was done talking with them. Later on, people realised that Old Dan was going to dig up Zhao Zhen's ancestral tomb.

The urge to fight to the bitter end had been stirred in Old Dan's heart. He dug day and night among the unmarked common graves. During these days, Zhao Zhen had gone out again. Someone told Zhao Zhen's wife what was going on. "I don't care," she answered. "After all, they're the graves of Zhao Zhen's ancestors." By the time Zhao Zhen came back to the village, Old Dan had finished his digging. He disinterred sundry pieces of bones and strung them on a rope and hung the lot on the wall of his home. He held one bone in his hand and struck those on the line one at a time.

"He is amusing himself by banging on your ancestors' bones," someone informed Zhao Zhen.

Zhao Zhen's face was first red and then white. After a while, it relaxed. He smiled.

"Let him bang away" was his considered reaction. "When people are dead they are dead. Death is the end of everything. What are the use of bones when the person is dead? He may as well use those bones to bang a gong!"

Zhao Zhen's words soon reached Old Dan's ears. Old Dan had, after a few days, grown tired of knocking those bones. On hearing what Zhao Zhen had to say, his heart clicked. He wouldn't carry on knocking anymore. He tugged the string in two and threw the bones into the gulley outside the village.

"I cannot conquer him," he thought. He was disappointed for a spell.

"I must find a way to conquer him." His two black pill-like eyes flashed with a wolf-like gleam.

Soon he hit upon a new method.

He went to Zhao Zhen calmly and at ease.

"I want to stand on the top of your manure heap," Old Dan said.

Zhao Zhen had a queer feeling. He looked at Old Dan like he was looking at a monster. Zhao Zhen's wife shouted angrily:

"No, if you stand on the top of the manure heap how can I pee and shit?"

"Is this OK or not?" Old Dan fixed Zhao Zhen in the face.

"Aren't you afraid of the bad smell?" Zhao Zhen asked.

"I'm not. I think I will grow into a tree. The manure heap is full of nutrients."

Zhao Zhen smiled and answered, "OK, go and have a try. I won't take care of your food, though."

"I won't eat or drink."

"Maybe you really can grow into a tree. Then I will fell you to make boxes and cupboards."

"That would have to be in many years time. Maybe you will already be dead by then."

"Then I shall let my son do it."

"When your son opens the boxes and cupboards, the smell he breathes in will be mine."

The next day, Old Dan did indeed stand on the top of Zhao Zhen's manure heap. Group after group, the folk of Double-Ditch Village came to the front of Zhao Zhen's privy and watched Old Dan like they were appreciating the scenery. The people carried their kids in their hands, led them by their hands and let them sit on their shoulders. They passed comments on Old Dan's demeanour, making animated gestures. Old Dan already had nothing to say to them. He could feel that the soles of his feet were cracking open. Something like root hairs were growing out of them and inching into the depths of the heap. Meanwhile, the hair on his head was stretching upwards. Had he been a tree, they would part into forks and boughs.

The Red Heat

Madam Yellow Plum's first experience of the red heat was brought on by the sparrows.

"That year," she recalled, "I was twelve years old."

Yellow Plum, then a girl of twelve, stood on the roof of her house, waving her hands and yelling out one round of cries after another. Her mother and younger brother were standing there as well, calling out in unison with her. Her grandparents, being too old to mount the roof, did their yelling in the yard instead. As for her neighbours – some of whom were as young as Yellow Plum – they were on their rooftops also. What about their neighbours' neighbours? They, of course, stood up on their roofs or down in their yards.

A greater height reveals to one a grander sight. From that roof, Yellow Plum was able to survey the Bell Tower and the Drum Tower, both of them teeming with people. Moreover, she also caught a glimpse of numerous tall buildings. Her father, as an ordinary worker, was likely to be standing at the summit of one of those lofty structures.

The city was too boundless for her to stretch her eyesight to gaze upon the suburbs. But, on the wings of her imagination, she could picture the fields and barracks on the outskirts of the city. There, diligent and simple-hearted farmers would be waving their hands and yelling in the fields together with her and respectable PLA soldiers would be waving their hands and yelling in the barracks together with her too.

They were all driving away the sparrows.

Subsequently, Yellow Plum turned her thoughts to the whole nation. Its boundless territories covered 9.6 million square kilometres and were crowded with workers, farmers, businessmen and students standing up on the roofs and down on the ground. At that moment, Yellow Plum could discern with some accuracy exactly how vast the area of her motherland was. The yelling resembled coruscating waves stretching from the coast of the Eastern Sea to the Pamir Plateau and from the river-riddled, lake-dotted lands of the South to the bleakness of Northern China.

Oh-shoo! Oh-shoo! The first round of waves subsided.

Oh-shoo! Oh-shoo! And then the second round rose immediately.

Even at so young an age, when tasked with trying to convey the vastness of her motherland, Yellow Plum was able to compose an elegantly-worded clause like "from the coast of the Eastern Sea to the Pamir Plateau and from the river-riddled, lake-dotted lands of the South to the bleakness of Northern China."

Oh-shoo! Oh-shoo! The yelling rang out from the coast of the Eastern Sea to the Pamir Plateau.

Oh-shoo! Oh-shoo! The yelling resonated from the river-riddled, lake-dotted lands of the South to the bleakness of Northern China.

Oh-shoo! Oh-shoo! The yelling burst forth from workers, farmers, businessmen, students and soldiers alike.

It was a moment filled with unprecedented exhilaration. Dressed in a short-sleeved blouse, Yellow Plum unconsciously exposed her tummy and her bellybutton when her waving and excited yelling caused her shirt and trousers to flap momentarily apart. Of course, it was not the fashionable thing for girls to display their navel in public. However, just because it was not fashionable did not mean that girls never, in fact, exposed their bellybuttons. In exactly the same way, just because it was not fashionable for girls to talk about sexual climax did not mean they did not experience orgasm.

The people's relentless campaigning dragged the miserable sparrows from the sky. One after another they sank to the ground out of panic and exhaustion. The whole world echoed with the tender sound of sparrows plopping to the ground. Every falling sparrow would stir a wave of cheers. And every wave of cheers would be followed by more frenzied *Oh-shoo*-ing.

Some sparrows fell onto the roof of Yellow Plum's house.

It was at that second that Yellow Plum was seized by a sense of dizziness and feebleness. *Pang!* One sparrow landed on the floor beside her feet. Intoxicated by a wave of cheers, she came over all dizzy and limp. Her red Young Pioneers scarf was lifted up from her bosom by the breeze. She bit hold of it with her teeth and then sank down.

No one paid any attention to the manner in which she squatted down on the ground. They only saw her eyes close slightly, which they took as a sign of her being tired.

Of course, after Yellow Plum had experienced that feeling of dizziness and feebleness it was quite feasible that she would feel tired.

Maybe her indescribable feeling of dizziness and feebleness coupled with her tiredness had nothing to do with being overcome by the red heat. However, it is an undeniable fact that during the process of sexual climax one is bound to feel dizzy, feeble and a little fatigued. So it cannot be absolutely concluded that this was a case of tiredness accompanied by sexual climax. It would be truly embarrassing for anyone to probe further into whether a girl of twelve is experiencing some peculiar sensation within her body as she is seized by a strange sense of dizziness and feebleness. If such inquiries were to be made, the questioner and the investigator would be taken as rascals. Nevertheless, nobody is able to confirm with absolute certainty that the female orgasm is exclusively related to contact with men and that it has nothing to do with banishing sparrows or any other activities. As a matter of fact, many years later when Yellow Plum came to disinter her sensation of dizziness and feebleness from out of her dusty memory, she admitted: "I did once have it; I had it when I was driving away sparrows from the roof of my house."

She told that to her husband while casting a hazy look in his direction. It was as though she were recalling something from the distant past.

Soon, Yellow Plum grew up and developed a fine shape. Now one metre and 64 centimetres in height, with a protruding bosom, she came to experience the red heat once again.

This time it was because of Iron Plum Li.

The sparrows had not been eradicated entirely. And yet, those who had been engaged in that pest control had already discovered a new source of excitement and enjoyment. Couldn't the opera heroine Jiang Shuiying excite the people? What about other opera heroines like the White-Haired Girl, Wu Qinghua, and Little Changbao?

Yellow Plum was once cast in the role of Iron Plum Li in the opera *The Legend of the Red Lantern*.

It was during her spell at acting that Old Cao fell head over heels for Yellow Plum and married her.

Think about it – during the act of telling the revolutionary family stories, when Granny Li illustrated the transformation from Zhang Yuhe to Li Yuhe through a lengthy passage of soliloquy and held the seventeen-year-old Iron Plum tightly in her arms, the latter was stirred. The girl lifted a signal lantern and sang the passage which begins "Follow my dad and fight the jackals" together with the audience who had previously expelled sparrows with her. These folks ranged from workers to farmers, to businessmen, students and soldiers.

Think about it – across the national territory of 9.6 million kilometres – from the coast of the Eastern Sea to the Pamir Plateau and from the river-riddled, lake-dotted lands of the South to the bleakness of Northern China – there were countless Iron Plums, sporting a typically long pigtail, clad in a red cotton robe and singing with a signal lantern in one hand.

She intoned lines such as, "the lifted red lantern blazes" and "we'll fight generation after generation," stretching out the sound of the word "battle" in the line "never retire from the battlefield till all the jackals have been wiped out." These lines made this particular and already long-excited Iron Plum Li dizzy and limp all over. It nearly caused her to sink to the ground. Of course, she couldn't do that, for she was not engaged in expelling sparrows on the roof of her own house. Granny grasped and supported her at the critical moment and they two together made the gesture of raising the red lantern on the stage.

Yellow Plum was very grateful for the choreography of this gesture. Without it, her dizziness and limpness would have rendered her too feeble to lift that red lantern for long enough. Thanks to Granny Li's timely support, she didn't squat down despite the fact that she was eager to do that. Were she not playing a role on the stage, she would probably have just squatted down on the ground so as to prolong that sense of dizziness and limpness.

For so many years, the gesture of raising a red lantern and singing the line about beating away the jackals stirred Yellow Plum to countless bouts of dizziness and limpness.

"Weren't these all sexual experiences?"

Yellow Plum fixed her eyesight resolutely upon her husband Old Cao.

She concluded, "I've examined strictly my sense of the red heat according to the characteristics of the orgasm as you described them. I do experience sexual climaxes. That is my conclusion."

Old Cao sighed, "Yes, you are definitely right. You not only have sexual climaxes but these are closely attuned to the pulse of the times. You make me want to cry!"

Yellow Plum soothed him, "Don't do that. I just hope that the red heat will come along when you want it to. Even so, you can't deny I have a history of coming off. I am not that type of person who can never reach it. If you need more examples of how this happened to me, playing Mahjong springs to mind."

After repeated exchanges with her husband, Yellow Plum could not only pin down what the red heat was, but could easily draw a connection between her playing Mahjong and reaching sexual climax. Recent years found her becoming fond of competing at the game. She was certain that playing it brought on the red heat. For example, in the act of touching and receiving the tiles, it felt as if the tiles were touching her back. This was experienced as a form of pleasurable and intimate contact. What is more, her mood would lift, and then slump when she mistook the tile she was feeling for the "seven *wan*" tile. That was until she found it was the "six *wan*" tile and not the "seven *wan*." Of course, if she wanted the "six *wan*" tile and got, it was then that the red heat put in its appearance. "*Oh, it is! Oh, Oh…!*" Her circulation had already sped up. She had already been overcome with dizziness and then grew limp and relaxed.

Yellow Plum recalled, "All these facts go to show that I not only come off but have done it many times."

Old Cao retorted, "But not you and me."

"I admit it," Yellow Plum replied.

Her husband made himself clear, "What I want is for you to get the red heat when you are with me. That's why I've gone to the trouble of having this word with you."

His request provoked some hesitancy in her. "I don't want to let you down. But to be frank, that will be quite hard. It must be said, you're not a sparrow or a signal lantern, and you are not a game of Mahjong either."

"Think about it," he urged. "Every night, across the territory of 9.6 million square kilometres, how many people are having sex and how many of them are coming off?"

After pondering for a while, Yellow Plum nodded. "Maybe this idea will work."

Having second thoughts, she added, "One question does bother me, though. You haven't brought this up in so many years. Why are you pressing me on it now?"

Old Cao answered, "In the past, I just felt that being between the sheets with you was a bit boring. I didn't know why. Now I know the reason I want it to stop being boring. I even have the urge to throttle you to death."

She agreed to give it a try with him because she didn't want to be throttled to death.

Actually, the secret of the female orgasm had been revealed to Old Cao by the masseuses in the sauna. He was first invited to that place by his friend, but afterwards, he visited it on his own a number of times. On each occasion, he discovered that the lady could reach a sexual climax. It is a pity that his wife never experienced this. She never groaned, she never twisted her body and she never cried out in excitement. "Finished?" Yellow Plum would merely utter that single word when Old Cao came on top of her. She would then open her eyes as if nothing had happened. Having realised the tedium that had been his sex life over so many years, he had the urge to wail bitterly.

Finally, Old Cao resolved to tackle the boring state of affairs between him and his wife. The massage girl, who got the red heat, was not boring but she cost him money. For Old Cao, spending the least money possible was his guiding economic principle.

Old Cao nearly succeeded. Once after his return from a business trip, he dragged Yellow Plum back home from the Mahjong house.

Old Cao said, "You told me you wanted to have a try with me."

Bringing to mind the promise she had made, Yellow Plum replied, "Oh, yes, I did."

Afterwards, she lay down on the bed and embraced him. At the outset, she seemed to be somehow absentminded but she soon got aroused. With her eyes open and her lips pursed, Old Cao could even hear her breathing. Old Cao asked her if she felt OK and satisfied and he even said so many sweet words to coax her. He said, "You must say something in return. I want to hear your voice, even if it's just *one* gentle grunt. My sweet."

She really did let out a grunt.

Then Yellow Plum said, "I should not have played that tile, I was really stupid!"

On hearing this, Old Cao stalled and stared at his wife. Then he rolled down off her naked body.

"I'll throttle you to death," Old Cao swore.

Scared, Yellow Plum wept and explained, "I know you were trying to arouse me. I am ready to be turned on by you. But I can't help thinking of the mistake I made playing Mahjong. That tile was really critical to me."

Old Cao still cursed, "I shall throttle you to death."

Sobbing, she pleaded with him, "Don't lose heart. Let's try again. Change needs practise to work. Be patient, please. I am able to make it, and so it's very likely it will come on when I'm with you."

Miracles did unfold as Old Cao tried to arouse Yellow Plum once again. At last, she felt the irresistible approach of the red heat and all of a sudden embraced her husband tightly with her mouth agape. She wanted to tell him, "I'm coming, I'm coming."

But she never had the chance, for her husband was not only pressing hard against her body but also gripping her throat firmly.

He screamed out of frustration, "You must be imagining I'm a Mahjong game or a signal lantern. I can't bear this."

At that moment, Yellow Plum was trying her best to twist her body.

The Billy Goat Pops In

I.

A HANDFUL OF chickens were scavenging for food at the entrance to the village. Their agile beaks worked several times every now and then but none knew if they had succeeded in getting any bounty. They gave the appearance of finding nothing since they simply pecked away without raising their necks. One rooster suddenly spread out his wings and swooped on a hen. The hen staggered to the apparent effect that it didn't want to do that business at present. But the rooster did. Therefore, he didn't stop clinging to the hen because the hen had lurched. With one of his wings outstretched, the rooster tried to draw himself close, time and time again, like a rascal.

At this moment, Full Victory Wang and his flock of sheep and goats were passing by the entrance to the village. The animals' leisurely hooves disturbed the rooster. He jumped to one side, retracted his wing and gawked at the flock of animals with reverence and awe.

The lead animal was a billy goat. A roll of eye-catching red satin was draped across his horns and a bell hung under his neck. With his head raised high, the animal sported an overweening air. His arrogance was derived entirely from his fine self-perception. He was of great importance. Not only was he a billy goat but also a breeding sire. Billy goats are ten-a-penny in this world but breeding sires are rare, and this beast could count itself among the few.

Full Victory Wang, who wore a length of straw rope around his waist, tailed the flock of animals. It was not that he couldn't afford or couldn't find the heart to sport a hempen rope or a leather belt. He did this out of habit. A straw rope had its advantages. When it was frayed, he could just dump it and weave another. Every day he was out on the mountains. When the flock started to graze, how was he to kill time? Roar a mountain ditty? Roaring a mountain ditty wouldn't hinder him from weaving a straw rope. For this reason, Full Victory Wang's waist was always bound with a straw rope. He was in his thirties and yet the wrinkles on his rough face were splattered with dust and dirt. His stubble was also smeared with dust and dirt, which had coagulated into grains and pellets; if they were dyed red, people might think that sour dates or goji berries were dangling there. His feet splaying in a V-shape, he strutted with his hands, gripping a shepherd's whip clasped behind his back. "Coming back?" "Yeah." He greeted a gaggle of fellow villagers while walking along.

Soon he reached the gateway to his compound. With a few more steps, his animals would throng in through the half-open gate. However, that billy goat remained still on the spot. Full Victory Wang felt a little surprised. He could see that the billy goat was listening to something with his ears pricked up. He too pricked up his ears. Immediately he heard a series of bleats let out by a nanny goat that was on heat. It was the property of his neighbour Security Hu. For sure, it was. Full Victory Wang looked at his billy goat again. Apparently, the beast's mind was running wild like a capering monkey or a galloping horse. He didn't want to cross the threshold.

Wang was quick on the draw. He twizzled the shepherd's whip in his hand and cracked it crisply in mid-air. The tip of the lash scraped past the billy goat's head, causing the beast to shiver as if cold and he ambled in through the gate like a thief.

"You son of a bitch – you want to nibble on something you haven't earned," Full Victory Wang cursed.

Wang picked up a huge bowl and started to have his meal. He put his mouth to the rim of the vessel and then rotated it, letting out a long drawn-out sucking noise. He felt that a mouthful of the lukewarm black bean and millet porridge had slipped through his pharynx like a small fish, dashed its head against the wall of his stomach and then halted somewhere in there where it was now bouncing gently. "Oh," he exclaimed. "Motherfucker, it is so comfortable. Oh," he continued. He no longer sucked. He dropped the huge bowl on the stone-slab top of the dinner table, seemingly wanting to savour the sweetness of that mouthful of softly-stirring porridge. He then said to his woman: "Security Hu's nanny goat is longing to be knocked up."

"Oh, oh," his woman responded.

"Didn't you hear that?"

"It doesn't seem to be bleating at the moment."

He darted a sidelong glance at her, explaining: "It is not a machine. Is it able to bleat incessantly?" He thought that his woman was pig ignorant. He snatched up the huge bowl and got ready to suck again. Barely had his lips touched the rim when it dawned on him that his billy goat was gone. He cast his eyes towards the sheepfold but failed to spot the creature. A kind of unpleasant feeling came bubbling up. "Son of a bitch," he cursed, put down the bowl, fetched that shepherd's whip from the wall of the sheepfold and scooted out like a gust of wind. He pushed open the gate of his neighbour Security Hu's compound quite confidently.

Full Victory Wang's billy goat had long since begun to ride Security Hu's nanny goat with his two hind legs pulled taut like a bow and his arse jiggling like a small chugging engine. With the red satin swaying and the bell jingling, he was working for all he was worth. Wang was on a knife-edge, not for the red satin across the billy goat's horns and the bell under the billy goat's neck of course, but for the billy goat's jiggling arse. Even squinting through half an eye he could tell that if the beast's rear moved like this for much longer, there would be serious consequences. He couldn't allow the animal to disport any longer. Flicking the shepherd's whip, he strode over to Hu's sheepfold.

Security Hu was squatting down in front of the pen watching with great interest as the two goats were indulging in their fun. He saw Full Victory Wang storm towards him.

"Your billy goat has popped in to see his neighbour," he said.

"The son of a bitch is nibbling on something he hasn't earned!" Full Victory Wang retorted.

Barely had Full Victory Wang raised the shepherd's whip when Security Hu stopped him. "*Ai, ai*, it hasn't finished yet," Security Hu gasped. "Let them finish doing their business."

"You can't use your whip all the time," he continued.

"I am my own master," Full Victory Wang croaked.

"You can't swish your whip now even if you are your own master."

Full Victory Wang persisted. "How would you feel if someone suddenly lashed you when you and your woman were on the job?"

Security Hu dissuaded him. "If you whip your animal now, it might affect its health. What if it isn't able to do the deed in the future?"

Thinking that Security Hu had a point, Full Victory Wang put away his lash.

"If I shouldn't swirl my whip now, I won't then. If you want to get your nanny goat knocked up, haul it over to my yard."

"They are in the middle of their fun, but you go on about taking them to some place else. Aren't you making things difficult for them? When you and your missus are on the brink of ecstasy, would you like someone to force you to move? Just think about it."

"This is really ridiculous. Why do you keep on lumping me together with the billy goat?"

"Then I'll compare the billy goat and myself. When me and my missus are on the brink, an emperor could come and command me to move to somewhere else. I'd sooner spit on his face. Look, look, it is done."

The business was indeed over and done. Having jiggled its arse violently for a while, the billy goat slid down from the nanny goat's back. The nanny goat turned her head and rubbed her lips against the billy goat's body several times. All smiles, Security Hu walked to his animal and interjected, "OK, OK, stop being so lovey-dovey." He then said to Full Victory Wang, "Fine, fine, now drag your animal back home." Seeing that Full Victory Wang didn't want to leave, he continued: "My nanny goat has been yearning for days to get knocked up. Your billy goat is really true to the name. Without so much as a 'hi,' he darted in and the moment he darted in, they got physical. *Hee-hee-hee-hee*." Security Hu's tone of voice and facial expressions bespoke a greater sense of comfort than his nanny goat was experiencing. He also spouted many other words. Later, fixing his gaze upon Full Victory Wang, he only smirked. He didn't mention the siring fee.

After coming back home, Full Victory Wang penned the billy goat in solitary confinement and, brandishing the shepherd's whip, gave the beast a good thrashing. Every lash sent the billy goat into a jump. The animal then regarded his master with a blank face, now knowing the reason for his being beaten.

But the siring fee required discussion.

A few days later, Full Victory Wang and Security Hu ran into each other in their respective outdoor latrines. It was morning and they were standing in their outhouses relieving themselves.

Wang let out a single cough.

Hu called out "Brother Full Victory," and continued: "I am convinced of your billy goat's power. The problem has been fixed once and for all. Every morning I went to the sheepfold to take a look and I did that just now. My nanny goat no longer bleated. Crouching down in the sheepfold, it was as quiet as a Bodhisattva."

Full Victory Wang cackled: "My billy can always seal the deal the first time."

"Yeah, yeah, I'm convinced of that from the bottom of my heart."

Security Hu fastened his waistband and got ready to go back

home. Full Victory Wang let out an *Ai* and also tied up his waistband. He strode to the front of Security Hu's privy and said: "My billy goat's efforts should not go unrewarded."

Security Hu raised a questioning eyebrow and queried, "What do you mean by this?"

Full Victory Wang explained: "My billy goat's siring job commands a fee. You know this." He followed Security Hu to enter his courtyard.

He went on: "I am not pressing you to cough up today. If you are feeling the pinch right now, you can have a few days' grace."

Security Hu's face turned cloudy. "It is true that my nanny goat was looking forward to getting pregnant, but she didn't go over to your home, did she? It was your billy goat that darkened my door. Now you want me to pay. This must be a little unconscionable."

Full Victory Wang demanded: "Judging by the tone of your voice, you don't want to pay the siring fee, do you?"

Security Hu argued: "It is not that I don't want to give you the money but it is not appropriate. After getting wind of this, other folks will laugh at me. My nanny goat has been screwed by your billy goat, but I still need to dip into my pocket?"

Full Victory Wang pressed, "Will you pay or not?"

"Ask your billy goat to pay."

Full Victory Wang knew that he couldn't get the money. Lowering his head to ponder awhile, he turned around and sprinted to Security Hu's sheepfold. By the time Security Hu came back to himself, his nanny goat had already received a hard kick from Full Victory Wang. Then another kick. Then another kick. Every kick was aimed in one specific spot.

Full Victory Wang was intercepted by Security Hu when he stalked outwards. Security Hu and his woman pinned him down in their courtyard and slapped him until his face was swollen.

Full Victory Wang didn't go back to his own home but to the home of the Village Head Perpetual Peasant Li. Perpetual Peasant Li poured him a cup of water and enquired, "What's the matter?"

Full Victory Wang thought hard for a time and replied: "Let me take a sip of water first." He drank one mouthful of water.

"Drink some more, drink some more," Perpetual Peasant Li insisted.

"There is no need. I will just take this one mouthful."

He then told Perpetual Peasant Li what happened between his billy goat and Security Hu's nanny goat.

"My billy goat knocked up his nanny goat. I requested a fee. Isn't that perfectly justified? He, Security Hu, not only didn't pay but slapped me across my face. Tell me what should I do?"

"What do you want to do?"

Full Victory Wang was a little taken aback and stared at the Village Head.

"Don't look at me like this. The moment you stepped in you fired off a string of questions. I'd barely asked you one question before you started glaring at me."

Full Victory Wang demanded, "You must intervene."

"I shall, I shall. Handing in the public grain, collecting impositions and fines, building the road, going on business trips, seeing that women are fixed up with a coil – tell me what business don't I have a hand in? I can imagine anything I should shove my oar in except that I should meddle in a billy goat knocking up a nanny goat."

Perpetual Peasant Li told Full Victory Wang to go back home first. "Do something to your face pronto. Your swollen face is an ugly sight and your jabbering words are agony to my ears."

Full Victory Wang waited for a number of days and consulted a number of people. It then dawned on him that Perpetual Peasant Li had not, in fact, sought out Security Hu. Badly pissed off as he was, he went to look for Perpetual Peasant Li again.

"You have put my trouble on the back of your skull, haven't you?"

Perpetual Peasant Li patted the back of his head and replied: "Yeah, yeah. No matter where I have put it, it is still there and hasn't been lost. The town government has dispatched several guys to enforce the family-planning policy. I have to escort them to grab a few women. Couldn't you see that? We also need to look for your woman."

"My woman has had a coil fixed in her."

"Then she should be examined to see if the coil is still there or not. If the coil is out of place, it is the same as not having one at all and the coil should be re-fixed."

"Don't drift off our topic. Stick to my business."

"Your woman's coil is also your business.

"If you wash your hands of it, I will tell my woman to take out her coil and then make her give birth to a gang of babies," Full Victory Wang bluffed.

"I dare you to," Perpetual Peasant Li answered back. "If you have one more baby, I will drive away all your animals."

"If you don't mind my business, I will go to the town court to file a lawsuit and lodge a complaint," Full Victory Wang threatened.

"*Ai*! This is a good idea. Going to the court is perhaps the right path."

Full Victory Wang did drop by the town court and then again entered Perpetual Peasant Li's compound.

"You have filed the lawsuit?" Perpetual Peasant Li queried.

"Filed my arse. The donkey-fucked court moaned that it is too trivial a matter and refused to pay any attention to it. I challenged them: if a life had been lost would they turn their eyes to it? Or if Security Hu had beaten me to death would they turn their eyes to it then? The bastards didn't say anything but only smirked. The donkey-fucked court."

Perpetual Peasant Li craned his neck and tittered.

"You are still laughing!" Full Victory Wang complained.

Perpetual Peasant Li sniggered another while. "Go back home," he said finally. "I will go to Security Hu's home tonight."

II.

Perpetual Peasant Li required Security Hu to take out 2.5 yuan.

"Though Full Victory Wang's billy goat paid the neighbour a visit, your nanny goat is now carrying a kid and so you should pay. But because Full Victory Wang's billy goat was the one who popped into your place, you only need to pay a half of the fee. You have slapped Full Victory's face swollen and I won't punish you for that," he added

Security Hu took out 2.5 yuan.

Full Victory Wang didn't agree and persisted in demanding five yuan.

"You should know what is good for you," Perpetual Peasant Li lectured him. "If I hadn't shown up, you wouldn't have gotten even one cent and perhaps your face would have ended up swollen again."

"It's precisely because my face was slapped swollen that I can't swallow that and, what's more, I want compensation for the pain."

"Your face is a thing of flesh. It's not been kneaded from clay. It is swollen but it will heal up, won't it? Of course, a swollen face hurts, but the pain broke out back at that time and it is no longer sore now, is it? Do you still feel pain? If you do, tell your woman to lick at it for you tonight."

Perpetual Peasant Li tossed the money onto the edge of Full Victory Wang's *kang* and went away with his hands clasped behind his back.

Full Victory Wang wanted to run out to catch up but was dragged to a halt by his woman. He looked at her. She flashed him a smile. On account of the billy goat incident, he hadn't touched her at all these days though she loved and cherished him.

"OK, OK, let's take it that he – Perpetual Peasant Li – has a point," Full Victory Wang said. His woman then stashed away the money on the *kang* and spread out the quilt. They had a good sleep.

Early the next morning, Full Victory Wang went out to the privy to empty his bladder and again bumped into Security Hu. Security Hu was also taking a leak there. They could hear the pitter-pattering sound of one another's splashing urine. Without looking at each other, they exchanged several words.

"Brother Full Victory, did you have a good sleep last night?"

"The moment I collapsed I fell fast asleep. Dead to the world. When I opened my eyes it was daybreak already."

Security Hu jeered: "All thanks to the 2.5 yuan."

"Yeah, yeah. So now you're 2.5 yuan out of pocket you don't sleep well?"

"At the very beginning, I couldn't but kept tossing and turning on my *kang*. But later on, I could. My nanny goat was carrying a kid and I'd also slapped someone's face. 2.5 yuan didn't amount to too much."

Security Hu went away with his hands hitching up his trousers. Full Victory Wang's flock also pressed out of the gate, that billy goat still being the lead animal. Full Victory Wang's woman handed him the shepherd's whip and the rations bag. He cracked the lash crisply as if putting on a performance and followed the beasts up the mountains.

At that time, neither Full Victory Wang nor Security Hu had expected that something further would occur between them.

Security Hu's nanny goat miscarried her kid. Crouching in front of the nanny goat, Hu didn't utter one sound or let out one breath for half a day. The nanny goat was lying in the sheepfold and her legs were slathered all over with a dirty bloody mush.

Two fellow villagers were squatting down side by side and wore a facial expression that was as grave as that of Security Hu's. They wanted to muster some words of comfort.

"The 2.5 yuan has gone to waste," one commented.

"On that day, I could see clearly from the back of my cave house how more than once, Full Victory Wang kicked the nanny goat's belly. Back then I thought that the she-goat wouldn't be able to conceive. Even if it could, the kid would be bound to be lost," the other one concluded.

"Perpetual Peasant Li could settle my prick's case. What if the billy goat were a human being? It would be convicted as a rapist," he added.

Unable to stand their words any longer, Security Hu sprang to his feet, paced out of the village and went up the mountains. He wanted to search out Full Victory Wang. He wanted to slap his face swollen once again and then inform him of the miscarriage. But he soon changed his mind. After scaling a gulley, he caught sight of Full Victory Wang's flock of animals. The grazing creatures were scattered all over the slope. He then spotted that billy goat and next changed his mind. At that moment, Full Victory Wang was lying in front of a boulder and seemed to be fast asleep. Security Hu walked past him, went directly to the billy goat, and scooped up the animal.

The billy goat's bleats startled Full Victory Wang out of his slumber. Security Hu had already strode some distance with the billy goat. Pulled up short awhile, Full Victory Wang then lost his voice. He staggered to catch up. Originally he could have made it, but in such a hurry, his foot slipped and he slid down the slope. When he crawled to his feet at the bottom of the gulley, Security Hu's shadow was already out of sight. He didn't continue to give chase because he still had a flock of animals on the mountain slope.

Three days later, Full Victory Wang again knocked the Village Head's door open.

"I would if I could, sink my teeth into the donkey-fucked bastard," Full Victory Wang complained. "His nanny goat lost her kid, but he went on blaming that on my kicks and asked me for a sum of compensation that was enough to buy two kids. I have rubbed lips with him for three days. With no other way out, I have to come to look for you."

"Oh, oh," Perpetual Peasant Li parried. "You go back first."
Full Victory Wang didn't go back home.

"Security Hu has mobilised all his relatives and friends to look for on-heat nanny goats throughout the world to be sired by my billy goat," he grumbled.

"Really?" Perpetual Peasant Li exclaimed.

"Hurry, hurry up," Full Victory Wang beseeched.

Perpetual Peasant Li reached his feet out to his shoes while commenting: "The son of a bitch Security Hu, that wasn't an idea he hit upon easily." He felt that things were suddenly becoming interesting.

III.

Security Hu's courtyard had become a breeding station. The billy goat was riding on the back of a nanny goat and throwing himself into the work. The nanny goat's master was fumbling in his pockets for money and getting ready to pay Security Hu. A clutch of others were waiting to one side, each with a nanny goat in tow.

The customer whose nanny goat had been serviced prepared to leave with his animal. Security Hu gloated while pocketing the money: "Spread the word among your fellow villagers. If their nanny goats are looking forward to getting serviced, haul them to my place. Three yuan a time. Neither the old nor the young will be cheated. NEXT ONE –"

The next customer dallied awhile and seemed to be unwilling to pull his animal towards the billy goat. "Security Hu," he doubted. "You must have overestimated your billy goat. The beast has to sire so many times in one day. It might have the staying power, but does it still have so much of that stuff?"

"Not much, not much. Yours is the third one. If the seed isn't planted, you will have your money back. So what are you afraid of?"

All those present looked at the billy goat, believing that he was already spent and broken. But they were immediately made to realize that they were wrong. The billy goat first rubbed his nose against the nanny goat's body. Perhaps he had picked up some scent, or probably the fun had reddened his eyes. He suddenly exerted himself and leaped up to rest his two fore legs on the nanny goat's back. "*Wow!*" the guys all let out a surprised exclamation.

"*One punch won't make a bull's dick grow and one push won't make a railway engine go,*" Security Hu cackled. "I am not blowing my own trumpet but today I would like to see him sire five times."

The others again let out a surprised exclamation.

"I would like to gauge. I want to see how good on earth a billy goat is," Security Hu explained.

But the billy goat's hind legs were apparently not as forceful as last time.

"This is normal," Security Hu said. "You seem to have never done this business before. If you were requested to do that three times in succession, let's see if you would be unsteady on your pins or not."

Full Victory Wang and Perpetual Peasant Li entered through the gate at that moment. The first thing that heaved into Full Victory Wang's sight was that poor animal belonging to his family. Letting out a cry as if his heart had been ripped broken and his lungs had torn apart, he meant to pounce over but was grabbed at the waist by Perpetual Peasant Li.

"My animal will be tired to death!" Full Victory Wang said.

He roared painfully and tried to struggle out of Perpetual Peasant Li's arm-lock. He wanted to stick his neck out to fight Security Hu. Perpetual Peasant Li held him tighter and whispered, "Look at the stone block –"

A stone block lay in the courtyard and a butcher's cleaver was put on the stone block. Security Hu was crouching in front of it.

"You pounce and pounce to get a taste of the knife?" Perpetual Peasant Li questioned.

Full Victory Wang immediately quietened down. He wanted to rescue his billy goat, but he was more afraid of taking a hack from the butcher's cleaver. Therefore, he stood riveted where he was.

What a poor wretch the billy goat was. He was straining himself.

Full Victory Wang implored: "I beg of you. Leave. He plans to torment the billy goat to the brink of death."

Security Hu responded: "You have belittled me. If I have tormented the beast to death, then what means do I have to make money? I want nothing more than to use it to knock a few more nannies up. Do you hear me loud and clear?"

Full Victory Wang turned his face to look pitifully at Perpetual Peasant Li. Perpetual Peasant Li waved a hand at him and enjoined him to leave. He wanted to have a word with Security Hu. Full Victory Wang didn't want to go. "If you don't leave, I can't find a way to kick the conversation rolling," Perpetual Peasant Li barked. Full Victory Wang left against his will.

"Security ..." Perpetual Peasant Li said.

"Wash your hands of it and let me settle it myself," Security Hu interrupted him. "You go and tell Full Victory Wang. I don't want to take advantage of him. I will return his billy goat to him after I have made enough money. His kicks killed my nanny goat's kid and I shall be compensated for my loss."

"The 2.5 yuan I paid last time also made me a sorry arse," he continued. "His billy goat darkened my door and screwed my nanny goat. The beast should be convicted of rape. You see: I know one or two things about the law. You are the Village Head and you don't have the foggiest idea about the law. Even so, you want to resolve the disputes between people. If you want to do that, you should quote from the letter of the law and let's solve it according to the law."

Perpetual Peasant Li's face was burning hot. Security Hu was right. He really didn't know the law. He couldn't pass sentence on the lawsuit.

Nonetheless, Perpetual Peasant Li the Village Head had made up his mind that he would settle the lawsuit.

IV.

Old Liu from the town court cocked his head and stared long and hard at Perpetual Peasant Li.

"I don't dare to say that I know you," he said. "I have been working in the court for so many years. I had never seen a Village Head who took the initiative to drop by and declare that he wanted to learn the law. I will be honest with you: There are many kinds of law books and there are laws on planting forests, on environmental protection and on family planning. Which kind do you want?"

"I want the kind on the affairs between men and women."

"There is no such a kind of special law."

"The indirect kind is also OK," Perpetual Peasant Li suggested.

Old Liu then gave Perpetual Peasant Li a stack of law books.

Perpetual Peasant Li shut himself away in a room and didn't permit anyone to disturb him. "I have some books to hit," he declared. Like a bookworm, he gnawed away at those small pamphlets page by page. He believed that these little books would provide him with a way of not only out-arguing Security Hu but also of convincing Full Victory Wang from the bottom of his heart.

During those days, Security Hu used Full Victory Wang's billy goat for a number of further inseminations. Full Victory Wang went to look for Perpetual Peasant Li but each time was blocked outside by Perpetual Peasant Li's woman. The woman smiled until her face changed into a walnut. "Perpetual Peasant is hitting the books and doesn't allow anyone to disturb him," she said. Full Victory Wang leaped into mid-air.

"Perpetual Peasant Li, listen," he snarled. "If you keep your nose buried in books like this, my billy goat will be tortured to death by Security Hu."

Perpetual Peasant Li's woman pushed Full Victory Wang out onto the street in a very friendly manner. "Perpetual Peasant will not come out," she sweet-talked Full Victory Wang. "You know his temperament. He won't come out."

Full Victory Wang was in no mood to go up the mountains. "My heart feels like it is being screwed by a prick" was how he put it to his woman. "I have no mood to go up the mountains."

During those trying days, nanny goats were hauled to Security Hu's home to be impregnated every day. Security Hu had succeeded in establishing the billy goat's prowess. The beast could sire three times a day at most. When it was the fourth time, he refused point black to mount the nanny even if he was whipped. There were billy goats in this world that could sire five or six successive times a day, but this one couldn't.

Whenever a customer hauled his nanny goat out of Security Hu's home, Full Victory Wang's woman would report it to her husband. Wang could stand it no longer. Gnashing his teeth, he jumped down from the edge of the *kang*. All along, he had been crouching there smoking a cigarette. Now, he jumped down.

"Motherfucker. I can't wait for Perpetual Peasant Li any longer," he barked. "Motherfucker. I will settle it myself!" he snarled.

He immediately summoned a gang of relatives from the Wang family including Full Room Wang, Full Light Wang, Best Scholar Wang and Scholar Wang. Toting long-handled agricultural tools such as pickaxes, iron shovels and spades, they blasted into Security Hu's compound.

"Hand over my billy goat!" Full Victory Wang shouted.

Letting out a startled shriek, Security Hu's woman crawled into her cave house and shut the door.

Security Hu had not expected that Full Victory Wang would opt for the tough way. He was caught on the back foot and had no time to make preparations. Taking grip of the butcher's cleaver in his hand, he looked daggers at Full Victory Wang and his gang.

Full Victory Wang commanded solemnly, "Put down the butcher's knife!"

"I will impale anyone who comes up, until blood flows all over. Until his intestines slither out," Security Hu threatened. "I will aim squarely at him and stab him into dead meat."

Of course, the dogfight didn't erupt. Many days later, people could still recall the scene when Perpetual Peasant Li charged into Security Hu's compound. Brave beyond words, he raised one hand and roared at everyone in the courtyard: "Stop, all of you!" Subdued by the Village Head's magnificence, Full Room Wang, Full Light Wang, Best Scholar Wang and Scholar Wang, who were by then getting ready to pounce forward, stood rooted there. Perpetual Peasant Li didn't lower his hand which had five outstretched fingers. He turned his head to look at Security Hu and ordered: "Drop your knife!" Not until he saw Security Hu had put down the butcher's cleaver, did he withdraw his hand from mid-air.

He stated: "Listen up, all of you. As long as you raise a finger, it will go beyond the jurisdiction of me, Perpetual Peasant Li. For days I've been trawling through law books. Look at my eyes."

Perpetual Peasant Li's eyes were indeed like a chicken's arsehole and a swipe of black soot from the bottom of a wok seemed to have been mopped under his nose.

He continued: "I burned the midnight oil. When the electricity was out, I stayed up late by lighting the paraffin lamp. Anyhow, I made it. The law isn't a scarecrow but something serious. If a life is lost, the parties concerned should go to the public security bureau to argue it out. Twice every three days, the county court sentences people to be shot. Aren't you afraid of that? If you are, shift your backsides out of here for me."

Full Room Wang, Full Light Wang and the others felt weak in the heart. The thought of being gunned down terrified them.

One after another they slunk out of Security Hu's compound.

Full Victory Wang was unwilling to leave. "I want my billy goat back," he insisted. Perpetual Peasant Li spat at him. Full Victory Wang also went out.

Perpetual Peasant Li walked to Security Hu's front.

"Tell me if I can settle the lawsuit or not?" Perpetual Peasant Li questioned.

"You can. Do it. You can," Security Hu replied.

"Here, first thing tomorrow morning, I shall settle the case. Apply the law," Perpetual Peasant Li promised.

All the villagers thronged into Security Hu's courtyard in the same feverishly excited mood, waiting to appreciate how Perpetual Peasant Li the Village Head would pass sentence on the lawsuit resulting from the billy goat popping in.

A huge circle was emptied in the centre of the courtyard. Two wooden pegs were driven into the ground there, to which Full Victory Wang's billy goat and Security Hu's nanny goat were tethered respectively. Unable to understand the farce-watchers' merry comments, the two animals accidentally raised their heads and pricked up their ears. Their masters, Full Victory Wang and Security Hu, crouched in front of them respectively with their heads lowered.

A wooden table and a long wooden bench were put on one side of the circle. Perpetual Peasant Li the Village Head and Old Liu from the town court marched in from outside the human circle and settled down on the wooden bench. Perpetual Peasant Li coughed and then dropped the stack of law books clamped under his arm onto the wooden table.

Silence descended on the crowd – even the crows and sparrows gagged their beaks.

Perpetual Peasant Li's face was a picture of earnestness. "This is Comrade Liu from the town court," went his introduction. "He has been summoned here to be a witness. He won't try the case. I shall."

The crowd guffawed. "Laugh. Laugh to your hearts' content and then I shall try the case," Perpetual Peasant Li said. The laughter immediately died down. Perpetual Peasant Li coughed again and then started the hearing.

He reasoned: "The households of Full Victory Wang and Security Hu both almost experienced the loss of a life, which was all down to those two troublemaking animals. I will talk about the animals first. A nanny goat yearning to get in the family way will surely bleat. It was hearing those bleats that encouraged the billy goat to pop in. The billy goat's master Full Victory Wang wanted to charge the siring fee. The nanny goat's master Security Hu claimed in rejoinder that the billy goat had committed the crime of rape. This is a contradiction. The nanny goat's master declared that since the billy goat came uninvited, the siring fee should not be charged. The billy goat's master riposted that the nanny goat seduced his billy goat by bleating and the money must be paid. This is another contradiction. One party has his explanations and the other party has his reasons. What about the law? According to the law, the crime of rape cannot be put on record unless it has been reported within twenty-four hours. Moreover, if the nanny goat didn't consent, the billy goat couldn't have made it upon its own conditions and abilities. Therefore, the crime of rape is not upheld. The only fact that can be inferred is: The two animals are neighbours. Affection was generated between them because they met each other frequently, could hear each other's voice and could smell one another's person during such a long period of interaction. It should by rights be an act of adultery. The law doesn't shove its oar into adulterous relationships. Security Hu, if you don't believe this, you can consult the law books."

Perpetual Peasant Li threw the law books from the table at Security Hu's feet. "If you can find out one article," he declared, "I will turn over the post of Village Head to you."

"I won't consult them and I don't buy your words, either," Security Hu growled. "If the law didn't stick its oar into adultery, then people throughout the world would all commit the crime."

Perpetual Peasant Li brushed him aside and resumed his settlement of the lawsuit. "Nonetheless, the two animals went against their family rules and took the liberty of dating each other in a clandestine manner, which resulted in disputes between the masters of the two families and caused certain consequences. The law will then intervene. According to the law, the guardians of children under the age of 16 and of mentally incompetent people should be responsible for the actions of the people who are their wards. By parity of reasoning, goats are animals, unable to tune into human businesses. Their masters should shoulder the responsibility for their misbehaviour. According to the afore-stated reasoning, the sentence on the case resulted from the visit paid by the billy goat is hereby pronounced as follows –"

Old Liu plucked at Perpetual Peasant Li's arm and whispered: "It is mediation, not sentencing."

Perpetual Peasant Li announced: "The mediation on the disputes resulted from the billy goat's visit to its neighbour goes as follows: First of all, since the charge that the billy goat has committed the offence of rape is not upheld, the nanny goat's family should pay the siring fee in full. Secondly, the nanny goat miscarried her kid because the billy goat's master kicked her. The billy goat's family should offer certain compensation. Thirdly, the billy goat was detained illegally and forced to labour in the nanny goat's home. The income from the forced labour should all be given back to the billy goat's master after the expenditure on feed has been deducted. This is an itemised account that we should sit down to settle slowly."

The lawsuit was tried like this. All present cheered after a *Wow*! in chorus and applauded Perpetual Peasant Li at length.

v.

Full Victory Wang and Security Hu bumped into each other in their respective privies again. Full Victory Wang shouldn't have had such a big mouth, but his throat just felt a little itchy. He greeted Security Hu and said: "I had never expected that you wanted to bring my billy goat to court on the charge of rape. Only you could hit upon that. Whenever I think about that, I feel it's queer. The law didn't recognise it as rape but as adultery. Your imagination was fantastic, but it was a waste of your efforts." He continued: "I should still thank you all the same. I didn't know that my billy goat could sire three times in succession. Now I do. But I let it sire two times only in one day. I am not as greedy as you."

Security Hu didn't say one word. During those days, he always had few words to hand. His mind was haunted by the expression "adultery." There seemed to be some obstruction in his throat which he could neither swallow down nor spit out. He had an unbearable feeling. On that day – one high noon after many days – he went to Full Victory Wang's home. He knew that Full Victory Wang and his animals were on the mountains. He told Full Victory Wang's woman that something was stuck in his throat and wanted her to see if she could gouge it out or not. He explained that his woman had gone back to her maiden home. Otherwise, he wouldn't have come to look for her. He was very serious and even coughed many times. Convinced, Full Victory Wang's woman asked him to open his mouth. He didn't open his mouth. Straightaway, he took hold of her wrist.

"Security," she protested, "your grip is hurting my hand. Be quick and let me loose."

"After a while, you will taste something tougher!" he growled. He exerted himself and wrenched the woman's hand around her back. The woman *humphed* and her belly stuck out. He pushed her into her cave house. The woman struggled. He added a little more force and the woman's belly stuck out higher.

"Security," she screeched. "You told me to help take out the stuff from your throat. Let me do that for you."

"I don't want you to do that now. But I want to screw you."

The woman turned her face to look at him.

"Don't look at me like this," he snapped.

"I want to see if you have a face or not."

"Fine, fine, suit yourself. I will screw you after you have watched me for a bit."

He again exerted himself.

The woman quit watching. She was panting heavily.

"I know you won't consent, but you can't shout and you can't cry. If you do that, I'll strangle you."

The woman didn't want to die. Security Hu got his way with her without much further ado. Before his departure, he cast one glance at the woman lying on the *kang*. The woman's head was cocked to one side and her eyes were opened wide and staring at the wall beside the brick-bed.

"This is *not* rape," he declared. "This is adultery."

VI.

Security Hu slept all the night with the butcher's cleaver on his chest. Perhaps Full Victory Wang's woman would spill the beans to her husband. Perhaps Full Victory Wang would never know that. It would be best if Full Victory Wang knew the truth but he wouldn't dare broadcast the disgrace visited on his family. But whether Full Victory Wang knew it or not, it was better to sleep with a butcher's knife on his chest than have none.

Full Victory Wang didn't look for him. Early the next morning when he went to the privy to take a leak, Full Victory Wang didn't pounce upon him, either. After he had emptied his bladder, Full Victory Wang herded his animals together to go up the mountain. He didn't even cast a glance at him. Security Hu's heart dropped back into his chest cavity. Then he became fired up. He jumped out of the privy and entered Full Victory Wang's home.

The woman was combing her hair. She seemed to have given him a smile.

"You are not afraid that Full Victory Wang might come back?" she asked.

Security Hu flashed the butcher's cleaver that was secreted about his chest and replied: "I have this equipment."

He didn't have the time to use that knife because Full Victory Wang pounded him flat with a pickaxe. When he rode on Full Victory Wang's woman, he heard a squeaking sound from the door. He turned his head back and spotted Full Victory Wang. Raising the pickaxe, Full Victory Wang charged at him from one side and struck out at his waist. He let out a moan and could no longer struggle to his feet. The woman withdrew her body from beneath Security Hu's and reported: "I have told it to Full Victory."

"Security Hu, get up," Full Victory Wang ordered. Security Hu struggled repeatedly. "My waist is injured." Pain was written all over his face. "You should go to look for Perpetual Peasant Li. He knows the law," he continued.

"I want to settle it myself," Full Victory Wang riposted.

He raised the pickaxe again.

"I thought that you didn't know. I want to screw her again," Security Hu said.

"Well said. I also want to pound you one more time," Full Victory Wang responded.

This time, he aimed at Security Hu's head.

"You have battered him to death," his woman said.

He tossed aside the pickaxe, squatted down outside the cave house, lit a cigarette and took one suck. "Go look for Perpetual Peasant Li," he instructed.

Perpetual Peasant Li had become a bit of a somebody by then. First of all, reporters from the county city came to look for him and then so did reporters from the district. They requested the opportunity to talk with him about his experience.

"I have no experience," Perpetual Peasant Li answered. "I do it according to the law. I have no experience."

The reporters were stirred up. "This is the best experience," they exclaimed and asked him to continue.

Encouraged, Perpetual Peasant Li told them how he burned the midnight oil under a paraffin lamp to wade through the law books. His deed was then broadcast by the radio and newspapers and most probably he would appear on TV. When Full Victory Wang's woman went to his home, he and his woman were comparing notes about what clothes he should wear when he was to be on TV.

"Hurry, hurry, hurry," Full Victory Wang's woman pressed. "Full Victory has pounded Security Hu to death."

Perpetual Peasant Li was taken aback.

"Say it slowly," he requested. "I haven't got you clearly."

Full Victory Wang's woman repeated her words.

Perpetual Peasant Li finally got it.

"Hurry, my prick. This should be reported to the public security bureau."

The policemen interrogated Full Victory Wang: "Why did you strike again after you had dealt him one blow?"

Full Victory Wang replied: "The first blow got his waist. I was targeting his head, but missed."

"Did you know that you might batter him to death?"

"I did."

"You did but you still struck out?"

"Your question is strange. His existence is an unbearable pain for me. Do you want me to always live in pain?"

The policemen laughed.

On that day when Full Victory Wang went before the firing squad, all the fellow villagers went to the county city to watch the farce. Full Victory Wang's billy goat again swaggered into Security Hu's sheepfold.

Buying Wives

I.

Orchid Root's belly became rounder under the full gaze of the folk of Rear-side Village. The other day, the Village Head Tiantai trod back from the river beach with Jade Rod carrying the tow-rope about their shoulders. Tiantai glanced at Jade Rod from time to time, wondering if he might say something about Orchid Root's belly, but any attempt was in vain. Jade Rod never made eye contact. Even though Jade Rod's attention was focused on Orchid Root's tummy too, he simply managed to dodge Tiantai's eyeshot. Jade Rod kept his head high, looking far into the distant sky. People are like that when they have agreeable things on their mind. They are apt to look far into the distance and talk to themselves. When they got to the entrance to the village, Tiantai slapped Jade Rod on the neck and exclaimed: "Look at your fucking face. I only want to have a word with you." Jade Rod retracted his neck a little, the pride on his face flipping over into a grin. *Hehe.* Jade Rod stared at Tiantai, who responded: "Don't grin at me. The whole village shares your happiness. When Orchid Root gives birth, you must share that with us."

The smile vanished from Jade Rod's face.

"What? Are you thinking of having a baby without letting us know? Not a dicky bird?" asked Tiantai.

Jade Rod hummed and hawed for a while, his face blushing.

"If, if…" Jade Rod started.

"If, if, my dick!" Tiantai snapped.

"If she's going to give birth to a dead baby again…"

Jade Rod stopped again.

Tiantai then understood. Orchid Root had been pregnant

once before but unfortunately didn't go full term; hence Jade Rod's reticence. However, Village Head Tiantai soon found his bearings and knew what to say. Twisting his eyebrows, he proceeded to lecture Jade Rod, "You are a man of seven foot tall! A snake bit you once and now a piece of rope scares you on first sight. Could it be … Er?" Tiantai felt it was awkward to say what he had in his mind so paused. He saw Jade Rod sniff with his lips closed, making a noise like a willow leaf being blown.

"Ah! Ah!" Someone called from his side. It was Tiantai's wife. She always addressed the Village Head like this. Tiantai heard, but still staring at Jade Rod, he didn't look back. "Can't we look on the bright side?" Tiantai asked.

Jade Rod told him that his 'sister-in-law' was calling.

Tiantai said, "Can't we…?"

"My sister-in-law called you!" Jade Rod insisted.

"Just fucking go, you fool. Go back to fondle Orchid Root's belly," Tiantai replied. When Jade Rod was about to leave, Tiantai said, "Ah, I'm asking you." Jade Rod paused again.

"How many days?" Tiantai went on.

"I don't know," Jade Rod replied.

"Pull your fingers to do the calculations. It should be 280 days after that day. This is the same as planting crops. Don't you know the exact date you knocked her up?"

"It's not a bit like planting crops – just burying seeds in the furrows and then watching."

Tiantai stamped his foot and said, "Oho, you really suck."

Jade Rod maintained, "No matter how many times you sigh, you can't lump this together with planting crops. I've been doing it with her every single night. Who knows on which night I pulled it off?"

"Then you ask Orchid Root."

Jade Rod still didn't understand. Tiantai's wife shouted again. Tiantai was a few years older than Jade Rod and adept at 'planting crops'. After his wife came, they had four sons in five years. Tiantai told him, "It's not easy to get to the bottom of these things in a few minutes. My wife is shouting. You'd better go and fondle Orchid Root's belly."

Tiantai shrugged his shoulders, repositioned the tow-rope and then went away.

Orchid Root had been brought over from Guizhou Province by Old Plum. Like Tiantai's wife, she too had beauty in spades. Every night, Jade Rod might caress Orchid Root's belly. Only he knew how fine that belly was. It was not simply that the baby in Orchid Root's belly grew larger day by day, but he could actually feel by his touch that it was getting larger. Lying in Orchid Root's arms, he placed one of his strong hands on her belly and stared at the wooden rafter in the roof, without saying a word, like he was shielding something fragile. He had made love to her every night before she fell pregnant. He abounded in strength. He loved how she moaned beneath his body as if she were forlorn and acted like a pool of mud.

He asked Orchid Root if she felt unwell. "No," she would say while hugging him even more tightly. Her face was like a red persimmon.

Now, he touched her. She was like a cat, lying quietly, and allowing him to caress her. Orchid Root detected something warm transmitted by Jade Rod's hand.

She asked, "You touch me like this everyday. When do you think you will feel you've had enough?"

Jade Rod answered, "I don't know why I can't get enough."

"My belly is so fine?"

"I think so. It's even better after I've touched it. You try if you don't believe me."

He then pulled over, Orchid Root's hand to have a try. Orchid Root resisted and moved her hand away. Orchid Root said she couldn't feel it.

"It's strange. I feel so good every time I touch it. Why can't you feel that?"

Orchid Root covered her mouth and smiled. Actually, Orchid

Root's mouth was rather pretty, but she loved concealing it when she laughed.

Jade Rod said, "Maybe a person cannot feel how fine her own belly is. A woman's belly should be touched by a man."

"Carry on touching. I feel good to know that you can feel it."

"It will come quite soon?" Jade Rod enquired. Orchid Root answered "yes."

"I heard from Tiantai that the date can be counted out." Orchid Root said that she had counted.

"Fucking Tiantai," scoffed Jade Rod.

Orchid Root asked why he was cursing him. Jade Rod answered, "No reason. He is not only good at farming but making his woman pregnant. Damn good."

Orchid Root laughed again.

"Orchid Root, this time …." Orchid Root immediately covered his mouth, not allowing him to continue: "Don't say that. I'm so frightened."

"Don't be afraid. Even if you lay an egg I will accept it."

He then recalled Tiantai's words. That damned Tiantai had asked him to look on the bright side.

Orchid Root then added: "Tiantai is so kind, but you curse him." Jade Rod asserted that he didn't actually scold him, but was, in fact, expressing his gratitude towards him. Orchid Root didn't talk anymore. Instead, she placed her hand on Jade Rod's hand which lay upon her belly until they fell asleep.

A few days later, Orchid Root declared that her tummy ached. Not forgetting Tiantai's words, he asked his elder brother Gold Beam to look for him.

"You tell him to invite someone over to screen a film in our village," said Jade Rod.

Gold Beam was five years older than Jade Rod. His wife had passed away and he was now a widower. Jade Rod had a more outgoing mind than Gold Beam. Originally Gold Beam had his own thoughts too, though the death of his wife made him spiritless. Despite being devoid of ideas, he was surprisingly even-tempered.

Orchid Root kept groaning on the *kang* in the back room. Gold Beam said he should go to look for Tiantai and Jade Rod, for Second Lady. Second Lady was a single woman versed in midwifery. Jade Rod told Orchid Root to hold on out and wait for him to find her. Gold Beam and Jade Rod both raced out of the main door. Orchid Root ground her teeth, lying on the *kang* with her eyes wide open like a dead fish.

II.

"Jade Rod wants to show a film," Gold Beam told Tiantai.

Tiantai was squatting on the brick bed, chewing pickled green radishes and slurping porridge. He turned his neck back and asked: "Has Orchid Root gone into labour?"

Gold Beam found that hard to answer.

"Oh oh," said Tiantai. "You are his brother, you can't spout drivel. Let's walk to the town."

Tiantai went to the town with Gold Beam and a couple of boatmen. There was a projector in the town.

By that time, Second Lady was already sitting on Orchid Root's bed. A basin of water and scissors used to cut the cord were near to hand. Orchid Root curled her legs and stuck out her belly, shouting and groaning. Second Lady wiped away the sweat from Orchid Root's face, goading her to exert herself.

"This is manual labour, Orchid Root," advised Second Lady. "You have to use all your effort. Some women need to have eaten heartily before labour so as to have the strength to give birth. Did you eat?"

Orchid Root tried to nod.

"Then you have to try hard. Don't begrudge using your strength."

Jade Rod squatted outside the door. He was not allowed to

enter the room. Second Lady said giving birth was not kissing and that men were surplus to requirements. Jade Rod wanted to enter several times because Orchid Root's groaning was so heartrending. Second Lady didn't let him in. Second Lady pointed out, "If you come in, then you must help with the delivery." These words were even scarier than Orchid Root's groan. Jade Rod had no choice but to squat down at the door. He bit his lip and became black-faced, as if Orchid Root was not giving birth to a child but committing suicide by hanging.

Orchid Root had been groaning for a whole day. Second Lady never had the chance to use her basin and scissors. Every sound produced by Orchid Root made Jade Rod want to rush in and slap Second Lady on her face, and then put his hand into Orchid Root's belly and draw out that thing that was so reluctant to come out. Of course, he did not rush in, he just imagined. He knew that having a child was not as easy as plucking an egg from the henhouse.

Dusk fell. Gold Beam and Tiantai came in carrying some silken cord. They had already left the projector and projectionist together in the yard of the Village Committee. They took one look at the closed door, alongside which, Jade Rod was squatting. They knew it was troublesome, so didn't say hello to Jade Rod. The husband acted as if he were suffering from a toothache. Gold Beam took a well-rolled cigarette from behind his ear and handed it to him. Jade Rod didn't accept it. Gold Beam put the cigarette in his own mouth then rummaged for matches in his pockets. Tiantai had already lit a fag, so passed his match to Gold Beam. Gold Beam shook his head and continued to search. Finally, he got it. Just when he was about to light-up, a sudden cry came from the room. The three men immediately lifted their necks and peered towards the door.

There was no cry from the baby.

Great excitement. The screen had been hung up. The projector was set amid the audience, with a light bulb suspended from a bamboo pole. The projectionist was a young man who was teaching another bachelor Wanquan how to generate electricity. Wanquan wrapped a piece of rope about the generator wheels and then tugged a few times, but in vain. Wanquan was not discouraged. Instead, he found it very amusing, wrapping and pulling again and again.

The children didn't have the patience to wait, shouting: "Show us! Show us!"

"Go to hell!" Wanquan cursed. "No electricity. You tell me how I can show it! If you keep on shouting I'll toss you up on the roof."

The kids stopped. They were all afraid of him. The bachelor Wanquan couldn't find a wife and so was irritable. He really would have thrown them if he was so inclined.

"Go and take a look in at Jade Rod's house," Wanquan told the kids. "Once his wife has given birth, come back and report it straightaway."

A group of children ran away. Wanquan again wrapped the wheels with hempen rope and gave a hard tug: the generator whirred.

The light bulb on top of the bamboo pole was lit up.

"Not bad, huh?" Wanquan looked at the projectionist, with a smug expression on his face.

"Cut the light first." The projectionist said, "We cannot show the film without the sponsor here to give the word. You can unwrap the rope. We can put it back when we want to start the film." He was shutting off the generator while telling that to Wanquan.

Wanquan was grouchy. He said that if the generator was turned off, the light bulb would go out.

The projectionist observed: "It is because we turned the generator off. It's inefficient."

"It's damn dark now. You should give them light."

"Watching a movie is not about watching the faces in the audience. If you just want to watch each other's faces, what am

I doing here? Just turn it off."

Several children came in from outside.

"Born?" Wanquan asked.

"Still in labour," the children answered.

"Damn you. I know she is in labour. Just go and ask her to hurry up."

The children described how Second Lady was using a rolling pin on Orchid Root's belly.

The projectionist commented that it sounded really bad. "Turn it off."

Another group of kids ran into the room, shouting, "Born! Born!"

"You see, you cannot turn it off now," Wanquan told the projectionist.

"Then I'm going ahead and showing the film."

With a rattling sound, the projector started up. The projectionist told Wanquan: "Look at the screen. Why are you looking at me? The film isn't being shown on my face."

The light went out; a beam was projected toward the screen. Wanquan, together with all the others in the courtyard, craned his neck like a wild goose.

"Shut it off!" Someone bumped into the yard, shouting.

It was Gold Beam. He cleaved his way through the crowd and planted himself in front of the projector.

"Shut it off!"

The projectionist blinked his eyes. He didn't shut the projector down as he couldn't get to it. The projector was making a clicking sound. The beam of light was directly on Gold Beam's chest. "Shut it off," Gold Beam ordered.

"Why?" asked the projectionist.

"The baby's dead."

The projectionist's eyes opened wide and were then narrow again. He swallowed a mouthful of saliva, appearing to be baffled.

"You see, you have paid. What are we to do now?"

The light shone on Gold Beam's chest. If it weren't projected onto his chest, the light would be on the screen.

"Fucking what?" Tiantai pushed his way through the crowd, turning on the electric light abruptly. "Just stop it. What can you do? Go back home and sleep! Did you hear that?"

Those in the courtyard all stood up, carrying their chairs and benches. Wanquan sat on a pile of bricks. He lifted his foot and kicked at the bricks, which tumbled down.

"Be careful of your fucking ankle!" Tiantai swore at Wanquan. "If it were your wife who had given birth to a dead baby would you still show the film?"

"I would invite a drama troupe if I had a wife!"

"There'll be a sow for you," Tiantai promised. "Wait for it on your brick *kang*."

Wanquan didn't dare answer back but only went out with an expression of pride, his hands put back and shoulders square.

"What a fool!" Tiantai scoffed.

The projectionist was still astonished. Tiantai muttered, "What on earth are you wondering? Pack up your stuff."

That evening, Gold Beam and Jade Rod dug a pit in the wilds outside the village and buried the dead baby. They squatted there for a long time.

"Jade Rod …" Gold Beam began.

He wanted to offer his brother a few words of comfort but couldn't find the right ones. For that reason, he appeared to be suffering a lot more than Jade Rod.

"Jade Rod …"

He repeated that a few times.

Later, Old Plum came.

III.

The river spouted out from the mountains and valleys and coursed gently until it reached the flats. It wound its way along with the mountains, flowing into the distance. As the sun beat down, flashing patches were produced by the waves, and the sunlight also added a layer of indifferent red to the sand and stones on the beach.

Besides planting crops, Rear-side villagers found themselves dependant on this river. They didn't fish; none was to be had in the river. Rather they ferried goods to the mountains. At the top of the hill stood an old pagoda which introduced a bustling atmosphere to the place. People flocked there to burn incense prayerfully and to take in the scenery. It was by means of shipping goods along the river that the villagers garnered their keep. They tramped across the sand and gravel of the beach, dragging the boat upstream. The boat was laden with food and general merchandise. The boatmen were young men. After having distributed the goods and been paid, those who had wives would return home whereas those with nowhere to go would tag along after the Village Head Tiantai and kill time at his home. It was not that those fellows had any physical impairment, only they simply didn't know why they couldn't find a wife. Men without wives are apt to become overly lonely and anxious. Thus, these chaps descended on Tiantai's place.

In those days, Orchid Root was the perpetual topic of conversation. At the same time, they would chatter about themselves, and then their thoughts would turn to Old Plum. Tiantai's wife was sitting on the *kang*, mending clothes. She worked relentlessly at those garments and trousers, with a contented smile on her face. Tiantai was flushed with satisfaction as well. He would squat on the edge of the bed smoking tobacco. Refraining from making interruptions, he just listened to the babblings of those single men.

"Is it that Jade Rod can't make a baby, or is it that Orchid Root can't give birth? Two dead babies already." They just couldn't think it through, so kept on revisiting this topic all the time. Then someone would retort: "The baby's inside Orchid Root's belly. She has to hatch the thing. How can you blame

Jade Rod? We're yacking on about bullshit." And then –

"I don't think that's total nonsense. Old Plum fetches those women from out of town. Not safe," someone else chipped in.

Wanquan was there, too. He stared at Tiantai's wife and observed, "Our sister-in-law was also brought by Old Plum. How come she pops out babies one after another? Could it be that our Head is just too good? Jade Rod has something to learn from him."

Tiantai's wife cursed his 'foul mouth,' but did so with a broad smile. She was not yet thirty years old and fine-figured, being the best-looking among those women brought by Old Plum.

"That damned Old Plum has water in his eyes. He picked the best for the Head," someone opined.

Wanquan didn't agree. Even with water in his eyes, he could tell whether a woman was beautiful or not. But how could he figure out whether the woman was fertile or not?

The bachelors said maybe. Probably Old Plum did have this insight. Those cattle dealers had the capability to judge whether a mare could whelp. Old Plum had been involved in that business for so many years. He must have such a sense. They wanted the Head to have his say.

Tiantai didn't add anything, he just laughed.

All of a sudden, four boys bumped in from outside the room, each one shorter than the last. They were all Tiantai's sons – his badge of honour. The tallest one shifted a bench and stood on it. He groped down a utensil that was hanging from the ceiling and grabbed one steamed bun, then another, and another. The buns were shared out among his brothers and he kept one for himself. Jumping down from the bench, he chased out with his siblings.

When the bachelors were thinking about Old Plum, they realised that he hadn't come to the village for a while.

"Why hasn't Old Plum put in an appearance for so long?" they asked.

"What? It seems as if you chaps haven't saved up enough

money." Wanquan answered. "If you have, you can just choose a girl and marry her legally. That way, you shouldn't have to worry about your wife running away or giving birth to dead babies like Orchid Root."

One man curled his mouth, grunting: "Money can't be picked up from off the street. It must be earned bit by bit. I've done my sums. To find a local woman costs so much from engagement to marriage." He made the sign of "six" with his fingers and mouthed "6,000." He went on to say, "If we buy from Old Plum, it is 3,000 tops."

In fact, all the bachelors had already worked out the same calculation. Therefore, when they had enough money, they would naturally think of Old Plum.

"You can get to know the background of a local wife easily," Wanquan explained.

"After you buy a wife, it won't take you long to find her background," reasoned the bachelors.

"Ask our Head how well he knows our sister-in-law's background." They badgered Tiantai to answer.

Tiantai just kept on laughing without saying a word.

A few days later, they got the news that Old Plum had returned to the village. They finished delivering goods and moored the boat. On their way back from the beach, Second Lady intercepted them at the village entrance.

"Old Plum is coming!" Second Lady announced.

"Is he?" they asked.

"Yes indeed," Second Lady replied.

With a rouge glow about her face, Second Lady was like a hen that had just finished laying an egg. Every time Old Plum visited, he would stay at her home. In his opinion, Second Lady was clean. Probably other things were going on between them. As soon as Old Plum came, Second Lady would act as if she had drunk something that filled her with elation. Even her thighs were atremble with excitement.

"Three," Second Lady ejaculated.

The bachelors let out a cry of "Whoa!" and scampered into the village.

"The same old place," Second Lady shouted to their backs.

Soon they caught sight of Old Plum and the three women he had brought.

They hadn't reckoned that Jade Rod would be there also.

IV.

If Old Plum were the hunter, then the women were rabbits. If Old Plum were a fisherman, then they would be the fish. He could always bag the rabbit or hoist up the fish. He gathered them together, trafficked them to Rear-side village, and assigned each one to the bachelors there. That was Old Plum all over.

Old Plum knew what the term 'commodity economy' meant. He said that a commodity economy required transactions. What was he to transact? Old Plum knew he should transact what sold best. One should purchase in the place where something was abundant and hawk it in the place where it was needed; one should also buy at the place where the price was low and sell it to places where a higher price could be realised. This was the circulation of commodities.

"In my hands, women find themselves circulated," Old Plum elucidated. "They are what you are in want of here."

"Indeed, indeed," the bachelors concurred. "We lack nothing except for women. You should circulate more for us."

Old Plum observed that it was becoming more and more difficult. "In the past, I could sport the title of 'matchmaker' but now they brand me a 'trafficker.' I even run the risk of ending up in jail."

"Shit!" the bachelors exclaimed. "Those who speak in that way must certainly have a wife already. Let them be bachelors for ten years and then see whether they will still be saying that. It is legal to buy from matchmakers and yet illegal to buy from traffickers? Matchmakers find women from nearby, while traffickers seek women from afar. It is just a matter of distance. What is the difference between 'nearby' and 'faraway'? One hundred *li*? Two hundred *li*? If it's illegal to traffic a woman from one hundred *li*, just make it ninety-nine."

"Of course, of course," Old Plum agreed. Old Plum would not be Old Plum if he let some iron hoop restrain him. He sucked in one mouthful of smoke, spat it out again, cocked his head, squinted, and let the smoke float up along the bridge of his nose.

That was Old Plum all over.

This time, he had got three. He promised each that he would find them a job. That is to say that they could go to the cookhouse at the mine and then might find work doing the books if they were literate. After many days in his company, the women didn't trust him any longer. They wanted to go back.

Old Plum's companion then turned his face. He was a young man with a very fierce countenance and a gash on his face. "Scarface" said that none of them could leave: "Do you think we led you here for sightseeing? How would you pay for the cost of accommodation and transport? There is the train and then the bus and the motor tricycle. You want to go back? Then leave one leg behind."

Old Plum didn't become mad. "Don't get angry," he said. "They've never been out of town. Getting homesick is just human nature, isn't it?" The women were frightened and kept on nodding at Old Plum. He then continued, "That's just it. How could you go back without working after having come such a long way?"

Old Plum could turn face as well.

At such times, he would let a woman take off her clothes and proceeded to remove his own. Then, his companion would take hold of the woman so that Old Plum could have sex with her. Thereafter, Old Plum would take hold of a woman; it was Scarface's turn to have sex. Old Plum felt it was dull to do that and he liked Second Lady. So he always preferred to be the one who held the woman for Scarface's benefit. He wanted to preserve the good mood for Second Lady. This was also Old Plum all over. He knew how to make women do what he wanted. He could render the disobedient ones obedient and the obedient ones more docile.

The 'old place' mentioned by Second Lady was an empty room at her home. Old Plum and Scarface pushed the women into the chamber, let them remove their blouses and trousers and stand by the wall, inviting the bachelors to have a look.

"Look," instructed Old Plum. "Look carefully."

On the other side of the room, the bachelors squatted by the wall, their eyes wide open.

"Tall, short, fat, or slim. Face, figure, breast, bottom, arm or leg. It's all here," Old Plum pronounced. "Literally, you only have to look."

By this point, the women had come to understand their situation and were seized with regret. But it was too late. They stood in front of a row of bachelors, trying to shrink, burying their faces in their hands and sobbing. Scratched onto the wall in white chalk above their heads was the price of each of them. The youngest one was the most expensive – 3,500 yuan.

"Her name is Little Ai," revealed Old Plum. "She is from the county and has a secondary school education."

The bachelors had started to calculate and select. Some were surprised by the price and decided not to buy. They just stayed there, judging.

"Such high prices. Are they made from gold or silver?" one of them asked.

"High prices don't necessarily mean they are practical. We are paying for a woman, not an embroidered pillow," another piped up.

"The 3,500 one might be barren," hazarded another.

Jade Rod entered at that moment. He pushed the door gently ajar, squatted in front of a bachelor, gave a nod to Old Plum and then focused his attention on the bodies of the three women.

"Why are you here? To buy a second?" the bachelors asked.

Looking intently, Jade Rod remained totally silent.

Wanquan didn't say anything from beginning to end. He was the most careful among the bachelors. Experienced as Old Plum was, he knew this was the real buyer. He approached Wanquan and pulled out a cigarette for Wanquan.

"Wanquan, don't be dazzled," he told him.

Wanquan refused the cigarette in Old Plum's hand and stood to size up to the older woman. She immediately buried her face in her hands.

"I am a married woman," she said, almost sobbing. "I have a husband and a baby. I've been cheated."

She started to cry.

Wanquan was not at all surprised nor was he angry, so acted as if he didn't hear what she had said. He looked at her from all angles, turned her round, inspected her again for a while, then stepped back and pondered.

"How is it?" Old Plum asked.

This time Wanquan accepted the cigarette. He lit it, inhaled and puffed white smoke.

"I'm taking her," Wanquan spoke, not so loudly, but firmly as though someone was delivering a punch.

"I'll have the 2,500 one!" another bachelor shouted, as if afraid that she would be snapped up by the others.

There was an expression of satisfaction on Old Plum's face. He glanced about at the bachelors.

The man next to Jade Rod touched him with arms, "Just one left. If you keep on thinking it could be too late."

Jade Rod rested his chin on his hands, still thinking.

"If cash-in-hand is a problem right now, you can pay later," Old Plum said.

Jade Rod was still thinking.

That night, Jade Rod kept on rolling in bed. He couldn't fall asleep and seemed to be obsessed by something intractable. His elder brother Gold Beam nodded off really early, snoring intermittently. Jade Rod sat up, staring into the darkness.

Bang, the light was turned on. Orchid Root sat up as well and slipped a coat over Jade Rod, looking at him, worried. She didn't know why Jade Rod was restless. She had recovered a good deal and now wore a red cloth on her forehead which was to keep off the wind.

"What?" she asked.

Jade Rod stared blankly, motionless.

Orchid Root touched his forehead. It wasn't hot.

"Do you want some water to drink? I'll get you some?" Orchid Root offered.

Jade Rod frowned and seemed very annoyed. Orchid Root didn't dare to ask. Jade Rod lay down again. Orchid Root tucked in his quilt and turned off the light. She didn't get into bed but propped up herself up on her arm, glaring at her husband. Jade Rod turned over several times. Orchid Root sighed in her heart and withdrew back to bed helplessly. She was too drowsy.

Early the next morning, Jade Rod got dressed, put on his shoes and went to Second Lady's home again. He didn't speak for a while but just sat on the edge of the brick bed. He rolled his cigarette carefully as if he had come for no other purpose than to roll tobacco.

Old Plum didn't speak, either. He smoked his cigarette, waiting patiently.

Jade Rod finally finished his rolling. He pinched the surplus paper but didn't light-up. Turning his head, he peered into Old Plum's face.

Old Plum just puffed one mouthful of smoke, his face becoming shrouded.

"You cut 1,000. I'll pay at once and take her away," Jade Rod proposed.

Old Plum mulled it over amid the smoke.

"Just give a reply – whether it is fine or not."

With the sound of a *clack*, Old Plum discarded the half-smoked cigarette onto the ground.

"Deal. You go get the money."

Things, however unwieldy, become simple when one's mind is made up. In this way, Jade Rod bought Little Ai, the youngest one.

"From the county and she has finished secondary school," Old Plum repeated.

v.

Jade Rod, brandishing a bamboo pole, lifted up a strip of firecrackers which popped out clouds of colourful paper flowers. Gold Beam, who was dressed up in new clothes, stood behind his brother smiling. It was hard to tell whether that was a smile of bashfulness or happiness. A few kids were picking up unexploded firecrackers. A couple of others shouted towards Gold Beam in the distance.

"Gold Beam, consummate the union. Gold Beam, take a wife."

Jade Rod swung the bamboo pole toward the kids. They jumped out of the way, then turned around and started shouting again in chorus.

Gold Beam just kept smiling.

Jade Rod didn't tell Gold Beam that he had purchased a wife for him. When Little Ai was brought back home, Gold Beam just blinked. Jade Rod handed Little Ai to Orchid Root and informed him, "Brother, don't blink. Come here. I need to have a word with you." Gold Beam was still blinking as Jade Rod pulled him into the room.

"How about her?" Jade Rod asked his elder brother, beaming.

"What? I don't get you," Gold Beam replied.

"The woman. How about her?"

Gold Beam still didn't catch on.

"I bought her," Jade Rod explained.

Gold Beam was even more confused.

"2,500. From Old Plum," he said, his smile expanding.

"To sell her on again?" Gold Beam was nonplussed because he thought Jade Rod wanted to set himself up as a secondhand dealer.

"How come you still don't understand? We need a woman in our house. Why don't you understand that?"

"Oh, oh. You bought her for me?"

"What do you think?"

"Not good."

Now, Jade Rod was the one who was unable to understand. He was annoyed.

"From the county and she has completed her secondary school education. Old Plum said as much himself." Jade Rod was getting anxious and spoke like a gun discharging, "You've seen her already. You think she's not good?"

"Ah!" Gold Beam stamped his foot. "I didn't say she wasn't good. Why should I be scornful? I meant that you should have talked over such a big matter with me."

"Oh," Jade Rod felt somewhat relieved. "It's not too late to discuss it with you now. You can't live your whole life without a woman."

"Indeed, indeed."

"Then what else is there to discuss? I have handed over money, you don't dislike her. Nothing else to discuss."

"Hark at you. Just let me finish."

"No discussions. Orchid Root, clean up the room and we'll hold the ceremony tomorrow."

Jade Rod left.

Gold Beam squatted on the ground for a long time, holding his head. He felt that all this had happened abruptly but was then greatly moved by his brother's concern. "Jade Rod, Jade Rod," he told himself in his heart. "How could your brother live his whole life without a wife?" He seemed to have swallowed a piece of hot bean curd which made him choke out tears.

Afterwards, they chattered on until the middle of the night. They had the feeling that they were the most intimate brothers in the world.

"We must keep the woman," Jade Rod said to his brother.

"Let Orchid Root keep her body well," Gold Beam told him in return.

"We must let off a string of firecrackers."

"You decide."

With a rattling and bursting sound, firecrackers were ignited. The din was so loud that the whole village appeared to jump. It was dusk. The two brothers had an agreement that after the firecrackers, Gold Beam would go into the room and consummate the union.

Gold Beam's room had already been cleaned up. Orchid Root took some new clothes for Little Ai to change into, though she was reluctant. Little Ai sat on the bed. Orchid Root sat on its edge.

"Anyway this is a joyous thing. Changing into new clothes, for good luck," Orchid Root said. She repeated that dozens of times.

Little Ai didn't say a word.

"As a woman, you will have to do this sooner or later."

"Orchid Root!" Jade Rod shouted into the room.

"Yes!"

"Out!"

Orchid Root told Little Ai, "We are one family from now on. I should call you 'sister-in-law.'"

"I'm coming," Orchid Root replied. She lay out the new clothes in front of Little Ai and smiled to her, "I'm leaving now."

The moment Orchid Root came out, Jade Rod pushed Gold Beam inside. He then closed the door, bolted it, and locked it. Turning around, he said to Orchid Root, "Let's go."

Orchid Root glared at the locked door, quite worried. Jade Rod, who was getting impatient, grabbed Orchid Root's arm and dragged her into their own room.

Jade Rod dragged her all the way to the bed. With him exerting such great strength, she could perch herself effortlessly down on the bed. He then closed the door.

"Look at you." Orchid Root stretched out her wrist to Jade Rod. His pulling had hurt her wrist.

"Why were you lingering in there?" Jade Rod quizzed.

"I worry about Brother Gold Beam …."

"Nothing to worry about. Take off your clothes."

"Let's listen a little bit to what they are doing."

"What is there to hear? If he's laid her down, it's sorted. Take those things off."

"You can say anything in a smooth way. Listen to your voice. It's like a plane gliding into the air." She blinked her eyes toward him and began to undo her buttons.

Jade Rod had already stripped off.

"Such a rash guy."

Jade Rod could scarcely wait for Orchid Root to remove her clothes. He laid her down. She let out a cry and grasped him tightly. Intertwined, they pulled out the light. They were very dedicated. Jade Rod lay on top of Orchid Root's body, gasping. Orchid Root let him do that on her body, groaning softly.

"Ah!" Jade Rod exclaimed.

"Oh!" So too did Orchid Root.

They lay there flat out, eyes opened, gasping for a moment. Then they turned their attention to the sounds of movement in Gold Beam's room. Jade Rod placed one hand on Orchid Root's belly, without saying anything.

VI.

Gold Beam didn't pull it off with that secondary school graduate from the county.

Little Ai's mother was the Deputy Director of the County

Health Bureau. She was the kind of woman who was by nature smart and tough. Her father taught music in a secondary school. He could play the accordion and possessed a loud voice. Nevertheless, he became inept in front of that smart and tough woman. Little Ai detested both her mother's shrewdness and her father's timidity.

Her mother told her to take an examination for Nursing School.

Little Ai retorted, "Why should I do that?"

Her mother insisted, "You're not capable enough to take the College Entrance Examination. I can't pull any strings at any other schools."

"That's my own business. Why do I need you to pull strings?" She stared at the Deputy Director. The Deputy Director was sipping a magnetised cup of water and on hearing that, planted the cup down on the tea table heavily.

She turned around to the music teacher in the kitchen: "Stop that." The music teacher happened to be playing *On the Outskirts of Moscow in the Evening*. He always liked playing that song and would pump the tune out while walking to the kitchen.

"Stop it!" ordered the Deputy Director.

The accordion stopped. The music teacher came out of the kitchen, confiscating the accordion. "What's wrong? I just reached the best part. Isn't it your favourite song?" His smiling face was so close to hers it nearly butted against her cold nose.

"Little Ai gets more and more ridiculous, simply to spite me."

The music teacher told Little Ai, "Don't run counter to your mum. That is not good for you."

"I don't want to be up against anybody," Little Ai replied. "I hate the way you two echo one other!"

She went out.

The shrewd Deputy Director and her inept husband stared at each other for a while. They had never thought that Little Ai would go out of town. They believed she would come back at supper time.

Little Ai didn't return. Upon exiting the courtyard, she turned into the alley and passed by the building where her apartment was. She heard the song again from that same accordion. She felt sick of it and went straight ahead until she stopped at the bus station. Then shortly afterwards, she met Old Plum.

Now, she was sitting on Gold Beam's bed. The light cast the shape of her body onto the wall and elongated it into a huge shadow. Orchid Root had put up a few paintings on the wall, turning it into a room fit for the newly-weds.

Gold Beam wasn't Jade Rod. He didn't go at her straightaway. He believed that if the woman was willing to lie down for him, he didn't have to resort to force; if she wasn't willing, there was nothing you can do about it. If you did it despite her unwillingness, you still couldn't make it. For that reason, he didn't force her. He poured a basin of hot water and put it in front of the brick bed, looking at her.

"You have a wash," Gold Beam suggested. "You intellectuals pay much attention to hygiene."

Little Ai never thought Gold Beam would treat her so softly that there was even a note of concern in the softness. She raised her face up and stared at him.

Gold Beam looked back at Little Ai's eyes, with absolute sincerity on his face.

"Well. Wash." Little Ai thought that and got off the bed. She took the basin over to wash her face. She really should have a clean. In a journey of over 1,000 miles, she had only washed her face a couple of times.

Gold Beam sat on the edge of the bed and watched Little Ai dousing her face. A feeling of warmth suddenly surged up within him. A woman was washing her face in his room. He was looking at her. Hence, the warm feeling in his heart.

Little Ai finished and wanted to go out and pour away the water. When she pulled the door, she realised it had been locked from outside. Gold Beam also thought of that. He had forgotten all about it because while he was busy watching Little Ai washing her face and his heartbeat had accelerated. He jumped off the bed, took over the basin and smiled at Little Ai shyly.

"Let me do it," said Gold Beam.

Gold Beam poured away water along the threshold. Little Ai walked over to the wardrobe and combed her hair in front of the mirror embedded in the door. When Gold Beam came back, Little Ai was already sitting on the bed with her hair tied back. She looked at Gold Beam, her face now apricot-like. It looked quite delicious but it would be a shame to eat it.

Gold Beam's stomach dropped.

Little Ai shut her eyes again. She heard Gold Beam step over to the bed and perch on the edge.

A shoe dropped onto the floor with a clatter.

Another clatter.

When Gold Beam was turning onto the bed, Little Ai started to shout.

"Don't come up here!" Little Ai raised her head and let out a cry. Ashamed and panicking, she started to bleed. Her face was suddenly persimmon-like and seemed to bleed.

Gold Beam was startled. Motionless, he looked at her.

"Don't …" She was almost crying. "Don't touch me. I'm only seventeen. I was cheated by Old Plum; he said he could find me a job. He cheated me. I want to go. I won't be your wife."

Gold Beam didn't know what to do.

"You climb down." Little Ai said.

"You can't let me stay on the ground all night!"

"Get down."

"I won't touch you, OK?"

"I'm scared."

Gold Beam waved his head and looked for his shoes.

"OK. I'm getting down."

Gold Beam poured a cup of water and leaned against the wardrobe.

"You sleep," Gold Beam said.

"I won't," Little Ai maintained, a little reassurance seeping into her heart.

"I'll drink water. You can sleep."

Gold Beam had a sip. Too hot. He blew on it and drank again.

Little Ai took off the clothes Orchid Root gave her and tore them into halves. Gold Beam stopped drinking and gaped at her. She went on ripping the clothes into strips and bound the waist and hems of her trousers with the strips. Gold Beam sensed his heart was beating so hard. He swiftly took a sip of water. After binding the waist and hems of her trousers, Little Ai shut her eyes again and sat there without moving. Gold Beam was so anxious that he kept on drinking. He finished the water in the cup but was still drinking, drinking the air inside the cup. All of a sudden he stopped. His eyes focused on a porcelain urn at the corner.

"Little Ai."

Little Ai was frightened, though raised her head.

"You cannot fall asleep, can you?" Gold Beam asked.

"I won't sleep."

"I'll show you how to lift a bowl."

Little Ai didn't understand. "Have you seen that in acrobatic shows? I can perform that for you," Gold Beam offered. In the meantime, he walked toward the urn. There were a few sacks inside the urn. He took the sacks out and grabbed hold of the urn with force. "Hey," he called as he balanced the rim of the urn on the crown of his head. He stretched out his arms and shook his body, trying to keep balance. His face twisted, convulsing red, his eyes remaining wide open. He was trying to keep watch on the urn on his head, while simultaneously looking at Little Ai.

Little Ai was astonished by his behaviour.

Gold Beam tried hard to smile but the urn was swaying on his head, and so he couldn't allow himself to be distracted by anything. He said to Little Ai, "You can see I have plenty of untapped energy. I am doing this for you." Tears welled up from his eyes as he told her this. He ought to have laughed then; somehow tears welled up instead.

"Little Ai, you look here, look at me," he implored.

He exerted his strength again, and with another shout, the urn swung up, turned over and fell down. He tried to pick it up from the other rim using his head.

But he failed. The urn was firmly planted around his head.

Little Ai shouted, with her head on her arms and didn't dare to look. She thought he must have been battered to death by the pot.

He wasn't. He was hit dizzy for a while. Not long after that, he crawled out from under the urn and squatted down by it.

He fell asleep.

VII.

Jade Rod slid the key into the padlock, unlocked the door and drew back the bolt. Gold Beam pulled it open and walked out. He opened his eyes and the sunshine lunged into them. He winked and walked to the latrine. The water he drank last night had turned into urine. Jade Rod pulled the door again, replaced the bolt and wanted to lock it. Orchid Root said, "Don't lock up. Brother and I are both at home. Can't we keep the woman safe?" Jade Rod then didn't lock it and put the padlock in his pocket.

Gold Beam came out from the latrine.

"You don't have to go to the river," Jade Rod told his brother. "You chisel out a stone mortar for us so we can grind chilli and spices."

Gold Beam looked at Jade Rod, a touch surprised.

"I've found the stone," said Jade Rod.

There was indeed a stone in the yard on which were balanced a hammer and a chisel.

"If she runs away, we've wasted our money," Jade Rod pointed out.

"Oh, oh," Gold Beam answered.

Jade Rod went to the river strand. Gold Beam sat in the courtyard, chiselling away at the stone. Orchid Root brought Little Ai some water to wash her face with and resumed sweeping the floor. When she had finished, Little Ai also washed herself and got dressed. Orchid Root asked her to accompany her to the kitchen, where she rinsed the rice and Little Ai attended to the kitchen fire. Little Ai didn't know how to blow the fire and did it quite awkwardly. Orchid Root told her to try a few times. Then she added solid wood into the furnace.

She quickly got started. She had never blown one before so felt it very interesting. Orchid Root told her a lot of stories of the village people, interesting stories. Orchid Root said there were rather a lot of women from other provinces. Those bachelors who had some money would certainly turn their thoughts to getting a wife. They all liked to buy wives from Old Plum. Even the wife of the Village Head had been purchased from him. So was Orchid Root herself. She explained, "My hometown is in Guizhou. I was tricked out of that place by Old Plum and then got spliced to Jade Rod."

"I ran away a few times but was captured and brought back," she continued. "Then I stopped running and accepted this fate. Why should I run? No matter who a woman is married to, that's her lot in life. Your parents sold you off as well. How is that any different from being sold on by Old Plum? Thinking like that, I set my mind at rest. I felt that Jade Rod is a good man as well. But he is bad-tempered. Not like Brother Gold Beam. It's a blessing for a woman to meet a good-natured man. Now there's nothing else. I just want to have a baby with Jade Rod."

It seemed as though those stories she told belonged to other people.

"My luck is poor. I had two but lost both." When she uttered this, her eyes turned red. Perhaps steam had gotten into them.

The water had come to the boil and she uncovered the pot, causing the rising vapour to disperse.

"It is boiling. You can stop now."

Little Ai stopped blowing the fire. Orchid Root filled two pots of boiled water and then put rice into the pot. Little Ai thought Orchid Root was very capable and pleasant.

She could also hear the sound of chiselling in the yard. Actually, Gold Beam was a good guy. Thinking of this, she tilted her head to him. He was under the wall of the front yard and couldn't be seen from the kitchen.

Gold Beam chiselled the stone hard. However, his mind was not in fact on that. He was thinking about the previous night and felt vexed about it. He thought he shouldn't have lifted the urn. He should have just got onto the bed, ripped off the strips and torn her clothes. If she shouted out, that didn't matter at all. It wouldn't have mattered even if the whole village had heard her shouts. He would have been removing his own woman's clothes. That had nothing to do with other folks. "It would be great if I could rip her clothes off. I'd clutch her breasts. I can clutch her breast any way I want to. If you clutch them and tear her clothes, things may be different," he thought while chiselling. So acute was his regret that he wished he could go back in time to the previous night.

At that moment, Wanquan squatted down in front of Gold Beam.

Wanquan gently pushed the door open, came in and gently closed it, squatting in front of Gold Beam. He glanced at the kitchen, with an expression of mystery.

"How was it?" Wanquan asked Gold Beam.

Gold Beam didn't speak.

"How about last night? How?" Wanquan asked again.

Gold Beam still didn't speak. He wouldn't lie to him but he also couldn't tell him about the urn. Therefore, he didn't reply.

"Not successful?"

Gold Beam had come over a touch nauseous and wanted to

pound Wanquan's head with the hammer.

"How come!" Wanquan exclaimed. "In your first encounter, you should teach her a lesson. My woman was the same. She was unwilling in every way. I struck her on the head. I said that if she didn't want to, she may as well die. After that, I got my leg-over."

Gold Beam still went on chiselling.

"Once a woman is underneath her man, she will obey without dissent."

"Try what I told you," he continued. "Everything's hard in the beginning. Once you start, it will be going well. It just depends on whether you can harden your heart."

Gold Beam stopped chiselling. But he didn't look at Wanquan, either. He looked at the stone. Wanquan thought what he said was useful and became earnest.

"You have had a wife before. Do you feel it's a pity that she's too young? She is still a woman, no matter how young. You can't screw a woman who is in your bed. Are you really a fucking man?"

Gold Beam banged his chisel against the stone. By that time Wanquan had noticed Gold Beam's facial expressions.

"Did I say something wrong?" Wanquan asked. "Am I wrong?"

Gold Beam started to talk, "I'll fucking brain you if you carry on with your nonsense."

"Look at you. I am teaching you how to do it and you treat me like this. My nonsense? Do I really speak nonsense?"

"Get out!"

Wanquan was a little scared. He stood up and looked at Gold Beam.

"Is this guy insane?"

"Go away!" Gold Beam bellowed.

Wanquan jumped away and stepped back to the gate. He was anxious about the chisel in Gold Beam's hand which he thought Gold Beam could thrust toward his head.

"Insane," he mumbled and jumped out of the gate.

Gold Beam raised the chisel and let it fall down hard on the stone. With a clatter, the chisel jumped out of his hand and far away. On hearing the noise, Orchid Root and Little Ai went out of the kitchen and stared at him. They didn't know what the matter with him was.

A few days later, Gold Beam gave Little Ai a lesson. Then he fought with Jade Rod.

VIII.

Little Ai didn't sleep with Gold Beam. He had no way around this. Little Ai swept the yard with Orchid Root, cooked together and even wore a smile on her face. But every night, she bound the waist and legs of trousers with a fast knot. That really made Gold Beam want to cry.

"Brother, do you seriously have no way? Can't you get straight on down to it?" Jade Rod shouted at his brother, apparently more anxious than he was.

"Some rope? A knife? Why didn't you use any of them?" barked Jade Rod.

That night, Gold Beam threw rope and knife on the cupboard cover.

Crash! The chisel followed.

Little Ai had already bound her waist and was just taking care of her legs. She stopped and looked at him. His face turned livid with rage. He seemed like a lion that was trying to ravage her. She drew back her hands from her ankle and was gripped with horror.

"Uncle Gold Beam …" she cried out timidly.

"Who is your uncle?" His eyes appeared ready to bleed. He roared, "I'm your husband! Did you hear? Husband!"

Little Ai immediately shrank back into her body, shaking.

"Take off your clothes or die. You choose."

She shrank even smaller, like a terrified lamb.

"Take them off!"

She shook her head in fear.

"Take them off!" He cried out with shouts and shrieks, giving vent to the sheer shame and resentment which were inside. All at once, tears blurred his eyes.

What he never anticipated was that his shouting awoke her from her fear. Her body gradually became relaxed. She stared at him with a kind of resolution.

"I don't want to die," she pleaded. "I don't like the idea of being your wife, either. If you really want me to die, you just kill me."

Gold Beam was astonished, tears seeping back.

"Just kill me."

They peered at each other, without any movement. He could feel the strength in his body fade away and his bones softening bit by bit.

Jade Rod, who was squatting in the yard, jumped up. He squatted there all the time, watching what was going on in the room.

"Useless!" he cried out.

It was quiet in the room.

He took a wooden bench and slammed it toward the door in anger.

"Useless!" he cried again.

He ran to the door, kicked it, and grabbed the bolt, shaking it. He was very angry.

"Gold Beam!" He called his brother by his name: "The woman on your bed was bought with our hard-earned money!"

Orchid Root ran over and dragged him away.

"Gold Beam!" He was still shouting.

Clank! Orchid Root closed the door of their room.

"Don't' be like that, Jade Rod. Let our brother handle that himself," she told him. She pushed him onto the bed and unbuttoned him. "Let's sleep. How is it that my warm body can't silence your mouth?"

By this point, all of the energy had been drained from Gold

Beam's body. He squatted at the foot of the wall and stared at one spot, as if in a daze. Sitting in the bed, Little Ai looked at the picture on the wall and seemed to be thinking.

Gold Beam mumbled something.

She turned over and looked at him.

"You go," he said. He didn't look at her. His voice was soft, but very clear.

She couldn't believe that he said so.

"I've had no luck when it comes to wives," Gold Beam murmured, seemingly to himself. "I had one. She died. Jade Rod was worried to see me always single and he bought you. I should blame myself. I'm muddled. You just go."

He spoke those words with pain, but with sincerity as well. Instead, Little Ai didn't know what to say. She faltered for a while.

"I, I will let my parents give you your money back." Finally, she had come up with a suitable line. "If you don't believe me, I can write a letter and ask them to pay to have me returned."

"Your parents didn't take the money. Why should they give that back? I caved in."

"Then, then you will lose both me and the money."

"You … If I don't let you go, I am much worse than that."

"Uncle Gold Beam, you are a good man."

"Shit," he cursed. "I don't want to be that sort of good man. You've forced me to be that. Don't call me uncle. It makes my heart ache."

Little Ai didn't understand why Gold Beam claimed she had forced him to be a good man. But she did not dare to say any more, being afraid that he might change his mind.

Gold Beam didn't. The next day in the middle of the night, he gently lifted the door open and led her out in the direction of the county. It was still dark when they arrived at the county bus station. Little Ai leant on the long wooden chair and fell asleep. Gold Beam squatted under the window of the ticket booth, taking a nap. He would stand up and be the first to buy tickets when it was open.

He didn't anticipate that anything would go awry, but it did. Before he had a chance to say a word, Jade Rod's fist banged against his face. He clutched a ticket and change and elbowed out from the crowd, trying to wake up Little Ai who was still sleeping on the wooden chair. He then saw a group of chaps led by Jade Rod dashing in from the outside. With a humming sound in his head, he stood up straight. Little Ai was rubbing her eyes while the men surrounded them. She was immediately awake and attempted to hide herself behind Gold Beam's body.

"Get her up!" ordered Jade Rod.

They dragged her onto the walking tractor by the station.

"You …" Gold Beam opened his mouth and hadn't even spoken a word before Jade Rod's fist fell straight on his face. Gold Beam heard something like a *clang* and then felt at once a burst of something spicy. He moaned out a cry and nearly fell down. He opened his mouth again. Another *clang!* The fist struck him in the face again. He let out a cry and fell. Jade Rod didn't stop but fisted and kicked Gold Beam simultaneously. He didn't talk, just lashed out crazily.

Gold Beam accepted this without putting up any resistance. A while after Jade Rod had left, he just got up slowly, walking with a wavering gait out of the station, allowing the dust to fall down from his body. He went to a restaurant to buy a basin of water. The man in the restaurant asked him whether he wanted to eat. He said that he would first clean his face. He washed his face. The man in the restaurant asked him whether he would eat or not. He said yes. Then the proprietor responded that he wouldn't have charged him for the water if he'd answered affirmatively before. He replied that he didn't care and asked him to bring over the food. The man in the restaurant asked him whether he would like some alcohol.

"Yes," he answered.

In the evening, he staggered back home. He got the key from Jade Rod and opened the lock. He lifted his foot and kicked at the door plank. The bolt fell off. He plunged in and locked the door. Then there came Little Ai's shouts and the noise of fierce fighting.

He raped her.

Little Ai lay flat on the bed, her eyes wide open, and stared at the roof.

"Gold Beam, you ruined me."

He flopped on the other side, snoring, with a smile hung upon his mouth.

Then winter came and with it heavy snow.

IX.

The blizzard fell quietly and then stopped silently. Mountains, rivers, and villages, were all turned into one colour by the snow. The snow had just ceased and children were going outside to play snowball fights in the wilds. They chased each other and pelted snowballs that scattered upon making contact with their bodies. But the sound of their play couldn't be heard. That had been muffled by the soft snow. It was extremely cold, but there was a kind of serenity in the chill.

Jade Rod whirled his axe with great concentration to split a tree stump.

The snow in the yard had been swept away. Orchid Root gathered snow with a shovel and Little Ai piled it into a snowman. She wanted to make it look better, and so dug out some eyes for the snowman with her frozen red digits. As she dug, she would step back a bit and exhale over her cupped fingers. She then went on digging again. At last, she took the ready-made nose off from the snowman's head and installed it. She was heavily engrossed.

Gold Beam came in, pushing a large bucket of water. He poured the water into a water vat in the kitchen with a smaller bucket.

"Brother, I found someone to dig the well," Jade Rod told Gold Beam.

"Oh, where from?"

"Shehui from Guan Village."

"Indeed, indeed."

"The price has been agreed," Jade Rod continued, "twenty-eight yuan for a well. He's coming tomorrow."

"Oh oh," Gold Beam said.

On overhearing this conversation and observing the situation in the yard, one might be convinced this was a happy household.

Out on the street, there was the sudden clatter of footsteps.

"Caught back!" came the cry.

Orchid Root and Little Ai bunched up their ears, listening to what was happening on the street.

"Wanquan's wife escaped last night," Gold Beam reported.

Someone rushed in and gasped, "Wanquan's wife has been caught back. They are pouring icy water onto her crotch." The gossip soon sped away. Little Ai showed no reaction and Orchid Root told hold of her hand.

"Go and have a look," Orchid Root suggested.

Gold Beam wanted to block them, but Orchid Root had already gone out with Little Ai. He glanced uneasily at Jade Rod, who said, "Just go." Gold Beam put down the pail and followed them out.

Wanquan's yard was engulfed with people and the snow had been thoroughly trampled. People's facial expressions were as intense as they were when watching movies. Wanquan's wife was being besieged in the middle, reacting shamefully and fearfully, with a bloodless face. Her legs were tied. Wanquan carried a bucket of icy water, put it in front of her, and began to loosen her belt. Women dodged and blocked Wanquan's hands with begging faces.

Clap! Clap! Two loud slaps on her face. She covered her face in pain and stopped dodging.

Wanquan easily loosened her belt. He scooped up a spoonful of icy water and poured it down onto her crotch.

She couldn't help but cry and her body immediately straightened up. Her livid lips trembled.

Another scoop.

"She deserves that," someone said.

"Pour her out a lesson," another one said.

Wanquan didn't speak. Instead, he just scooped cold water from the pail.

Freezing water kept raining down onto the woman's crotch.

"Is she from the same place as you came from?" Orchid Root asked Little Ai.

"No. We met up halfway."

"No wonder you don't speak in the same accent."

The woman's face was quite livid. Her body trembled as if she would collapse at any time.

"Let's go." Little Ai touched Orchid Root.

"What's the matter?" Orchid Root asked.

"Nothing."

"Hold on. Let's watch some more."

They watched for a moment.

When Gold Beam took off his clothes that night, Little Ai was sitting on the bed, not saying a word. He thought that she was still thinking about what had happened to Wanquan's wife. He said that damned Wanquan was not a man. She seemed not to hear. He instructed her to sleep and pointed out that since the well was to be sunk the next day, having fresh drinking water would make their lives more convenient. While he was talking, he slid under his own quilt and was the first to fall asleep. They slept on the same brick bed but didn't share the same quilt. Apart from that time, Gold Beam never touched Little Ai again. He even felt regret. Though Little Ai never said anything resentful to him, he still had some regret. To Little

Ai, it appeared as if nothing had ever happened. She cooked and swept the floor with Orchid Root. She also tidied up the room, held the washing water for Gold Beam and sometimes joked with her sister-in-law too, which made him really warm in heart. Nevertheless, once they were on the bed, she would tie up her waist and ankles. At that juncture, something like a cat's claws seemed to scratch his heart. Little Ai left Gold Beam with such feelings: at one moment he was warm in his heart and at another time it was as though it was being scratched.

In the few days which followed, Gold Beam didn't chisel away at the stone but helped the diggers to drill the well. Orchid Root and Little Ai worked together on the cooking. Jade Rod, meanwhile, repaired the boat on the river beach. The delivery boat had been damaged. It was impossible for him to get back home at noontime, so he let Orchid Root fetch food for him.

It was in delivering the meals that matters went awry.

Shehui who was drilling the well was a weird sort. He was about 25 or 26, always bold. He even shaved his head in winter. He said he had an overabundance of internal heat. He owned a black and white television and carried it wherever he went to drill. Every time he came up from the well, he was coated with dust and mud but was never hasty about cleaning himself up. He would first turn on the television and then wash his face and hands. "I like watching the news" he told Orchid Root and Little Ai. Orchid Root said there was no news broadcast in the daytime. She thought that was a waste of electricity and wanted to turn it off. Shehui disagreed.

"Wait a minute. It will come on soon," he maintained. He stubbornly watched his TV while eating.

While he was doing that, Orchid Root made her delivery to Jade Rod.

"You eat. I'll take Jade Rod his lunch."

She did that for two days. On the third day, when she had just said that, Little Ai put down her bowl and proposed, "I'll go with you." This put Orchid Root in an awkward situation, but she felt it difficult to refuse. She took a glance at Gold Beam. Little Ai knew that they didn't trust her. She picked up her bowl and didn't speak. Orchid Root felt it even more difficult.

"Go! If you want to," Gold Beam responded.

She came over uneasy and insisted she was not going. Orchid Root, who was very embarrassed, took her hand and commented, "I'm afraid Brother Gold Beam doesn't like to let you go. But since he gave permission, let's make tracks." She dragged Little Ai away.

Nothing happened. Little Ai left together with Orchid Root and they came back together. This made Gold Beam relieved and a little shameful. Then there came a spot of excitement. He borrowed a bike, rode dozens of miles to the store in town and bought several packets of instant noodles and bottled fruit. In the evening, he took them out one after another, put them on the cupboard cover and invited Little Ai to eat.

"You are not used to the food here. Allow yourself a change," he told Little Ai who was sitting on the bed.

Then, he took out two books and put them together with the food.

"I asked for a few books from a primary school teacher. You are an intellectual. You can read them if you are upset."

Little Ai peeked at the two books and wanted to laugh, but withheld.

The books were textbooks for Year Two pupils.

"This place is remote. Few people go to school," he explained.

When he got onto the brick bed, Little Ai didn't tie her trousers as usual. Those strips were laid on one end of the bed. He noticed this. His heart seemed to be bitten by ants. Not much. Just one bite. He threw the strips at Little Ai and then took off his clothes.

He was about to get into bed. She still sat there motionless. He didn't know what she was thinking about or maybe she thought nothing. He opened his mouth and wanted to say something. But when he spoke up, it turned into something else.

"You eat the bottled fruit," he urged.

She kept sitting there like that, with no movement.

"I'm going to sleep," he said.

Every night he spoke those same words and then drifted off. Only he himself knew they were not redundant at all. He didn't want to sleep first. He thought it would be great to be able to sleep with her. He thought that maybe one day, she would pick up on his words and say something back. No, she didn't pick up on his words. He always climbed into bed forlorn, wallowed in glumness for a long time, and then fell asleep.

Now, he said it again. The same mood and the same quilt. And he knew he would still feel sad after getting into bed. But –

She called out his name.

"Gold Beam …" Though Little Ai called softly, he heard that. He couldn't believe it. He thought he was mistaken.

"Gold Beam …" Little Ai called again.

This time, he heard it distinctly. He pulled out his nose from inside the bed and looked at her.

It was indeed Little Ai. She was indeed calling him. She didn't look at him, but she did call, with very light voice.

He didn't know if he should reply.

"You, you called me?"

Little Ai turned around. Her expressions were hard to fathom. She just peered at him.

"You don't want my body?"

Gold Beam immediately panicked. He didn't expect her to say that. Her eyes made him a little terrified. He remembered that night. His tongue seemed to be tethered up with a hair.

"I was drunk last time. I was out of my mind."

He dodged her view.

"I will never do that again."

"Gold Beam ..." she called again.

He raised his head and looked at her face.

"Tonight I would like to."

She said that very sincerely, though Gold Beam didn't believe her.

"Don't tease me, Little Ai."

"I'm not teasing you. I will."

"You've come around?"

She nodded.

Gold Beam was startled for a period. Then he lifted the quilt up to the corner of the bed, jumped up, knelt down and took her hands.

"You..." he began, "have come around?"

Little Ai nodded again. Excited, Gold Beam let out a cry and was all tears. He held her and babbled a string of words to her amid those tears. He asked, "How could I not want your body? I never stopped thinking about it until my heart dries up." He buried his tearful face in her bosom and wept. "Every time I think of the fact that you sleep on the same bed but don't want to be my woman, my heart aches as if it's being cut by a knife and I just want to die."

That night, like all the submissive women, Little Ai let Gold Beam rub her body in every way and with every effort. He called her name once and then again, hoping that he could melt himself into her body.

How could he know why she was treating him like that!

He soon knew the reason.

x.

Orchid Root carried the bamboo basket of food and took Little Ai's hand. They walked along the valley, and as they went she pointed out to her the names of the surrounding mountains and places.

"You see, that is the Ostrich Peak. They say it resembles an ostrich. I've never been able to see it. Who knows whether that's true or not? This valley is called Ram's Horn Valley. We must hurry. I'm afraid Jade Rod has been waiting for too long. There is enough time for you to take all of this in. This is a remote place but has very beautiful scenery, more beautiful than the mountains and waters in movies," Orchid Root declared.

It appeared that Little Ai couldn't take it all in – too many things for her to look around at. She was so curious.

Suddenly she stopped and stared down at the bottom of the valley. Orchid Root thought she must have seen something novel, and also looked down.

Nothing good to stare at.

"Nothing at the bottom of a valley could be absorbing. If you want to have a look, ask Brother Gold Beam to take you sometime…"

Orchid Root hadn't finished when she was shoved by Little Ai. She let out a cry and turned around but didn't have time to see Little Ai's face clearly before she fell over. The bamboo basket reacted like a sparrow, shooting up and then diving down and rolling together with Orchid Root.

Little Ai watched Orchid Root as she rolled down into the ditch; there was no expression on her face.

"Sister Orchid Root, I'm not like you."

That was all she said, then she turned around and ran away.

Orchid Root was still rolling down, like a garment with something wrapped inside.

When Jade Rod and Tiantai managed to carry Orchid Root back, she was smeared with blood. Gold Beam appeared as though he had been bashed on his head. Then his eyes straightened up and his body stiffened. Jade Rod informed him, "Little Ai ran away. She knocked Orchid Root down and fled. I'm chasing after her now."

He climbed onto a walking tractor with a group of people

in tow and then left in a rush. Before he got out of the compound, he had some words for Gold Beam – "Brother, don't be afraid. Orchid Root will be fine. Little Ai cannot run either." There were tears in his eyes. Some people, when they are really angry, not only turn red-eyed but become watery-eyed. Jade Rod produced tears of rage.

After they had gone, the yard became quiet. Someone was cleaning Orchid Root's wounds for her inside the house.

Shehui who was drilling down the shaft called and nobody answered. He then climbed up from the well. He soon knew what had happened. He wiped off the dust and mud from his bald head with his hand and walked to the steps to pick up his TV, ready to go.

"What!" Gold Beam suddenly yelled. He had been standing stiff as wood. He suddenly shouted toward Shehui.

Shehui said that he was going and the well couldn't be finished as a family drama was unfolding there.

"Bullshit," Gold Beam cursed.

"Oh, oh, you still want me to drill," Shehui retorted. He didn't collect the TV. "I'll do as you say. Half-shifts are troublesome to tot up."

Gold Beam fell silent. He came over very fierce looking, balled his hands slowly into fists in apparent readiness to beat someone.

He didn't beat anyone. He let out a cry and punched himself in the face. His nose bled. He knew that but didn't want to care. It seemed that he was intentionally letting out surplus blood. Shehui couldn't just watch this anymore. He gouged out two hard and tiny clods and bunged them up Gold Beam's nose.

"Even if you have too much blood, that's not the right way to tackle it. I think you should have a good sleep. When people are overly-worried, they feel better for a good sleep." He pushed Gold Beam into the room and closed the door.

Gold Beam really did sleep. After a night's rest, he seemed like another man, neither angry nor anxious.

Little Ai was recaptured the next morning. She was made to kneel in front of Orchid Root's bed. She didn't manage to get that far. On her way to the county, she was intercepted by Jade Rod. They tugged her hair and beat her really hard. Then she was thrown onto the tractor. She was drenched with dirt and her face was black and blue. Someone advised Jade Rod to strip her and parade her through streets; some said he should smash her leg so she would have to pull it along behind her for the rest of her life. That wouldn't prevent her from warming Gold Beam's bed and she would still be able to have babies with him. Jade Rod didn't speak. He took her to Orchid Root's bed and let her kneel down. She did likewise. He asked Orchid Root to decide whether to cripple her hamstring or leg. He thought he should comply with Orchid Root's decision. But she shook her head and asked him to get out. She said she wanted to have a few words with Little Ai. Her head and hands were wrapped in gauze. The woman stared at Little Ai and didn't say a word for a long time. Little Ai couldn't bear this and opened her mouth first.

"Sister Orchid Root, I'm so sorry."

Orchid Root's eyes became wet. She took her hand and murmured, "You've really got a head of iron."

"You'll let them kill me."

Orchid Root didn't answer. She advised, "If you went away and I fell to my death, how could Gold Beam and Jade Rod carry on living? They are not easy people. They look rough but are kind in heart. I must have a baby for Jade Rod. I thought maybe you could have one before me."

"With kids running around in the yard, the family would be complete."

Little Ai also had a face full of tears. However, she was not of the same mind.

"I want to go."

"You can't. You saw it with your own eyes how they punished Wanquan's wife. Not many people in this world may live as they want to. That's not for you to decide. You can't follow your heart."

Little Ai cried in deep sorrow, clinging to Orchid Root's arm.

"Brother Gold Beam may not have the luck of owning a woman in his life," Orchid Root sighed. "It seems it's impossible for him to lasso your heart."

Gold Beam and Jade Rod were squatting in the yard eavesdropping on the conversation. They didn't know what to do.

Shehui walked towards them, holding a cup of tea and he joined them in crouching down.

"I think." He gulped a mouthful of tea. "You can't keep this woman."

Jade Rod stared at him with red eyes. He wanted to slap him on the face or grab the tea cup and fling the tea in his face.

Shehui didn't notice Jade Rod's face and swallowed another mouthful.

"I don't think she'll stay."

"Bah!" Jade Rod spat towards Shehui.

Shehui dodged the saliva. He didn't get angry.

"Jade Rod, what I said is the truth. People are not willing to hear the truth. That's most people's problem."

Jade Rod wanted to spit again but was prevented by Gold Beam. Gold Beam told him he shouldn't fight with Shehui as his words were correct. "Let her go if we can't keep her."

Jade Rod's eyebrows jumped. "You only know how to let her go! If she goes, what about the money?"

Gold Beam fell silent.

"Money?" Jade Rod asked.

Shehui chipped in again with something Jade Rod and Gold Beam would never have expected.

"If you like, you give her to me and I'll pay you."

Jade Rod and Gold Beam's eyes straightened and they stared at Shehui. Shehui was not joking, his face being the picture of sincerity.

"This is something to discuss," he counselled. "She wants to go. You can't prevent her. You'll lose both the woman and the money in the end."

"I break her legs and let her lie on the bed. I'll raise her."

"That's all unnecessary," added Shehui. "It may seem that you can't get through to her. Actually, you can't get over yourself."

"Drill the well. It has nothing to do with you," Jade Rod instructed. "If we can't prevent her, how can you? You've got almighty powers?"

"Maybe I have."

"As your wife?" Jade Rod asked.

"Don't mind." Shehui wasn't revealing everything. "You'll get your money. If you don't trust me, we can ask the Village Head to be our witness. This is not a good place to talk. Let's go to the Head's house and talk it through. If you don't let her go, she'll still be yours to keep. Nothing to worry about."

Matters had really taken a serious turn.

In the beginning, Jade Rod wouldn't even entertain the notion. Gold Beam said that he had already given up and maybe what Shehui said represented a way out. Jade Rod now loosened a little.

But he insisted that Gold Beam should talk about it himself as he couldn't just swallow that up. Gold Beam said they should go together and he must swallow that, no matter how difficult it was. Jade Rod asked him whether he had decided not to keep her. Gold Beam was adamant that he wanted to, but she was not a moggy or a puppy that could be kept easily. Jade Rod didn't speak anymore.

The second day early in the morning, they went with Shehui to Tiantai's home. The Village Head surmised that if she wouldn't stay put they should just give her to Shehui. But they two should think it through as once they had taken Shehui's money they couldn't rue the decision. Shehui suggested they could write an agreement. Neither Gold Beam nor Jade Rod put up any opposition, and Tiantai composed a draft. He read it to them. They all said yes. Tiantai asked them to make the mark of his fingerprint to show they all agreed. He took out a box of ink paste and asked each of them to press a red fingerprint on the agreement. Tiantai then said, "OK, Shehui, you should pay the money." Shehui replied that as the Head was their witness, he should also leave his print. Tiantai agreed. He pressed his fingerprint and told them, "I'll fetch the official seal of the Village Committee for you. That looks more stylish." They all thought that was a good idea. Tiantai then sealed the agreement with the official stamp and told Shehui to cough up. Shehui replied that it was too much of a rush and he could only pay in part, leaving 1,000 yuan to be handed over a few days later. Tiantai asked Gold Beam and Jade Rod. Jade Rod refused. Shehui looked at Tiantai. Tiantai told Gold Beam that Little Ai was not suitable and he could wait for Old Plum to bring new women and just give this one to Shehui. Tiantai said Shehui had a family and so couldn't up sticks and there was also the agreement, so they should just wait for a few days. Gold Beam took the money.

That evening, Shehui fetched Little Ai away on a donkey and handed the TV set to her, letting her hold it as they went out of the village. She asked him where they were. Shehui explained that they would first go to his house and then he would take her to the county the next day. She thought Shehui was preparing to send her home. She asked why he was such a chivalrous man. Shehui said he had inherited that from his parents. She asked why Gold Beam and Jade Rod felt they could let her go. Shehui said he gave them a little money. She pointed out she would let her parents send the refund over when she got home. Shehui insisted that it didn't matter whether money was sent or not. Money was just meaningless shit. She told him that she hadn't ridden a donkey before and felt like she'd fall off. Shehui advised her that she should hold on tight or he would lose a lot if it was broken.

Once they arrived at Shehui's house, a few people manhandled Little Ai into a food sack. There was a well in the backyard and Shehui was already down there. "Slip it down," Shehui called from the bottom of the well.

They chained the sack on the rope and slipped it down.

XI.

There was a kiln at the bottom of the well which was used to store sweet potatoes. At present, that cavity contained a pile of hay covered with plastic sheeting and bedding. On it sat Little Ai. Shehui admitted, "To be honest with you. I bought you from Gold Beam to be my wife. I'm in the same boat as him; I've been single for a long time." Then he deposited her down on the bedding and tore her clothes. She clutched at his face with both hands which were stretched into talons. Shehui let out a cry and jumped away. Immediately, a number of prints had been left behind. He touched his face and it ached a lot.

"Rascal!" she cried.

"Yes yes. If I wasn't a rascal, how else could I have gotten you here? Your time at school stood you in good stead – you figured it out quite right."

hose above ground asked him if he was coming up as they were tired of waiting. Shehui's head reached out from the kiln and up toward them and he cried, "You go now. I can clamber up myself." The people went away. He turned round to Little Ai and smiled.

"This is the well for my own house. We dug the kiln for storing sweet potatoes when drilling the well. I never thought I could put a wife in here. Even I feel a little strange."

"You let me out!"

"Going out means having to sleep with me on the same bed. My ma has already cleaned up the house and the bed, which is heaven and earth compared with the bottom of the well."

"Shame on you."

"Not being shameless will never get me a wife. I'm quite clear about that. As long as you become my wife, you can call me 'Shameless' every day. I can also change my name to 'Shameless.'"

She could not produce a word and so just breathed very hard. Shehui drew closer to her and realised that her hands were about to turn into talons. He stopped. He asked, "Do you want to scratch me again? I won't touch you. If you don't think it through, it will never be done even if I strip you. This is not like nailing a wooden peg into the wall."

"Clean your mouth."

"Peasants' mouths are bound to not be as clean as you city folk's mouths. Peasants don't brush their teeth because it's too troublesome. But if you like, I can brush my teeth every day."

Little Ai didn't speak. She sensed the man was so shameless, shameless to this extent. She surmised it was just a waste of breath.

But Shehui still wanted to talk. He said, "I'm not like Gold Beam. What he did is what I despise. I have my way. I got this when I drilled the well for them. I've given you a blanket, a plastic cloth, bedding and a quilt here. I would like to see where you can run unless you want to plunge into the water."

Little Ai's head was about to burst. She embraced her head and started screaming:

"Let me go!"

Two strings of tears fell out from her eyes.

"Then you cry for a moment. Sometimes crying can take away some sadness. That's what my mum does. Cry out and do what should be done."

Little Ai did indeed start to cry, her head in her arms, and wept very sadly. Shehui squatted very patiently by her side, listening to her sobs.

"If you want to cry, then let it all out."

She cried for a while and stopped.

"Not crying anymore? Then let's get on with it. In fact, there's nothing else to say. You sleep with me and become my wife then I'll let you out of the well."

"I'm hungry."

"Oh oh, I am hungry too." Shehui touched his belly. "I'll go up to get something to eat, and then come down here again and talk to you. Of course, I won't bring you anything to eat. Maybe letting you be hungry for a few days will make you think about the consummation."

Shehui spoke a few more words cheekily and then climbed up the well. He had something he needed to do. His ma and his pa asked him if this would work. He said the way it was, it could not possibly work at the moment, but would in a few days. His ma boiled him two eggs and asked him to take them down to Little Ai. He replied, "Ma, you're wrecking it. If she feels she has food and bed, how can she be my wife?" He ate the two eggs. His mother looked at his father. He said: "let's just listen to him this time."

The next morning, they didn't give her anything to eat, nor did they shout out at noon. At supper time, his mother found she couldn't agree with this. She held her bowl and shouted at Shehui: "Are you going to starve her to death?"

"You are wrong. If she starves to death, where else can I get a wife? This opportunity is so slim."

"If she dies, let her ghost be your wife."

"I read in a book that it takes seven days and seven nights without food and drink for a person to die."

"Bullshit! I'm sending her food right now."

His mother let his father send her down to the bottom of the well. Shehui's father took out the sack, tied it to a rope hook, and allowed his mother to sit inside it.

"Let me do it." Shehui realised his mother was in fact determined to go down there and he proposed he should go down himself. His mother spat at him and asked her husband to slip her down.

"Wrecked." Shehui lifted back his head and said.

"Wrecked," he repeated.

"And off," his mother requested.

His father swung the windlass.

Things really were wrecked, but not because Little Ai ate the food sent by Shehui's mother. There were other reasons. First of all, his mother found that Little Ai felt had come over sick and wanted to vomit. Then, Gold Beam visited Shehui's home, followed, later on, by Director Zhao, the chief of police in the town. Cumulatively, these factors piled up into a huge case.

On another trip down the well, Shehui's mother found that Little Ai had the uncontrollable urge to wretch. She asked her a few words, and then let Shehui's father haul her up in a panic. Once she got onto the ground, she proclaimed: "Little Ai is pregnant." She didn't know what had transpired above ground while she was talking with her down below.

"She's pregnant!" she insisted.

After that revelation was shared, she happened to notice that Gold Beam too was standing at the edge of the well.

They were all astonished.

XII.

Gold Beam came to Shehui's house on account of Director Zhao, the chief of police in the town.

That day, Director Zhao rode his decrepit motorcycle over to Rear-side Village. Its engine stalled before he arrived at Tiantai's house and couldn't be started again. That motorbike often had this problem and might grind to a halt anywhere, causing considerable nuisance to Director Zhao. But then, he was Director Zhao; somehow he could always make it start again, so he would still ride it no matter wherever he went.

"Tiantai, Tiantai, ask someone to push my motorcycle." He

stood at Tiantai's door and shouted. He was about fifty years old, and bared a mouth of yellow tea-stained teeth.

Tiantai walked out and inspected both sides of the street; no one was there.

"Well, well. I'll give you a push," Tiantai proposed.

They pushed the motorcycle forward into Tiantai's house. Tiantai's wife served the tea. His four boys wanted to sit on the motorcycle but were shooed away.

"Go, go away. You can't touch the motorcycle. If it's broken, your dad can't afford that."

"Don't tease me, Tiantai," Director Zhao said while repairing the motorcycle.

Tiantai insisted he wasn't teasing Director Zhao and his four boys really could turn it into a write-off. That would cause trouble for Director Zhao. He then smirked and squatted on the other side of the bike.

"You have been the director for a few years. Why not change it for a new one? It's better that it's broken down here as I'll offer you a bit of hospitality. You just take your time to repair it. But what would you do if it's broken down halfway?" Tiantai said.

"It's quite nice that I still have a full tank of oil. Change it for a new one? Last month's salary still hasn't been paid," Director Zhao replied.

"Then what the hell are you working for?"

"You think I love the errands? I look forward to retiring all day long. But my age doesn't make me eligible yet. What can I do except for work?"

"You must have come here for some reason."

"Nonsense. A few more wives have been sold to your village, haven't they?"

"No."

"You shouldn't play the goat with me. Your villagers bought so many out-of-town wives. Did I ever ask? I'll butt into other matters even if no one tells me. But I won't deal with this until folks beat a path to my door."

"What is it?" Tiantai became somewhat nervous.

"Is there one named Little Ai?"

"So what if there is?"

"Her parents have been to the county public security bureau. You tell me whether I should butt in or not? If I don't, they will cause trouble for me."

"There's no such person."

"I am talking to you very seriously this time, Tiantai."

"There's no such woman in our village. If you find her, I'll go with you to the jail. If you don't believe, you can just look for her here."

"I didn't say that she must be in your village. The business I'm involved in is a matter of hearsay." He handed Tiantai a cigarette and got one for himself. Tiantai came closer to light it for him.

"You can catch whatever you want. But why must you catch others' wives?"

"You are a Village Head and you don't even know the law. According to the letter of the law, this is 'trafficking.'"

"The law was made by human beings."

"Yes, the people made the law. But not you and me, right? We can't allow their parents to cry every day in the public security bureau."

"If you take these women away, the families of the buyers will also wail like mourners."

"Is it possible for you to show a little humanity?"

"It is so wrong to say that. It's not that I am not human, but that the two of us aren't the same."

"That's true," Director Zhao agreed. He stood up, clapping his hands.

"Ready?"

"Just give it a try."

The motorbike started up again. Director Zhao got on it and was about to go.

"Won't you have something to eat?" Tiantai asked.

"I will. I'm just off out for a ride. You prepare the food." Then he went out pushing the motorcycle.

He dropped by at Gold Beam's house. Orchid Root was at home alone. He asked the whereabouts of Gold Beam and Jade Rod and was told they were on the river strand. While he was talking, he glanced at the rooms. Orchid Root asked if he had come about a matter. He said nothing specific. She asked whether he would sit and wait. He said no and asked her why she was wrapped up like that. She answered that she had fallen on the stone. He replied "Oh, OK." and left. He went back to Tiantai's home for a meal, chatted a little and then returned to the town.

That night, he came back with a few people from the police station. They knocked on Gold Beam's door. They didn't find the one they were looking for.

"Where is she?" Director Zhao asked Gold Beam and Jade Rod.

"The only two folks here are standing in front of you. The third one is my wife – in bed – want to have a look?" Jade Rod asked.

"Hey, you. Your wife. Don't you think I dare not look? I do want to. Lead the way." Director Zhao said.

There was only Orchid Root in the room.

"Sorry, sorry," Zhao apologised.

"Is it OK just to say sorry?" asked Jade Rod. "You let us open our door in the middle of the night. Don't you see I only have one shirt? What if I catch a cold? Come with some cold medicine next time. Anyway, you are entitled to free medical care."

"OK, sure."

They didn't find Little Ai. They went to Wanquan's house and took his wife away by motorcycle. Wanquan wailed for half the night as if he had been stabbed with a knife.

The next day, Gold Beam got up very early. He claimed he

didn't sleep for the whole night and he wanted to see Little Ai as he felt uneasy.

"Shehui is not a decent person," he commented.

"You are asking for trouble," Jade Rod warned.

Orchid Root proposed that if he really wanted to take a look he could go to retrieve the 1,000 yuan Shehui owed them. She knew that Gold Beam was fretting about Little Ai.

'We can't take the money!" Jade Rod exclaimed.

"Just take a look!" Orchid Root said. "Brother Gold Beam, you go alone."

Thus, Gold Beam went to Shehui's home and discovered that Little Ai had been put down the well. He wondered aloud how Shehui could get her into a place like that. Shehui was initially annoyed to see Gold Beam at his home. Shehui asserted that wherever he chose to place her was his own business entirely. Gold Beam told him to get her out. Shehui replied that he should just go away. Gold Beam slapped Shehui on the face. Shehui dodged and took up a stick: "Do you want a fight?"

"Get her out of the well."

"I don't want to fight. Don't come any closer."

In the meantime, Shehui's mother shook the rope from down the well and wanted to be lifted up.

Hence, Gold Beam learned about Little Ai's pregnancy.

XIII.

Flushed with agitation, Gold Beam dashed back home. He grabbed Jade Rod by the arms and shook them, not saying a word for a long time.

"What is it?" Jade Rod was getting anxious too.

"Little Ai's pregnant!"

Orchid Root immediately ran out from the kitchen.

"Little Ai's pregnant!" Gold Beam repeated.

After the meal, Gold Beam and Jade Rod went to Shehui's

home and conducted intense negotiations. Shehui's father was there as well. They all spoke very directly.

"Yes, yes. I owe you 1,000. I'm not a deadbeat. I'll give you it," Shehui promised.

"I don't want the money I want her," Gold Beam replied. "I'll refund your money. I've brought the cash with me."

"I won't accept the money. We have an agreement. Find your Village Head if you want to take her back. Let him do the asking."

"It wouldn't work even if the Head did," his pa said.

"Dare he come? I'd slap his face!" Shehui grunted.

"She's pregnant with my child," Gold Beam complained.

"How can you say that it's your child? I also slept with her. You shouldn't talk bullshit. She's in my house, how can she bear your kid? If you go on with that, I will be blunt with you."

"How dare you!"

"I'll do anything if you push me hard enough."

"Bastard!"

Shehui stood up at once but was dragged back by his pa.

"Sit down, sit down," his father told him. "We won't quarrel with him. Don't talk to him. We'll pitch in the money and send it over tomorrow."

"I'm not taking it," was Gold Beam's response.

"That's your own business," Shehui's father pointed out.

Gold Beam trembled all over with anger.

"Gold Beam, this can't be solved with anger. This is a reasonable thing," his father maintained.

Jade Rod had been silent. He had been staring at Shehui and his father's faces. He knew there was nothing more to say. He just stood up.

"Go," he told Gold Beam.

"It has not been solved. How can we go back?" Gold Beam quizzed, not willing to budge.

"Go!" Jade Rod cried at Gold Beam.

"Jade Rod is more sensible," Shehui's father observed.

"Tomorrow morning, I'll ask Shehui to send the money."

"You wait at home. I'll come and pick it up," Jade Rod volunteered.

"I don't want the money!" Gold Beam winced.

Jade Rod pulled his arm and went outside.

"I won't take the money!" Gold Beam turned and cried.

That evening, Shehui and his father stumped up enough money. The next morning, they didn't go anywhere, instead waiting for Jade Rod and Gold Beam to collect the cash. They waited till breakfast time came around.

"They won't come," Shehui predicted.

"Wait for a moment. If they don't come after breakfast, we'll send it over," his father replied.

"Mum, you cook."

The door burst open with a *pang!* Someone ran into the yard and shouted:

"Shehui be quick! Gold Beam and Jade Rod are coming with a big pack of people!"

Shehui jumped into the yard at once.

"Where are they now? How many people?" he asked.

"They are approaching the village entrance. A lot of people. All of them have weapons."

Shehui's face turned pale at once. His father stuffed the money into the flue inside the brick bed and jumped through the doorway.

"Call all our family members to the entrance. As many as possible," his father commanded.

Shehui answered and lifted the pickaxe down from the eaves, then ran out to gather people.

By the time Shehui and his family members rushed to the village entrance, the people on Jade Rod's side just arrived. They carried a stretcher too in readiness to transport the wounded.

Shehui and his father waited, undaunted.

Gold Beam and Jade Rod came to the front and stopped. The folk on both sides looked at each other, gripping their weapons in their hands.

"What are we gawping at?" Jade Rod suddenly asked. "Charge!"

Hence, the fighting began. They immediately stirred into action. Pickaxes, shovels, clubs, and sticks were swung toward the heads, waists and legs of the other side. Stones, bricks and fists produced all kinds of strong noises. Once labour tools had become weapons for fighting, their owners were no longer bodies, but flesh – something either strong or fragile that came under attack. And only at this time would an inhuman madness be engendered in a strong body. Originally they knew each other, greeted one another warmly when they met, and would also greet each other warmly later when they met again. But at the moment, they were warriors. They were trying to beat each other. Beat! Beat those damned! They were beating themselves dizzy and dazed. Some even beat those on their own side. When that happened, the one who was beaten would jump up and scold: "you fucking beat me!"

Someone bit others, his hard teeth ripping off pieces of flesh.

Soon there were moans because some were already beaten onto the ground, bleeding here and there.

Jade Rod's opponent was Shehui. He rapidly beat him down. He rode up, seized the ears of Shehui, and knocked Shehui's head to the ground. Shehui screeched: "Jade Rod, you let go of me. We can talk." Jade Rod wouldn't. Jade Rod knew if he let him go, Shehui might jump up, let him down and knock his head. So he couldn't let go of him. He pummelled his head one strike after another. He felt holding his ears was no more useful than tugging his hair, though as Shehui was bald, his ears were all he could grab.

Gold Beam targeted Shehui's father from the very beginning. Shehui's father knew he was not his equal and just ran. He shouted while running, requesting people's assistance in warding off his adversary. That deprived Gold Beam of the chance of giving him a proper pasting. Undeterred, Gold Beam set his mind on beating the guy and making him lay low. Gold Beam was not to get that opportunity, for a whack from a stick caused his leg to cave in and he was forced to his knees. Shehui's father smiled and threw himself at Gold Beam, but he caught him first on the shoulder with a brick. The old man let out a groan and crumpled onto his knees as well.

If it wasn't for Shehui's mother, the brawl would just have continued. However, his mother came.

"Don't fight! Stop fighting! Little Ai's been seized by the police!" she caterwauled at the mob, bursting into tears.

The din of the fighting attenuated.

"The cops took Little Ai away on a motorbike!" his mother continued.

No more noise.

Gold Beam, Jade Rod, Shehui and Shehui's father all climbed up from the ground and stared at Shehui's mother. Then, they fixed each other.

"Must've been Director Zhao," Gold Beam said.

"From the backstreets," his mother added.

"What shall we do?" Shehui looked at Gold Beam and Jade Rod.

"Hurry up and give chase!" his dad piped up.

"After them!" Jade Rod ordered.

All those who could climb up, rose to their feet, raised their respective weapons and ran with Gold Beam, Jade Rod, and Shehui. That way, they were united as a single unit.

"Take the shortcut!" Shehui's father shouted toward them.

They soon saw the three-wheeled motorcycle.

XIV.

Like a dog, Director Zhao had quickly sniffed out the whereabouts of Little Ai. He was excited for a while, and then launched his three-wheeled motorcycle to Shehui's house. He didn't waste any time because Shehui's mother spied him. Her teeth chattered as she made a confession without any questions being asked. She took out the sack, tied it to a rope hook, and together with Director Zhao, lifted Little Ai up from the well.

"Director Zhao, they are fighting at the village entrance," the old lady reported.

"Oh, oh," the Director muttered.

"You ask them to stop. Your words will wash because you are the Director."

"Oh, oh."

He didn't go to the village entrance. He went away via the backstreets. He wanted to escort Little Ai into town, and would then come back to break up the rabble. He looked down upon their guts. He did not pay due attention to his motorcycle either. The vehicle faltered again at the least opportune time. It couldn't be started no matter how hard he tried. He caught sight of Gold Beam, Jade Rod and Shehui and numerous others rolling down from the slope with all kinds of weapons. Getting very close. His ankle became limp and he just couldn't get his motorcycle to budge. He knew it would be a while before it could be fixed so he just left it there, lighting a cigarette and waiting for the crowd to surge towards him. Little Ai called out nervously a few times. Director Zhao comforted her by saying: "Don't be afraid. We have right on our side; we are protected by the law. They daren't do anything to you." He wiped off a head-full of beads of sweat.

With a burst of footsteps, he was surrounded. Gold Beam, Jade Rod and Shehui, who were at the vanguard, stared at him angrily. He wanted to give them a smile in return, but his expression was neither a grin nor a mope.

"Put her down," Shehui instructed in a very harsh tone.

"Why?" Director Zhao tried to make his voice soft.

"I bought her, fair and square."

"You see," Zhao said. "I am duty-bound. I have no other way. What's say we go to the town together and have a talk there?"

"Cut the cackle! We'll fight if you don't get her down."

"You are breaking the law."

"We have no chance to consider that. Why don't you hand her to us?"

"No." Director Zhao took down a pair of handcuffs from his belt. "Whoever interferes will be cuffed."

"Grab her back!" Jade Rod let out a cry.

Director Zhao raised his handcuffs and shouted, "Don't move!"

"Beat him!" Shehui cried.

With a roaring sound, the mob swamped Director Zhao, his motorcycle and Little Ai. He was beaten from all directions; his justice and law were pounded into oblivion.

"Don't aim for the bones. We will be in big trouble if he ends up disabled!" Shehui cried out to the crowd.

No one hit his bones. They knocked him down. They trampled on him and took Little Ai away, then overturned the motorbike. By the time Director Zhao clambered up from the ground, Little Ai and the crowd had disappeared; only his sneaking three-wheeled motorcycle lay on its side, on fire. No one knew who torched it. He looked at the burning vehicle, and finally broke into a smile. Just then, he wanted to give them what for but didn't do it well. Now he had made it. He felt some pain in his forehead, and examined it. There was a swelling and it became more painful on being touched. He remembered what he had said to Little Ai and felt very funny.

At that time, Little Ai was flanked by Gold Beam and Shehui. They each took hold of one of her arms and burst into an argument.

"Little Ai can't go to your house," Gold Beam said.

"She can't go to your house, either," Shehui replied.

"No matter where she goes, Director Zhao must not know," Jade Rod insisted.

"Yeah," agreed Shehui. "For the time being, Little Ai temporarily belongs to two families. When we've talked it through, she will go wherever she ought to go."

This time they didn't quarrel, nor did they fight. They reached a temporary consensus. They placed Little Ai in a secret place and resumed their negotiations.

The negotiations were conducted in Gold Beam and Jade Rod's home. Orchid Root made several dishes that went with alcohol and let them eat, drink and talk. Their chopsticks didn't move. Their minds were not on the dining table.

Almost crying, Gold Beam blurted out to Shehui: "You give her to me. You are younger than me. You have plenty of opportunities."

Shehui didn't agree.

"I am younger than you, but my parents are getting older. If I don't marry a woman, they can't rest in peace."

"Why don't you just do battle over the same woman?" Gold Beam suggested.

"I have no way. That's our fate." Shehui surmised.

"She's pregnant with my child."

"Why are you saying this again?" Shehui was not happy. "If this goes on, in the future when the baby is born, how will I be able to face others? People will say that Shehui's child is Gold Beam's. How can I keep face in front of people?"

"You can't tear her into two," Jade Rod commented.

"That's what I was going to say," Shehui said.

"I want her no matter what" was Gold Beam's resolve.

"Same here."

They talked for a night and a day and it didn't work.

"We have the agreement." Shehui suddenly thought of the

contract. "Let's solve it according to the agreement."

"Fine. Let's take the agreement. It was signed by both of us. Either side shouldn't have the exclusive right to decide," Gold Beam concurred.

They called for the Village Head Tiantai. Tiantai asserted he couldn't judge this case. Shehui was turning nasty. Shehui chimed in: "After all, you are the Head. You can't act like this. What did you say when the agreement was signed?"

"I was endeavouring to do good by the two of you. Now it's like this. What should I say?"

"Then let's go to the town."

"This is one way. The Mayor of the town has a higher rank than me. Maybe he can solve this."

"You must go with us."

"Of course, of course, I'll go with you. I'll speak up when I should."

They worried that Director Zhao might find out about their trouble but soon they were not afraid. Little Ai was in their hands. What trouble could he find?

They then headed for the town.

XV.

It all went off very quickly. This was something they hadn't counted on.

The Secretary of the Township Government led them into a room, poured them each a glass of water, and informed them, "The Mayor asked you to wait a minute. He has a meeting with a few folks from the county."

"Who?" Shehui asked.

"I didn't ask. You just wait here."

The Secretary shut the door and went out. A few minutes later, the door opened again. It was neither the Mayor nor the Secretary, but Director Zhao. The swelling on his forehead had disappeared, leaving just a purple patch.

"I heard that you were coming."

When Director Zhao started talking, Gold Beam, Jade Rod and Shehui were not nervous anymore. Tiantai stood up and wanted to shake hands with Zhao. Once he got to the Township Government, he shook hands with everyone he met.

Director Zhao didn't shake hands with him.

The door was wide open. A few police officers came in, each holding a pair of handcuffs. They cuffed Gold Beam, Jade Rod and Shehui. They also cuffed Tiantai.

They were all goggle-eyed.

"What on earth is this, Director Zhao?" Tiantai asked. He was much more experienced than them, appearing to be the picture of calmness.

"You are avenging your personal grievances in the name of the public good!" Shehui shouted at Director Zhao.

"You were involved in trafficking and broke the law," Director Zhao responded.

"Was I?" Tiantai didn't get it.

Director Zhao nodded at him.

"You wronged me," Tiantai accused.

"As you'll surely grasp when you are sentenced," Director Zhao explained. "The official seal of the Village Committee is not a toy. You can't just use it at will."

"Oh, oh." Tiantai now appeared to comprehend.

Director Zhao took a cup of tea, drinking it in a leisurely fashion.

"When we pick up Little Ai, you will all be sent to the county," he went on. "This time it really is a big deal. The Chief of the Public Security Bureau has come along too, with Little Ai's parents. Her mother scolded our Mayor for a long time. That is one tough woman, with words like knives. She said our place is so backward and that even after years of spreading the word of the law, the common people don't even have an ounce of basic legal sense. The Mayor must also take his share of responsibility for this. The Mayor's face flushed. The Mayor said 'yes of course, but to be honest, in this place, even if the Provincial Governor descended on us, he could hardly make matters better.' The Mayor was unconvinced. Little Ai's mother said that she cherished her daughter, but was even more angry about how the people here rode roughshod over the law. That damned woman."

Director Zhao talked to those in handcuffs like he was chatting casually.

A few motorcycles drove into the yard. Little Ai was picked up. She cried for a long time in her mother's arms. They then watched the police bundle Gold Beam, Jade Rod, Shehui, and Tiantai into a van.

"Little Ai," someone called her.

It was Orchid Root. No one knew when she arrived.

Little Ai approached her, wanted to say something but didn't speak up. She took Orchid Root's hands and called out: "Sister Orchid Root."

"You see, how many people you've done harm to ..." Orchid Root uttered.

Little Ai just felt like crying.

The van started. Little Ai's mother told her to mount onto the motorcycles. So she did.

Gold Beam was sitting in the van, looking at Little Ai on the front of the motorcycle carriage. He was unconcerned about what they would do to him. He only thought of her.

"What will you do to Little Ai?" he asked Director Zhao.

Director Zhao thought the question ridiculous.

"Didn't you see her parents?"

"She's pregnant with my child," Gold Beam revealed.

"She is with your baby. But the baby is illegal and should be aborted," Director Zhao answered.

"Bullshit!" Gold Beam stood up, flushed.

"You sit down. If the car moves, you'll fall down."

Gold Beam slowly sat down and buried his head. He didn't

say a word.

When it reached the county, the motorcycle carrying Little Ai and her parents drove to the county hostel while the van with Gold Beam and the others headed for the detention house. Gold Beam suddenly jumped up and ran out from the door.

"Little Ai!" he gave out a heart-rending cry.

Little Ai turned to look at him. He fell down, climbed up from the ground and staggered toward her.

"Little Ai, you are pregnant with my child."

She nodded. She immediately felt sorry for him. She sensed that the feelings in her own heart must be convoluted. She didn't want to deceive him.

"You want to get rid of it, right?" Gold Beam eagerly looked at her.

This time, she didn't nod or shake her head. She didn't want to hurt him. She wanted to convey something to him.

The motorcycle suddenly let out a cry and revved up.

"Little Ai!" Gold Beam cried in despair.

"You can't…" he cried out.

Two policemen set him upright and dragged him into the van. Gold Beam stubbornly twisted his neck, tracking the motorcycle that was driving farther into the distance.

In the detention house, they met Old Plum and Second Lady. Old Plum took out a box of cigarettes, distributing them in a very relaxed manner. Jade Rod and Shehui smoked. Gold Beam didn't. He was still thinking about Little Ai and the baby. Tiantai didn't smoke, either. He was filled with grievances, so squatted on the other side and chewed little by little, unwilling to say anything.

A month later, they were found guilty and sentenced to hard labour. The longest penalty was for Old Plum – five years. Second Lady got three years. Gold Beam, Jade Rod and Shehui were assigned one year each. Tiantai got off the lightest – he was sentenced to half a year under house arrest.

A year later, Gold Beam, Jade Rod and Shehui lifted their bundles and trod out of the gate of the work farm together. Gold Beam didn't want to return with Jade Rod and Shehui. He said he was going to find Little Ai. Jade Rod knew he couldn't be stopped, and didn't say anything. Shehui told Gold Beam to get his heart back and accept it. Gold Beam was again silent and went alone.

He did find Little Ai's home. She recognised him. She gave him a glass of water and said: "Gold Beam, you sit down. I didn't expect you would come."

Gold Beam didn't sit down but asked, "Where is my child?"

She looked down and shut her eyes. She said she was sorry.

Just then her mother pushed the door open and walked in. She saw Gold Beam and asked him to get out. He said he was coming for his child. Her mother screeched: "you get out. None of our family knows you."

Gold Beam flashed her mother a smile.

Her mother scolded, "Don't grin cheekily at me. You must have learned that on the work farm."

Gold Beam's face suddenly changed. He drew a knife from his luggage and plunged it into Little Ai's mother's belly.

"This is something I also learned from the work farm."

Eyes wide opened, her mother tumbled over, holding her stomach.

Gold Beam didn't stab again. He turned to Little Ai and said: "I see your face every day in front of my eyes. I can't help."

Little Ai held her head in her arms and let out a scream.

Gold Beam was sentenced again – this time for fifteen years. When Jade Rod and Orchid Root visited him in prison, he claimed that now his heart was clean and he didn't have to think about having a wife anymore. He told them to live well. Jade Rod nodded at Gold Beam. Orchid Root was continuously wiping away her tears.

By that time, Old Plum had already been released from

jail. Through bribery, he managed to get his punishment cut. He tried to change professions but after several times in vain couldn't manage it. He resorted to his old business, passing on women. Of course, he didn't go to Rear-side Village. He moved to a province further north. Hence, he didn't know about Gold Beam's second conviction. He laid his hands on a few more women and was in the process of bringing them up north.

The Road from Sandy Terrace Town

At 2pm, the market-goers started to disperse. Within the time it took to smoke two pipefuls of tobacco, they had skittered like abacus beads into those dozen or more gulleys in the adjacent few score square miles. The street gradually emptied. Three old men were sitting on the boulders in front of the purchasing station, talking nonchalantly about something or other and a number of dogs were strutting to and fro purposefully. The wind poured in from the western entrance and slid through the street. A school stood at the end of the street. It had no perimeter walls. A piece of iron hanging down from a locust tree served as a bell to signal the beginning and end of classes and the school building was flanked by a canteen that didn't open for business until market days.

A man with a number of paper-clad parcels in his hand came out of the canteen. He turned to enter the school. After a while, he came out again with a roll of bedding on his back and a twelve-or-thirteen-year-old boy in tow. As the trio of old men sat staring on the stones, raising their necks again and again, the chap and the kid approached and then went down the earthen slope at the entrance to the street.

Having mounted a vaunted slope, Sandy Terrace Town now seemed to have been transformed into an empty matchbox, discarded without a dicky bird among the shadowy mountain ridges. It appeared so minute that a pair of fingers could pinch it into smithereens.

No human shadows could be seen, nor could trees or crops. Nothing besides mountain ridges and slopes heaved into sight. A few of the slopes were peppered with terraced fields. Maize stalks minus their already-harvested cobs stood bolt straight against the sky. Wheat fields bald as barren caps covered the mountaintops. It still took another while for the sun to plop behind who-knows-which mountain ridge. Illuminated by the sunshine, the caps shone gold and their bared nakedness sent chills into people's hearts. Some grass-like foliage had attempted to spring out of the northern face of the mountains but was already withered into patches of crusted dirt.

The man narrowed his eyes and cast a glance at the sun suspended in the sky.

"Take the short cut," he said.

The kid neither said anything nor looked at the man but followed him as he made a beeline for a small path that led to a zigzagging gulley. A stampede of wind emanated from the gulley, introducing a draught of cold.

The road led only to Sky-jacking-up Hill, the westernmost village under the jurisdiction of the town. The man and the kid had more than thirty miles to trudge. Time and again the path disappeared at a turning and then crawled out after a distance. Such was the character of the roadway.

"You said you'd fetched me steamed buns and wouldn't force me to go back home, but you went back on your word again," the kid moaned. "It's not my fault if I'm not any good at my lessons."

The man gagged his mouth as if he had not heard those words.

"I'm not following you back home," the kid continued.

"Your mama misses you," the man explained.

"Is she a bit better now?" The kid didn't bend his cocked head back but simply stared at the surface of the road.

"She says she misses you."

"I'll come back to school after I have seen her."

The kid turned his head back to look at the man's face. Unable to anything figure out, he held his tongue and kicked a pebble carelessly to the bottom of the gulley.

They again caught sight of the sun.

"The sun's dazzling my eyes," the kid complained. Some

wormwood-like plant-life was visible on the edge of the cliffs opposite. Not trees. Or perhaps they were small trees in the process of perishing.

Having nothing else to grasp his attention, the kid scanned those things and aimed especially at the tall vegetation. He wondered when he could turn his back and leave this hole behind.

"It's too hard a trudge. I don't want to walk anymore," he grumbled.

"This is a short cut."

"Loads of gulleys. I hate gulleys – so many of them."

"They are formed by rainwater."

"I don't believe that."

"Washed away at by water, day after day."

"I don't believe that."

The kid raised his head to stare at those overlapping mountain ridges – they appeared to have been cast in the same mould.

"You didn't let me go back home but you went back on your word again," the kid grumbled.

A string of thick songs came from some unknown place, but the singer held his tongue after only two lines:

Come, come and come again.
He has come down from the opposite gulley – yao-he!

Not until they had trekked a great distance did they find out that singer was a cowherd. The cowherd's face couldn't be seen clearly, but the white towel wrapped around his head was especially striking. Wielding a long whip in his hand, he roamed about the slope. He seemed one moment to dart a look at them, only to turn around and declaim another two lines:

Come, come and come again.
He has come through the Crystal Water River – yao-he!

Neither time was he through with his song. At the end of each rendition, he shooed at his animals. Apparently, that was the correct way to sing this song. The tune was simple and had only these two lines, which he repeated again and again. But he did it in a very special manner. He sang extremely slowly; the sound not being produced by his throat but rather some organ slightly lower down. The noise butted its way out and after it left his mouth, it was again ripped into tattered cloth strips of different lengths and widths by the dry wind. That voice came across as laborious and hoarse. Consequently, the song was tinged with a flavour that should be described as neither passionate nor reserved and as neither bleak nor heroically moving. According to those lyrics, the skies were as poor as poor could be and the impenetrable hills appeared more monotonous and lonely. Though his voice was hoarse, its reach was vast:

Come, come and come again.

He has come through the carved gate – yao-he!

"Father, he is singing," the kid said.

"It is a cowherd."

"What is he singing?"

"A sour ditty."

"What is a sour ditty?"

"A song he's cooked-up himself."

"Why does he sing all the time?"

"He feels miserable."

"When he sings, he feels miserable?"

"Yeah."

"Are singers all miserable?"

"Yeah."

The kid fell silent. After another turn in the path, they spied that singer again. He was still chanting, his hoarse voice swinging to and fro in the dry cold air like torn strips of cloth. Those strains sank down into the gulleys and onto the crossroads and then percolated underground. Everything they touched became icy cold.

"I really didn't want to follow you back. You said you would fetch me steamed buns," the kid muttered.

"I told you, your mama misses you," the man replied.

They had reached the bottom of the gulley. Mountains surged

up on both sides and darkness seemed to be gathering. The sunshine could only spotlight the crown of the topmost hills. The wind haphazardly plucked at the desiccated grass on the slopes. A small river tumbled into the depths of the gulley and, faced with this obstacle, the small path again extended towards the highlands opposite.

"I didn't want to take this road to begin with, but you insisted. You're entirely to blame."

"Let's take a break," the man said. He put down the roll of bedding and stood beside a cliff with the kid next to him. The man sat down on the bedding and ducked his head to look at the tip of his toes, becoming lost in thought. The kid lingered there awhile and then ran to the river to splash in the water. A short time later, he returned to his father.

"Look, you summoned me to go back home. Originally I didn't want to," he muttered.

The man looked up at the kid and tugged at his hand. Not knowing what was going to happen, the boy stared at the adult's rough face, which now appeared rougher because the man was sitting with his back to the sun.

"Third Kid, you are a grown-up already," the father murmured. He drew the child close and put the youngster's head against his chest.

"You've been drinking again?" the kid enquired.

The man didn't answer but rubbed his face against the kid's.

"Third Kid, your sister's gone."

"Gone where?"

"I don't know … Some bloke passed through our village and she left with him. He stayed in our home for one night. The next day, your sister followed him away."

"Why did she leave?"

"…"

"You didn't stop her?"

"No."

"And my mama?"

"Your mother didn't try to stop her, either. Your mother cried."

The kid, who was wrapped in the man's arms, looked up at the sky. The sky resembled a huge cloth parcel engulfing everything down below tight. The cloth parcel was preternaturally blue. Not a string of wind could be hung up there.

"I overheard the conversation between your sister and that man. She took the initiative to look for him. They talked through the night. I heard all their words. I drifted off to sleep, but your mother shook me awake. I got up to eavesdrop again. Your sister and that man were in the courtyard. They went away without a bye or a leave and didn't even bother to come back to the cave room again … Your mother then caught a disease. I went to buy some herbal medicine for her and to bring you back home."

The sunshine faded from the mountaintops and shadows first extended to those sinking places. Those zones assumed a layer of thick armour as if to resist the hacking of a knife. Silently, the tall cliffs pressed against the bottom of the gulley. But if one were to take a second look, they seemed to have been frozen by ice. The fields on the mountain ridges had hidden their heart-freezing yellowness. Darkness was burying everything. Be they gulleys or slopes, everything was changing into a blur.

"Where do the mountains stretch to?" the kid raised his head to ask.

"To somewhere faraway."

"Can we find a way out?"

"Yeah."

Night fell like this. The wind in the gulley scratched their faces back and forth as if it had fingernails. They had stayed there for quite a long while. The man stood up and again put the roll of bedding on his shoulder. The roll of bedding was not worthy of its name.

"It is getting dark," he said.

"I didn't want to follow you home. You promised me but you

broke your promise." The kid bleated as if he had been wronged, yet he still tailed the man. They waded through the nameless river at the bottom of the gulley and started to climb upwards. Only this snaky path could be figured out in the gulley.

They heard a bark from a dog.

"It is an animal from our village," the kid cheered.

They also spotted several orbs of lamplight. Their paces slowed down. The man sneezed in the cold and the kid leaned against him as if he was frightened, taking grip of the hem at the back of his father's jacket.

The lamplight seemed to be near, though in fact, it would still take them quite a while longer to reach there.

Dark Scenery

I.

THE STORY ITSELF started simply enough; well, as simply as it could do given the things that happened afterwards. That day, the melon farmer stood in front of his shed watching over his field. As usual, the sun rose in the east and set in the west. As usual, the melons continued to swell plumper and plumper as they did day in day out. It seemed that nothing could cause him to become excited or agitated. The light from the sun intensified the moment he took a second glance at the melon fields. He then searched for a spot on the edge of the field where he could lie down.

The melon field was spread across the top of a mound. Dirt roads swung from both sides of the elevation rather like the ends of an untied trouser belt dangling down to the floor. This gave the mound the appearance of a suspended shelf set up purposefully to hang this belt. The pits outside the melon shed contained some discarded rinds. It was incredible that watermelons could be grown on such barren land, let alone such a hefty crop be yielded! Row after row of the fruit nestled quietly and peacefully across the ground. Peering into the distance, one's view would be filled with nothing more than ridges and gulleys, making your eyeballs feel as dry as if they had been crammed with dirt.

He laid his head down on a small protuberance, covering his face with a straw hat. He did not fall asleep. Instead, he sensed something on his leg. Lifting that limb, he slapped skillfully at it and immediately felt something sticky. He was proud of his aim.

It was a bug.

Later, he heard some pack animals walking towards the top

of the mound. They hoofed along the belt, wending their way slowly upwards. All of a sudden, he had a desire to howl.

Coming, coming, coming again.

He sang out those words and then realised, in one peep from below his hat brim, that a group of livestock traders were standing at the end of the field. They wore unclean faces and sported high-waisted black or blue trousers with wide legs, tied with woven belts. The men came into the melon field, bending down to select watermelons with their hands. They went from one fruit to another, like they were touching something which pleased their hearts.

He heard that they were nearby. He remained still, his ears pricked up. After a while, he felt a hand on his hat.

"Cut a melon."

It was the hand of a man with a moustache.

He didn't respond and stayed motionless. The strong sunlight probed into his eyes as soon as the moustachioed fellow removed the hat.

"Cut a melon," the man with the moustache repeated.

The melon farmer still didn't move. He was fighting against the fierce sunlight. The moustachioed man placed the straw hat under his posterior and plumped down there next to his head.

The farmer heard the sound of a melon cracking.

Then came a whole burst of cracking watermelons.

The melon farmer squinted and saw a gaggle of livestock dealers striking at and eating his watermelons joyfully. He wanted to close his eyes, but kept them open. He watched as they manhandled the fruit. Anger crept onto his face and he began to breathe audibly. He even huffed out a few breaths.

The cracking sound came again.

"Pack of bastards," he exclaimed.

He suddenly sat up.

"Stop it!" he called out. He shook his head vigorously with all his strength.

"Stop it!" he said again.

"I'll give you money. Let them crack away," the man with the moustache said and then gulped down some watermelon.

"Stop it!" he shouted. For all his stubbornness, he seemed to be shouting for his own benefit alone. He was still sitting on the ground.

The livestock dealers paused for a moment.

"I said 'stop it'!" the melon farmer repeated.

The cracking sound coming from the melon field became even more vigorous.

The farmer saw a dealer hold a big watermelon in his arms and smash it down on the head of his pal who was squatting eating a melon. The watermelon ruptured on his bald head, coating it with pulp. The bald-headed one twitched, but went on eating the melon.

"Stop it!" he growled.

The dealer took no notice of what the melon farmer was saying and smashed that half-melon down on his bald pal's head, nonetheless. He sensed that his throat could be about to rattle out a burst of laughter, but he wasn't able to laugh because something seemed awry. He turned his head only to find the farmer standing behind him. He then burst into laughter at the farmer, unassumingly.

"I said 'stop it,'" the melon farmer enunciated in a low but firm voice.

Unassumingly, the dealer laughed a second time.

The farmer suddenly swung his melon knife, which had a crescent-shaped blade. There followed a sound almost indistinguishable from the sound of rupturing watermelons. This time the dealer didn't laugh. With a wrench of his body he pitched over, that unassuming smile still on his face.

The others dealers came over to see their partner who had been slain by the melon farmer. They then crooked their faces to take a look at the killer.

"Bastard," one of them said.

"I told him not to crack open the melons, but he didn't

listen!" the melon farmer defended.

"Don't you grow them for money?"

"Of course. Why else?"

"Then why did you kill him?"

"I said 'stop it,' but he didn't listen!" The farmer, failing to understand those dealers, tried to explain with a wink. In his mind, the melons were indeed grown for money, but why did they have to crack them?

The bald-headed dealer, with melon pulp on his pate, stepped closer to examine his face carefully. He was a stocky man.

"You killed a guy, you son of a bitch," the skinhead said.

"He swiped my watermelons."

The skinhead grabbed one of the farmer's hands and screwed it to his back until he yelled out with pain. Then, the bald man yanked the melon farmer's legs up to the tip of his nose. The victim, putting up no resistance, lay on the ground, with his eyes fixed and looked at his feet being folded over bit by bit towards his nose.

"Supple muscles," the dealers commented.

"They are."

Finally, there came the noise of bones cracking and the melon farmer's cry of pain. So they toyed with the man, very carefully, just like they were doing something perfectly normal. Presently, they took down a rope from the melon shed, bound his ankles and suspended him upside down from a rafter so that his head thudded against the soft earth. Later, they slipped his head into the crotch of the faded blue pants he was wearing, transforming him into a round ball, hanging up there from the rafter of the shed. The bald-headed guy tugged at the rope little by little so that the round ball swirled upward.

"You killed our man, you son of a bitch. You should cough up 3,000 silver dollars together with a virgin girl before the week is out. Otherwise, we'll kill everyone in this village."

The village lay at the foot of the slope, like a pile of old but warm clothes slung there casually by folks.

Those dealers left, carrying the dead man on the back of a pack animal.

They were a flock of bandits accustomed to buying and selling on such beasts.

At that time, the melon farmer was still swinging from the rafter in the shed. Several watermelons sat upended in the field, their oily surfaces gleaming in the sun.

II.

Grandma Six was the most attractive woman in the village. In her living room there gathered a group of men with expressions of apathy on their faces. They were here to discuss a burning issue; some were squatting, some sitting, and others leaning against the wall. A hum of flapping wings emanated from the flies which rested on the pickle jars outside.

Grandma Six was leaning against the door frame, with half a carrot in her hand. She was aged and haggard but still had a very fine set of teeth for munching carrots. The light cast from within the room spot-lit half of her thin face. Another oil-lamp balanced on the lid of the jar.

They had just finished dinner. In front of their feet was a dish of pickled vegetables. Some stretched their tongues, trying to lick the last grains of rice out of their bowls, generating a melodious sound from the porcelain.

"This is such a big village but we can't stump up a suitable tribute. I don't believe it," someone piped up.

There came the cry of "Tether-tight!"

Tether-tight lifted up his eyelids to take a look at the man who had called out his name.

"My daughter is only twelve years old. How can you insinuate that?" Tether-tight exclaimed.

"Whose daughter do you think is right?"

"Morality Liu's little Laurel is good," Tether-tight proposed.

All of them cast their gaze at the head of Morality Liu.

Tether-tight's words seemed to have wounded him to the extent that he could hardly mutter a word. A moment later, he blurted out, "I should have told you the truth beforehand. Laurel has been used already by a man – that pot-mender, who lived in my house for a few days. He did a shameful thing. At the same time, he managed to fix all the broken pots in the village, he fixed my girl, too. She's now a used woman with a huge belly. Go and see if you don't believe me. He left on the hush hush, not asking for the fee for mending my pot. He didn't even say goodbye. Son of a bitch! You folks go and see if you don't believe it."

Morality Liu was choked with sobs.

Grandma Six didn't say a word. She kept on chewing that carrot.

"Offertory Rice's dad," a younger man shouted loudly. It was Virtuous Wang.

The people turned their heads to the corner. Offertory Rice's father seemed not to have heard. He didn't look up.

"Your Offertory Rice is suitable," Virtuous Wang said.

"Offertory Rice's dad, say something."

Offertory Rice's dad remained still.

They turned their heads to Grandma Six, signifying that: we have chosen the right person – Offertory Rice – but her dad didn't respond to us.

Grandma squinted. It appeared from the smile she was wearing on her face that she was laughing. She stopped chewing. Her mouth stopped moving too, with her two lips closed like a withered flower.

"Offertory Rice is suitable," one said.

"Let Grandma Six decide," some of them said.

The flies on the jar lids vibrated their wings excitedly.

Offertory Rice's dad raised his head, looking at Virtuous Wang for a good while. He abruptly stood up.

"Virtuous Wang!" he shouted.

Virtuous Wang looked suspiciously at the face of Offertory Rice's dad.

"I'll screw your wife!" Offertory Rice's father retorted.

"I'll screw your wife!" he cursed.

He elbowed aside the crowds, walked out from the corner, and came into the yard, heading in the direction of the gate. He turned around halfway.

"I'll screw your wife!" He seemingly jumped a bit.

They watched him leave out of the gate. He dragged along his cloth shoes, the soles clapping against his feet, making a *Click! Click!* sound.

Someone suddenly woke up and hurried out with him.

"Don't go, hey, what a person you are!"

A cat jumped out from the threshold. Grandma Six reached out her hand to grab it skillfully, throwing the pussy, which let out a high-pitched squeak, onto the *kang*.

She resumed chewing the carrot. She took a bite, making a crisp sound which all could hear.

Things were sorted.

Her chewing became extremely noisy.

That very second, the moon was bright in the sky. On the top of the mound, the melon farmer hanging from the rafter of the melon shed looked like a nondescript piece of kit. The watermelons in the fields seemed to be somehow animate and strangely green in colour.

In the distance lay nothing but bun-like mountain after mountain.

III.

Castrating pigs was what that Turtlish Kid did for a living. He squatted in front of Benevolence's house, his back propped up against the stone roller. Inserted into his vest between his neck and shoulder was a small bamboo stick with two red scraps of cloth tied to it. That was the symbol of his trade. On his deathbed, his dad pointed at that stick and told him never to look down upon the cloth because it would be the "bowl" he relied on for a living. Turtlish Kid cast a glance at the "bowl." His dad added that people would treat him well if he wore the bamboo stick between his neck and shoulder. Turtlish Kid nodded to his father. The old man took out a castrating kit in a shiny case and stuffed it beneath his chest-covering cloth. His dad said that when slicing the testicles, he should be speedy and put his back into it, not being deterred should the pig thrash and bleed. Turtlish Kid nodded again. Later he grew to be an expert in the field.

At that moment, Turtlish Kid squatted in front of Benevolence's home, a half-smoked fag between his lips. From Benevolence's yard came the sad and shrill cries of the pig.

Benevolence ran out with a piglet in his hands.

"Where? Where will you do it?" Benevolence asked.

Turtlish Kid pointed at the ground with his feet. "Just here," he said. He took out a sharp knife from the case. Pressing the pig's hind legs under one of his knees, Benevolence grabbed the wriggling swine's ears.

"Press on the head," Turtlish Kid instructed.

Benevolence watched Turtlish Kid's face, feeling that he was too merciless and used too much strength. Why did he expend so much strength when fixing such a little pig?

"What are you saying! Press tightly, it isn't your pig? Is it? Be tender." He looked at Turtlish Kid's hand.

Turtlish Kid took no notice of him. He was shaving the hair from the pig's stomach to reveal in no time a patch of white skin. He made an incision, the skin splitting apart like a white mouth. Another cut helped the blade dive through the skin. Holding the knife between his teeth, he thrust a finger through that opening into the abdomen, then fumbled around inside. The other hand took down the knife from his mouth and plugged the hooked end into the body following the route of the finger. Out came a bloody thing, which plopped into his hand when he cut it free with the other side of the blade. He then raised his arm and flung the bloody thing onto the street. A dog appeared. With one curl of its tongue, the mud-soaked piece of flesh and blood entered its mouth. Soon afterwards there came the noise of chewing.

"You cut the hole too big," Benevolence said.

Turtlish Kid went about stitching up the hole with a needle. A sound could be heard each time the needle penetrated the skin.

"I said 'you cut the hole too big,'" Benevolence complained. "You cut so big a hole on such a little piglet! You are being this merciless because it is not your pig, aren't you?

Turtlish Kid threw a look at Benevolence.

"You asked for seven coins, but I just want to give you five since you cut that big a hole," Benevolence complained.

Bang! Turtlish Kid severed the end of the thread, and then stood up.

"I don't want your payment," Turtlish Kid said.

Benevolence's eyeballs stopped moving and the pig pummeled at his legs; he could no longer hold it.

"Look, look at you," Benevolence replied. "It is OK to cut a hole that size. I was simply making an observation. Look at you."

"Eight coins," Turtlish Kid demanded.

"Look at you." Benevolence seemed to shed tears.

"Eight."

"Look at you; we agreed on seven."

"Eight."

"Eight is OK. I'll give you eight."

"Gimmee then," Turtlish Kid said.

"Look at you. I didn't grow this old wanting to cheat you. Eight, eight," Benevolence insisted. He pulled out a handful of coins from his pocket. "Look at you. Can't I afford to have a pig fixed? What kind of a person do you take me for?" he asked.

Turtlish Kid finished off the sewing and they released that little pig.

"You took that thing clean out of it?" Benevolence checked.

Turtlish Kid slid the knife, needle and thread into the case.

"You are supposed to pay me something if you botch the job," Benevolence said.

Pah! Turtlish Kid spat squarely and with great accuracy into Benevolence's face. He then left.

Watching his back, Benevolence didn't return to himself for a long time.

"Son of a bitch," he muttered.

He pulled up his sleeves to wipe the dirt from his face. The little pig came into his mind.

"Here piggy, piggy, piggy," he cried out.

The running pig disappeared. He saw Tether-tight coming over from another end of the street, beating drums.

"Bring out your grain–" Tether-tight shouted.

Carrying bags of grain on their shoulders, the villagers stepped out of their houses and headed for the Rice family home. Kids who were kicking around shards of broken tiles ran along behind them.

IV.

Inside the Rice family courtyard there stood piles of bags of grain, with names of the donors on them. Beside them were the donors, who hunkered down there without saying a word. They made the wise decision to live rather than risk death, even though they were attached to their grain in a big way. They would always say "Better to live than to die." Those folks smoked tobacco, occasionally drawing the saliva from the mouth of the pipe into their stomachs, with their ears erect, fully expecting a response from Offertory Rice's dad, who was in one of the wing rooms.

From outside there processed a crocodile of villagers carrying bags of grains on their shoulders. Meanwhile, Offertory Rice sat on the steps in front of the main room, picking peppers. She had single eyelids and was in good health. She seemed not to care what was going on in the courtyard of her house. She even stepped into the pigsty to pee and empty her bowels, which she accomplished after a painful but happy effort. While she was fastening her belt, a carefree sound whipped up. She knew the pigs were eating what she had produced and deposited there. Her face aglow, she passed by the grain bags to sit down on the steps, picking up a bunch of peppers.

"Did her dad say anything?" someone asked.

"No, not yet."

"That son of a bitch wants more," Virtuous Wang said. Like the others, he was hunkering down in front of a bag of grain.

They looked into the wing room where Offertory Rice's dad was.

There was a dead silence in the wing room, as dead as a stone. They had been waiting for a good long time, and were still waiting. They had adequate patience and waited there staring at the rafters up on the roof and the grain in the wood of the cabinet cover. Once in a while, they directed their gaze at the face of Offertory Rice's dad. They didn't want to say anything, since they had said too much to him.

Offertory Rice's dad sat on the edge of *kang*, with one leg lying on the brick bed and the other dangling freely. Since his old woven belt no longer rode properly about his waist, he thought it was a cheerful thing to weave a new one right now. He was working on one end, with the other end wound around his toes. He was now the most carefree among all those present in his house. They were begging him! Were he to lean back against the wall, he could see what was going on in his courtyard through the window. However, he didn't do that. He focused on weaving that belt, as if he had the answer. Other people might not be as confident as he was at that moment.

More and more bags of grain were piled in the courtyard. A few kids were running among them and counting: "seventeen, eighteen, nineteen, twenty ..." Other kids were jumping from one pile to another.

He continued to fashion his belt. Seemingly, it would turn out to be the most stylish example in the world. It was dead silent in the room, silent enough to hear the sound of the air circulating. Everyone in the chamber was staring at him, with anger crawling about their bodies. How they wished they could bite him! How they wished they could grab that belt from his hand and fling it into the faeces in the sty.

Virtuous Wang elbowed his way into the room, walked close to Offertory Rice's dad and whispered to him.

"Yes or no? You should let us know, yes or no," he insisted.

He was still working on his belt.

"Go bring more. Go and bring more again. Empty out your grain bins." Virtuous Wang, standing on the doorstep, shouted to the villagers in the courtyard.

"He wants us to starve," someone said with fury.

"No more. Let the bandits lynch us."

"What have you said? I don't want to be lynched," one of them responded.

"Let's go, go to bring more to him."

Offertory Rice took a look at them. She had picked two piles of peppers: one was fresh red and the other dark green. She took a red pepper and dragged it under her nose to take a sniff. Then she took a bite of it. The strong stimulation made her open her mouth wide to exhale, her eyes immediately welling up with tears. Some of the assembled turned their heads and took a look at her.

"Donkey's bollocks would plug that problem," they roared.

Offertory Rice heard nothing. Maybe she did. She was still there, with her mouth open.

"You please take a look into the courtyard, only a look," Tether-tight said to her father.

The courtyard was now filled with containers of different shapes with various types of grain in them. Several brought over baskets of eggs.

The room was filled with a tense silence.

"It is time," Offertory Rice's dad said to himself.

He looked out of the window and into the courtyard, his eyes stopping on the gateway, on the frame of which was leaning Grandma Six. They heard the sound of chewing carrots.

"Ahh!" Offertory Rice's dad burst into tears all of a sudden.

"I feel so sorry for her mum who died when she was little… How can I tell her about this when I meet her in the netherworld…" Tears streamed down his cheeks.

Grandma Six left.

People felt greatly relieved. They walked one after another out of the gate of Offertory Rice's home.

"Ahh!" Offertory Rice's dad was still wailing in the kitchen.

Offertory Rice watched the piles of grain in the courtyard, silently. Later, she straightened her clothes and sat on the steps, with the gesture women adopt when they cry before graves. She proceeded to open her mouth, from which came out her cry:

"Ahh! My ma, you left me all alone…"

The crying voice dragged out longer, so that it sounded like singing, having cadence together with a combination of unspeakable joy and grief. It was a narrative chant, being simultaneously descriptive and lyrical. She inhaled twice then resumed her singing cry. A voice rose in her throat as she was about to inhale.

"You left me alone…"

Offertory Rice's singing cry vibrated in the air.

v.

Benevolence had been wrangling with his wife for a whole day. His wife asked him to send grain to Offertory Rice's dad, but he didn't want to.

"I don't want to give it away," he complained.

The eyes of his wife slanted down onto him. She was portly, with stout legs, a chubby posterior and big breasts balancing on her chest like two heaps of fat. Nearly all of the men-folk coveted the latter.

"All the villagers have handed in their grain except you. You are taking a risk," the woman said.

"I am a risk-taker," Benevolence replied.

"You'll be asked to go to Mule-and-Horse Village if you don't give any grain. The bandits will kill you for sure."

"I won't give any grain and I won't go to that village either. I don't care what will happen."

"Risky, you are running a risk."

"Yes, I am."

"From this village only one risk-taking bean has grown: you."

"I have no grain to give."

"I've filled one bag with grain."

Benevolence opened his eyes wider. He spied a grain sack standing in the corner. He turned his head to look at his wife's face, which was dirty and unclean.

"Fuck your mother!"

His woman opened her mouth.

"Why did you fill that with grain?"

The woman was still there, with her mouth agape. Benevolence came over to her with the intention of grabbing her by the hair. She knew Benevolence was about to beat her like he always did. Benevolence seized her hair and tugged it so her face was pointing towards the ceiling. Her eyeballs sank back into her skull, leaving only the whites of the eye protruding nest-like. Her body was bent back, with her belly bulging out and the two heaps of fat on her chest stretched taut. Benevolence didn't touch them. Instead, he reached his hand into her clothes and poked down along her neck across her belly to the part between her thighs. Then with a firm grab he took hold of a handful of fat. After that, the woman cried as he exerted more pressure with his fingers. A river of tears poured out from her eyes and nose, with two rows of dirty teeth becoming exposed.

At this moment, Benevolence grabbed tighter, channelling more strength into his fingers.

"Fuck your mother," Benevolence growled ruthlessly.

The woman bared her teeth, enduring the terrible pain.

"You dump that grain back into the bin," Benevolence ordered.

"No," the woman retorted.

He applied yet more force and this was followed by another agonized cry.

"Yes or no?" Benevolence asked.

"Yes," the woman wailed.

Benevolence took his hand from the woman's thigh. The woman touched that part of her leg and moaned a few times. Benevolence watched as she dumped the grain back into the bin.

"They will ask you to go to Mule-and-Horse Village," the woman warned him.

"Who has eaten leopard gall and is daring enough to let me go?"

"Let's wait and see."

"Let's see what happens. I don't care."

"I won't give any grain and I won't go to that village either," he repeated.

Later, they overheard Offertory Rice's singing cry. They listened quietly, both feeling the need to pee.

"I don't care," he said, while looking at the wooden rafters in the roof.

VI.

Offertory Rice cried until it was dark. She still remained in that posture, sitting in the same place where she had let out her singing cry. Her single eyelids were somewhat swollen.

The grain bags in the courtyard had grown fewer in number

since Offertory Rice's dad had emptied some of them, pouring the grain into his bin, which was now fit to burst. He threw the empty bags out of the room and into the yard, where a pile of them was mounting up.

"Stop feeling wronged," he told Offertory Rice.

"It's women's fate to live with men when they grow up," he explained to her, planning to further enlighten Offertory Rice.

"Is there any good man in this poor village? Have you ever seen any? Those bandits are human beings, too. As they grow up they are fed on grain and take women as their wives. They eat people, don't they? But it depends. Suppose the bandit head does eat people, but he will not eat you, should you be obedient as his wife. Instead, he just wants you to be his wife, doesn't he? You see?"

An empty bag was tossed out of the room. He passed Offertory Rice with his shoes dragging along as per his custom.

"I asked you to give me a hand but you haven't," he said, once again holding a bag of grain. "If you don't help me, I'll tire myself to death. Is your heart really so hard, as hard as a stone? Your mother's heart was like a stone. I told her that she shouldn't die. 'If you die, what will me and Offertory Rice do?' But she closed her eyes to kick the bucket. Her heart was harder than a stone."

He came to stand on the step of the grain bin.

"Isn't this better than farming? We're not having to grow grain or collect it. We are just pouring grain. When have we ever seen so much grain before? This is proper grain. It isn't earth or cow dung. You sit quietly and listen to me. Your dad has thought this matter over until it's crystal clear. How could I make you suffer such a loss? You think about it this way: stay with him if you like, come back home if you don't. Can he force you to live with him? Can a person's heart be forced for one month, a year or two, or even a whole lifetime? Can such a forced marriage last for long or be happy? The bandits' leader was raised on grain, not grass. He is supposed to know this.

Look, look at the grain here. We are going to consume it when you come back. Eating it will do no harm to your stomach. Look at you, you don't like to listen to what I am saying to you, acting like you are the one that's been made to give grain to others! Alas, you silly girl!"

Lifting her behind, Offertory Rice entered another room. Her dad crooked his neck to observe her closing the door.

"Look, look at you," Offertory Rice's dad said.

Offertory Rice blew out the lights in her room. The courtyard was engulfed with moonlight. With his hands crossed behind him, Offertory Rice's dad trampled on the moonlight to see if he could crush it into pieces. Later, he stopped and listened carefully with his ears erect, but heard nothing from Offertory Rice's room. He crept over to latch the door and then fumbled out a lock from his body and locked the door.

"You sleep, Offertory Rice," he said to the door. "Sleep well. Once they decide who will escort you to that village, you'll have a long trip ahead. Sleep, you sleep. "

"I shall go to bed, too," he added. "Tomorrow, I have to do what I didn't finish doing today. I've been kept busy my whole life, and can't ever live idly. "

Offertory Rice's dad entered that wing room, casting a glance at the woven trouser belt. He removed the old one from his waist, chucking it out of the door. The belt landed precisely on the fence of the pigsty, where it swung to and fro.

He blew the lights out.

Only moonlight was left in the courtyard, lying on the ground like a layer of water. A few bags of grain were soaking in the water-like moonlight. The *twit-twoo* of random nocturnal birds cut through the sky. These were as horrifying as the feeling of something worming its way into one's scalp.

Offertory Rice's dad repositioned the brick pillow under his neck to the right place and fell asleep.

VII.

Tether-tight was beating drums again, the unhurried sound of which was like a death knell being delivered. A terrible foreboding was spreading throughout the village.

All of the residents were gathered in front of Grandma Six's house. They stood or hunkered down there, disheartened. Beside them were sundry trees, a haystack, and a heap of dung and dirt. Chickens were not afraid of the villagers, foraging with their talons around the haystack and dung, where clods and crushed grass sprang out from the ground. In the ditch by the street, a pig was foraging in the earth with its snout. Perhaps it was Benevolence's castrated piglet.

On the wooden table shone several ingot-shaped silver dollars, alongside a women's sewing basket. Instead of having needles and thread inside, there were many wads of hempen paper.

It was high noon. Amid the sunshine, there was the sound of dry hay stalks rubbing themselves into pieces, which made the people quiver with panic.

Grandma Six sat on the threshold, squinting. She did not eat carrots, her hands instead clutching her knees.

No one paid any attention to the wooden table. They didn't know what they were looking at. Maybe nothing. Their eye sockets were like pairs of round pits stricken by walnuts.

Someone coughed and rose from the crowd.

It was Tether-tight.

"Benevolence," he shouted.

Benevolence didn't move. He stared angrily at Tether-tight.

"You didn't give grain, did you?" Tether-tight accused.

"I have no grain," Benevolence answered.

Tether-tight turned to the crowd.

"Benevolence wants to dip oil without giving millet, beans or money, so he is the one who should accompany Offertory Rice to that village," Tether-tight proposed.

Benevolence got into a spin.

"No, I am not going because of my poor legs," he maintained.

"You must go," Tether-tight said. "Everyone must try his best to help – to give money or give a hand – that's the rule."

"Benevolence, you've been chosen from among us and stand out!" Tether-tight reminded him.

People fixed their eyes on Benevolence, compelling him to do whatever he was asked. Benevolence dared not disobey Tether-tight's words to stand out of them. He tilted his body and said to Tether-tight:

"I won't go, no matter what you say."

Tether-tight announced: "A volunteer is still needed. We shall have to draw lots if nobody is willing to go."

"There should be no fumbling around. You take the first one that your fingertips touch."

"I won't do this," Offertory Rice's dad said as he walked out of the crowd, somewhat complacently. Walking up to Grandma Six, he planted himself down next to her.

"Do as you are told."

People stood up one after another, crowding towards the wooden table.

"One after another," Tether-tight ordered.

People then lined up in single file.

Benevolence was still recalcitrant, crouching down beside the table.

"I won't go. Whichever son of a bitch is willing to go should go," he wailed.

Standing with his butt poking out, Offertory Rice's dad enjoyed watching people's facial expressions while they were drawing straws, as if he were the most carefree person in the world. He said to himself that this is how people should live. It occurred to him that Offertory Rice was still locked in her room, a situation of which Grandma Six should be informed.

"Grandma Six," he began. "Please put your heart at ease. Don't worry, I have locked Offertory Rice in her room. She won't starve because I've left her food to eat, nor will she run away."

Grandma Six didn't respond, narrowing her eyes into slits.

The lots were drawn, but nothing was reported back.

"Tell us – who is the one?" Tether-tight asked.

The silence fuelled the people's anger.

"Whoever it is should stand out, don't hide yourself away," they chorused.

"It must be Turtlish Kid," someone surmised.

Turtlish Kid was holding his head, without saying a word.

"You are unwilling, just to act as an escort. What about Offertory Rice? What should she do?" her father asked. "Don't be so dark-hearted."

"Fuck!" Turtlish Kid stood up, tearing the wad in his hand into minute pieces, as minute as milled rice.

VIII.

Tether-tight and Turtlish Kid were standing in front of Benevolence's house.

"Benevolence!" Tether-tight shouted.

Benevolence came out from his room.

"I won't go there. Whoever is willing to go there should go," Benevolence insisted.

"We are willing to give grain, right now." Benevolence's wife stepped out from behind Benevolence and said.

"Too late," Tether-tight answered. "Why didn't you do this days ago?"

"I won't go there," was Benevolence's refrain.

Benevolence cried out with pain the moment Turtlish Kid took hold of the thing in his crotch. He then fell to his knees, his belly sucked in.

"Don't move," Turtlish Kid commanded.

Benevolence straightened his body.

"Lie down."

"No," Benevolence protested.

Turtlish Kid directed more strength into his hand, making Benevolence cry out with unbearable pain. "I will lie, will lie," he shrieked.

Benevolence lay on his back, looking up at Turtlish Kid's face.

"Go or not go?" Turtlish Kid asked.

"Don't," Benevolence replied.

Turtlish Kid took out the knife he relied on for his living from his waist.

"Tether-tight, untie his belt. Let me fix him," Turtlish Kid said.

With a surprised exclamation, Benevolence's wife threw herself at Turtlish Kid and gave him a kick with nearly all her energy. Turtlish Kid didn't move, but she was thrown back to the ground as the result.

"I can't go on living," she wailed.

"Take his trousers off," Turtlish Kid instructed.

Tether-tight untied Benevolence's belt while Turtlish Kid brandished the knife before him. Benevolence continued to lie on the ground, apparently in readiness for their treatment.

An ice-cold feeling shot through Benevolence when the blade made contact with him. He couldn't prevent his legs from shivering in fright. He knew very well that Turtlish Kid would emasculate him for sure and would feed the stuff he cut out from him to the dogs.

"I will go," he whimpered to Turtlish Kid.

"I wouldn't have been born and raised by my parents if I weren't to go," he wheezed.

Turtlish Kid removed his hand from Benevolence, putting his knife away in the box. Benevolence stood up, and patted his clothes to get rid of the dust.

"You dare to do to people what you do to pigs?" Benevolence asked.

Pah! Turtlish Kid spat onto Benevolence's forehead.

Pah! Benevolence's jaw was now gobbed on, this time the projectile coming from his wife. He cast his wife a glare, without saying a word.

That evening, Benevolence, having become more obedient, squatted inside the threshold of Grandma Six's house with Turtlish Kid. Grandma Six brought out many silver dollars, putting them on the cabinet cover.

"This should cover your expenses on the way to that village," Grandma Six said.

They took a look at that pile of money.

"Set off after suppertime," the old lady ordered.

At the moment they were about to leave, she added:

"Kill Old Eyes."

They turned their heads with fright.

"Kill him," she repeated.

Leaning against the wooden cabinet, she seemed sleepy. That cat was sitting in the quilt atop the earthen *kang*.

Grandma Six began to eat another carrot, with the crisp sound of chewing reaching their ears as they stepped out of the gate.

IX.

The melon farmer hanging in the melon shed didn't swing anymore. There was no wind. A hill ridge lay not far from the shed.

There was the creak of wooden wheels.

Out of the pass on the hill ridge came Turtlish Kid, Benevolence and Offertory Rice. Benevolence was pushing a single-wheeled wooden barrow followed by Turtlish Kid. On the barrow sat Offertory Rice, with one quilt under her body and another rolled up behind her to form a backrest.

Offertory Rice wore a red upper garment, as red as a chilli pepper. She tilted her head down and looked nowhere, not caring about how the barrow bumped and shook.

Behind Benevolence was Turtlish Kid. He walked with his hands crossed as he surveyed the scenery along the road. Plugged beside his neck was the sign of his trade: pig castrating.

They stopped the moment they saw the melon farmer. They heard someone singing on the hill opposite.

Coming, coming, coming again.
Coming from the flowery gate…

They looked into the direction from which the singing sound was coming. Benevolence salivated, filled with a feeling of panic.

"You people have treated me unfairly!" Benevolence suddenly shouted out.

"Why did you people ask me to go? You people have treated me unfairly!"

Benevolence jumped once. The creak of the wooden barrow rang out again. They headed down the slope of the ditch.

There was a long journey ahead of them.

They arrived at the bottom of the ditch. A river cascaded down itself from a company of large stones and ran along the ditch. Offertory Rice stretched one of her legs and jumped down from the barrow. She asked for some water to drink.

"Drink, drink, everybody drink," Benevolence called out.

Benevolence and Turtlish Kid knelt on their knees, sucking water from the river. After taking some refreshment, Offertory Rice began to braid her hair. Turtlish Kid and Benevolence sat on a stone, listening to the sound of braids being unpicked.

"It's your turn to push the barrow, isn't it? We are meant to swap every few miles," Benevolence reminded him, looking at Turtlish Kid's dirty face.

"You can't always be so selfish and willful to take a mile when given an inch. You should keep your words that I've not been hired by you to work like a pack donkey or servant mule. Offertory Rice, you say something."

Offertory Rice was braiding her hair. Her manner was extremely detached and she didn't care whose turn it was to push. Therefore, she didn't say a word and went on braiding.

When the pigtail was done she flung it elegantly over her shoulder onto her back. With another stretch of her legs, she seated herself back on the barrow.

Turtlish Kid took hold of the handles and began to push the barrow while Benevolence pulled. After they had crossed the river, they left behind some wet footprints on the bank. After studying those wet footprints, Benevolence decided to follow the barrow with his hands crossed behind his back. He thought that he should cross his hands behind him. He went on processing in his heart that: "*men have their turn at being a grandson and their turn at being a grandpa. Whichever it is their turn to be they should act that role properly.*" He wanted to do what Turtlish Kid was doing: walking and taking in the scenery.

"Yes, I am right," he thought to himself.

Later, Offertory Rice's dad crossed his mind, so he wanted to exchange a few words with the girl.

"Offertory Rice, your dad was so smart that he was able to become a wealthy man in our village," he observed.

"At this very moment your dad must be making and eating white steamed buns. Do you believe it?" he asked.

Despite her body jolting as the barrow went along the rough road, Offertory Rice's eyes remained perfectly still.

"Believe it or not. Were I your dad, I would do that," Benevolence said.

He squinted into the distance, daydreaming that he was Offertory Rice's dad, imbibing the aroma of those white steamed buns.

Mountains stood on both sides of the long narrow road, which snaked through the ravine.

On the road were three of them, walking.

x.

Offertory Rice's home was busy as never before. Her dad wanted to have his house renovated. Now, not only could he afford to make it happen, but had the mood to do so, too. Morality Liu, Tether-tight and Virtuous Wang were asked to assist him in building a wall. He boiled jars of tea and poured it out into bowls for them.

"Drink," he declared. "Don't be in a hurry to work. Drink first. I have prepared plenty for you to eat and drink."

"Oh, Oh," Virtuous Wang and the others smiled at Offertory Rice's dad, watching him walking away with vegetable jars.

"Dark-hearted. How dark-hearted that guy is!" Morality Liu commented.

"He's become the rich upstart in the village," Tether-tight said.

"After giving our grain to him there's nothing left but the northwest wind for us to eat," Virtuous Wang complained.

"I just want to throw this bowl on the ground and smash it into pieces," Morality Liu exclaimed.

"Do it," Virtuous Wang cajoled.

"Smash this son of a bitch's bowl!" Tether-tight repeated.

Bang! The teacup in Morality Liu's hand was thrown down onto half a brick. Morality Liu wore an exaggerated expression on his face.

"Look what you've done," Virtuous Wang and Tether-tight said, both looking at Offertory Rice's dad.

"Fuck, I didn't have a proper grip," Morality Liu lamented.

Offertory Rice's dad glanced at the broken pieces of bowl on the ground, but didn't come over.

"Fuck, a broken bowl, fuck," Offertory Rice's dad cursed.

Virtuous Wang and his company felt something oppressive in their stomachs.

"We can't bear to watch him living better than the rest of us," Morality Liu droned.

"My wife's fallen out with me," Virtuous Wang explained.

"She scratched my face, scolding me as a turtle egg and went back to her parents' home."

On Virtuous Wang's face there were several finger-marks.

"There should be a way," Morality Liu said.

"We're gonna find a way," Virtuous Wang promised.

"Go and see Grandma Six," Tether-tight proposed.

They downed tools and headed for the middle of the village. Offertory Rice's dad thought they had all gone to the toilet.

"I do have a pigsty in my house you can use," he called out.

"Pack of bastards," he muttered, dissatisfied.

It was at this moment that Virtuous Wang chanced upon someone stealing chickens from his house. We don't know this person's name, so let's tentatively call him "Skedaddle." He entered the gate of Virtuous Wang's house with a cloth girdle on his shoulder, shouting: "Give me something to eat, aunties, uncles, grandmas or grandpas." A pair of washed cloth shoes had been left out to dry on the windowsill. These he slid under his girdle as quickly as he could. "Aunties, uncles, grandmas or grandpas…," he carried on shouting. Later, he spotted a hen. There was a chicken coop on the short wall, inside which a hen was laying. He plucked it out of the nest, and proceeded to wring its neck with the intention of slipping the dead fowl under his girdle, too.

"Thief!" Virtuous Wang stood at the gate, growling.

Skedaddle was taken aback. He stuck one of his fingers rapidly into the bird's rectum.

"Eggs, you see. It's really a hen. I can feel the eggs." With a shameless look on his face, he smiled at Virtuous Wang and attempted to slip out.

"Put it down!" Virtuous Wang ordered.

Skedaddle let go of the hen, which flapped its wings a few times.

"I came to see whether it is with egg or not. Yes, it is. I'm not cheating you," Skedaddle defended.

"You are thievish-looking," Virtuous Wang said.

"Get out of the way!" Skedaddle suddenly changed his face and bellowed loudly. Half-crouching his body, he ran towards Virtuous Wang in an attempt to flee in that direction while he was in a daze. It was in vain. Virtuous Wang took hold of him by the lugs. He was made to turn in a circle with his neck tilted.

"I wasn't stealing. I just wanted to see whether it could lay eggs," Skedaddle screamed in defence.

Virtuous Wang's hand lifted Skedaddle's ear, forcing him onto his tiptoes. They went out of Virtuous Wang's house and walked onto the street. Skedaddle would howl when passersby were near and beg for mercy when nobody was around.

"Let me go. I won't ever come back to your village again. If I did that'd make me a beast. Grandpa, please let me go," Skedaddle pleaded with Virtuous Wang.

Virtuous Wang put all of his strength onto his fingers, tearing Skedaddle's ear.

XI.

Grandma Six sat, cross-legged, on the earthen *kang*, smoking her long copper pipe. Besides eating carrots, she loved smoking her pipe. The cat was cradled in her arms.

Besides Tether-tight and Morality Liu, many other villagers descended on Grandma Six for help.

"I cannot live my life," Tether-tight wailed.

"He is neither virtuous nor righteous. We can't treat him as he wants us to," Morality Liu bemoaned.

"Grandma Six, you give us an idea," Tether-tight beseeched.

"Kill him" was the advice of a number of those present.

Grandma Six tapped the ashes from her pipe and lifted her arm to reach for half a carrot left on the cabinet cover.

They heard Skedaddle's screams. After a while, Virtuous Wang came into sight, tearing at Skedaddle's ear.

"He stole my chicken," Virtuous Wang announced.

"No, I didn't," Skedaddle countered. "I just wanted to see whether it could lay eggs."

Virtuous Wang gave Skedaddle a firm pinch. Skedaddle cried with pain again, still standing on his tiptoes. Virtuous Wang put his hand into Skedaddle's girdle and produced a pair of shoes.

"He stole some shoes, too," Virtuous Wang added.

Virtuous Wang slapped Skedaddle on his face with the soles of the shoes.

"Tie this son of a bitch up," someone shouted.

They trussed Skedaddle to a tree in front of the house.

"Fetch a knife!" one of them suggested.

"Chop him!" another said.

Skedaddle stopped shouting and closed his eyes.

"Let me die. Deliver me to death," he pleaded.

When matters take a complicated turn, ordinary folk feel astonished. Here was a thief who was not afraid to die.

Grandma Six came out from behind the crowd.

"Let him go. I'll give him a piece of my mind."

Skedaddle opened his eyes and stared at Grandma Six. Tether-tight having untied him, he stretched his arms and legs, looked disdainfully at the others and then followed Grandma Six to the room.

What happened next was that Skedaddle was dispatched to shave the head of Offertory Rice's dad.

Offertory Rice's dad washed his head with hot water, wrapped a towel around his neck, and sat down on the wooden stool, watching Skedaddle sharpen his razor, skillfully.

"You said you can shave? I wouldn't have taken you for a barber," Offertory Rice's dad admitted.

"You cannot judge a person by his appearance," Skedaddle retorted. He tried the blade with his fingers and walked towards Offertory Rice's dad.

"I've been shaving others for years. I am best at shaving heads bald. Haven't you seen Virtuous Wang and Tether-tight?

I shaved their heads. Haven't you seen them?"

"I still wouldn't have taken you for a barber."

Skedaddle pressed down on the head of Offertory Rice's dad with one hand while the other hand raised the razor. He looked outside the gate. He knew very well that at this crucial moment he needed to calm himself down.

The razor sizzled on Offertory Rice's father's head and then a strip of white skin appeared. As it moved hair fell out. Skedaddle's hand seemed to shake a little.

Another sizzling sound came as he traced a second stroke along the white skin. More hair fell down. Skedaddle wore a serious, even terrified look. Offertory Rice's dad didn't notice what was going on with him. Instead, the disgusted faces of those villagers flashed across his mind.

"They envy me!" Offertory Rice's dad blurted out to him. "I had to sacrifice my daughter when all they had to do was to give over a bit of grain. How come they envy me? What is this world coming to? Is it easy to raise a daughter that old? I regret it. Wasn't it a great loss to swap a virgin daughter for some grain?" Offertory Rice's dad turned to Skedaddle, with his eyes fixed on his face.

Succumbing to a sense of guilt, Skedaddle's hands began to shake more violently. He took another look outside the house. He knew they were waiting for him.

"You shave, shave on. You are actually quite good at it. I can tell that from the sound the razor's making."

The razor sizzled again. White tracts of skin appeared one after another. Skedaddle's face was awash with sweat. A cough was to be heard from somewhere, followed by another. Both of them heard that hacking sound.

"Those jealous villagers must have eaten lime. Those sons of bitches must have eaten lime," Offertory Rice's dad surmised.

The razor moved faster and faster. Later, it shook a tad, nicking him on the neck and causing him to cry out. Skedaddle jumped out of the gate and stumbled up the street.

The villagers who were squatting on the street suddenly stood up, watching Skedaddle bumping into the crowds and running out of the village to the hill mound, where the melon farmer was still hanging in the shed like a bag of kit.

"Ah, ah," he shouted, looking behind him from time to time. No one ran after him. They didn't have to give chase.

A sound came from Offertory Rice's father's wing room. It was emanating from the master's own throat. After that, the onlookers saw him drag half of his body over the threshold, pink bubbles foaming from the cut on his neck.

They held their breath as they stared at him, keeping fixed to the spot as all the bubbles ran out of the gash.

"He is dead," they judged.

Tether-tight rotated the dead man's head. They caught sight of a fearsome pair of eyes, with one ball close to hanging out of its socket. Despite being caked in dirt it was still fixed on them.

The crowd was disturbed. Droves flocked to the grain bin. Offertory Rice's dad had tossed away those empty bags after pouring out the grain onto the steps in front of the main room. They rummaged about trying to recover their own bags.

Tether-tight took a hempen notebook out of his shirt pocket.

"Aren't you going to obey the rules?" he asked.

"Fill your bags with grain one after another," he instructed.

He began to read the words from the hempen paper:

"Morality Liu – three *dou* of millet, two *dou* of wheat."

Morality Liu walked up to the grain bin with his bag.

"Virtuous Wang – eight *dou* of millet."

They lined up and took turns at filling their sacks with grain. Before very long, the grain bin Offertory Rice's dad had once patted gleefully was now empty like a hollow eye socket.

The courtyard was quiet. Nobody knew that when the pigs nosed the fences open, they would come out of the pigsty, and snaffle at the grain spilled on the yard, around the threshold and up to the front of the grain bin.

XII.

They stopped in front of a cave dwelling. Since it was nearly dark, they looked at the cave, wanting to bed down inside.

"You go in and check it out," Turtlish Kid told Benevolence.

"You go, you go and see," Benevolence replied.

It was an empty cave, and a spacious one at that, which shepherds had left abandoned. The leftover hay suggested that somebody had bedded down there. Turtlish Kid kicked at it with his feet, gathering the strands into order, and then stamping them level.

"We can sleep here," he said.

"How?" asked Benevolence with his eyes on the hay.

Offertory Rice lay down at the other end of the hay-strewn area. Turtlish Kid removed the bedrolls from the barrow. He reached out his hand and groped around. Some of the silver dollars were still there. He placed his bedroll under his head as a pillow and lay down next to Offertory Rice, leaving one strip of hay vacant. Benevolence knew that was left for him. Holding back what he wanted to say, he sat down on the hay, took off his shoes, emptying the dirt out from inside them and then lay down to sleep.

The smell of hay and sheep dung pervaded that cave.

Moonlight sneaked in through the cave entrance. They lay there with their eyes open.

"It is strange that I can't fall asleep," Benevolence mused. He heard Offertory Rice shuffle her body. All of a sudden, he seemed to remember something. He straightened his body up, supported by his two arms and took a look at Offertory Rice first and Turtlish Kid second. He then found that the gap between Offertory Rice and Turtlish Kid no longer existed. In fact, their bodies were drawing very close to each other.

"I can't fall asleep," Benevolence repeated.

"Let's switch over," Benevolence said to Turtlish Kid. "I can't fall asleep near the cave mouth."

Turtlish Kid remained still. Benevolence lay down again.

"I can't fall asleep, it's strange."

He sensed some changes going on in his body, which immediately brought his fat wife into his mind. At night, as he thought of her, the woman's special smell would assail him. He would then become hard in readiness to do something. Thinking about this caused him torment. At that moment he just wanted to do that thing. But all he could do was think about it. The more he thought about it, the more torment he suffered.

Turtlish Kid was so naïve that he was able to sleep next to a virgin. Benevolence always believed that a male virgin was simpleminded and required more sleep. Thinking on in the darkness, he drew towards sleep himself.

The hay rustled abruptly. He saw Offertory Rice stand up, walk past his feet and out of the cave. He elbowed Turtlish Kid awake.

"Offertory Rice is trying to escape," he asserted.

Turtlish Kid followed Offertory Rice out of the cave and witnessed her squat down behind a stone. He felt like a part of his body was being touched. He watched the stone, and then heard the sound of a thread of urine. Benevolence stood behind him, listening to the sound together with him. When standing up Offertory Rice saw both of them. She, twitched her eyebrow once, said nothing, and passed by them.

"You watched her pee!" Benevolence yelped. He thought Turtlish Kid was utterly shameless.

"Shame on you watching a virgin pee!" he accused.

Offertory Rice seemed to have overheard Benevolence's words. She didn't turn her head back but walked into the cave with Turtlish Kid's eyes still on her.

"You, I think, have evil intentions," Benevolence opined.

"How dare you, Turtlish Kid!" he scolded.

The staring face of Turtlish Kid scared Benevolence.

"OK, OK, I'll say nothing. Carry on looking. You can only

look, but you are not capable of doing anything!" Benevolence said.

Not entering the cave straightaway, they sat down on a stone. It was quiet in the valley.

"How can we kill Old Eyes?" Benevolence asked. "Is it possible for us to kill the one who always kills other people? You say something."

"We won't do the killing ourselves. We'll leave the second we've dropped Offertory Rice off there. We won't think too much about it," Turtlish Kid reasoned.

"How will they deal with us when we've dropped off Offertory Rice and filled their hands with money?"

"I have no idea."

"What about Offertory Rice? How will they deal with her? She will be …"

"I couldn't tell."

"Let's run away. We won't go there," Benevolence suggested on the spare of the moment, looking at Turtlish Kid's face.

"We have 3,000 silver dollars in hand. Let's travel somewhere, without thinking about the future consequences," Benevolence said.

Turtlish Kid remained silent.

"Or, you let me go. There is something wrong with my legs. We can share the money and go our separate ways anywhere we want," Benevolence proposed.

"Do you agree?" Benevolence wanted to know.

"I will fix you," Turtlish Kid croaked with a sudden change of face.

Benevolence heard the sound of the knife box on Turtlish Kid's waist.

"Look, look," he pleaded. "We won't split. I have a wife and kids at home in the village. We won't split."

Inside the cave, Offertory Rice was choked up with sobs. They listened to this for a while.

"She is missing her dad" was Benevolence's diagnosis.

On entering the cave, they saw Offertory Rice sitting sobbing on the hay. She didn't miss her dad. Even she herself didn't know what was wrong with her. She had not thought the whole issue over at all. She sat on the barrow when asked; she would go to Mule-and-Horse Village when asked. She knew her way forward was dark. She sometimes thought of her mum, but she couldn't remember how she looked. She thought she might have been a woman older than her. On thinking of her mum, she could feel nothing was good and wanted to shed more tears. She found it strange. People sometimes were overcome by such strange emotions.

At dawn, Offertory Rice stepped out of the cave. Benevolence saw her going out and followed her quietly, without disturbing Turtlish Kid. He got into a panic when he saw Offertory Rice heading down the slope.

"Offertory Rice has escaped!" He kicked Turtlish Kid's leg. Turtlish Kid woke up and stood up quickly.

"I saw her walk down along the slope. She's running away," Benevolence exclaimed. He didn't go out with Turtlish Kid, but took the money bag out from the bedrolls. He was a little taken aback when Turtlish Kid unexpectedly returned.

"What are you looking at? She's run away. You didn't believe me when I told you so."

"1,500 each, then we go our separate ways," Benevolence whispered.

Turtlish Kid remained unmoved.

"You want a bigger share? No, let's split in half," Benevolence said, loosening the rope on the money bag.

They heard the sound of footsteps. It was Offertory Rice who was coming back from the slope, with an armful of mountain fruits. She watched them, without knowing what they were doing.

Some silver dollars fell out from the untied bag and rolled along the ground. The coins were large and round like Benevolence's eyes.

"Bastard," Benevolence scoffed, smiling at Turtlish Kid.

With Offertory Rice sitting atop the barrow, they resumed their journey. She popped a bright red mountain fruit into her mouth and chewed a few times.

Later, they met up with Skedaddle.

XIII.

Skedaddle had gone into self-imposed exile for several days and nights, ranging about the valleys and slopes. He thus came to forget the business of shaving Offertory Rice's dad. He was very hungry when he saw Turtlish Kid and Benevolence tramping along the valley. He thought he should stop them for some food, so he unfurled his arms and climbed down from the top of the mound.

They glimpsed Skedaddle as they entered the valley, but didn't recognise him. They sat down on the roadside and were a little surprised to chance upon a person in such a desolate wasteland. They wanted to say hello to him, but didn't. Instead, they walked by in front of him, without even turning their heads.

Skedaddle had been keeping his eyes on them as they passed by. He felt it unreasonable that they should not greet each other.

"Hi!" Skedaddle shouted.

Turtlish Kid and Benevolence looked back at Skedaddle, waiting to see what words would follow. But Skedaddle fell silent. Without feeling any danger, Benevolence walked up to Skedaddle.

"You were calling out for us?" Benevolence asked.

"Yes," Skedaddle answered.

"Why shout?"

"I was just saying hi!"

"Have you eaten too much that you have time to waste?"

"I am actually hungry," Skedaddle pointed out, "I have been starving for days. No water or rice has touched my teeth."

"Do you have the strength to shout when you are hungry?"

"I was just saying hi!"

"Let me touch your belly." Benevolence reached out his hand.

"Go touch a woman's belly," Skedaddle said, taking one look at Offertory Rice.

"You have such a rich imagination, you son of a bitch," Benevolence barked, punching Skedaddle on his neck. Skedaddle jumped up.

"You hit me," Skedaddle whined.

"I want to amputate your legs from your body," Benevolence replied.

"How daring you are to hit someone whose teeth haven't been touched by water and food for days. Even so, you want to amputate my legs," Skedaddle said while retreating all the way back to the cart. His eyes swept over Offertory Rice and her face left him stunned. What a beautiful face! The red and white are picked out perfectly. He smiled at Benevolence.

"You are escorting a bride, aren't you?" Skedaddle deduced. "Let me feed myself before working for you."

"I'll push the cart." Skedaddle glanced at Offertory Rice.

"Do you know where we are heading?" Turtlish Kid asked.

"I don't care. Are you going to kill some folks?" Skedaddle wanted to know.

"You are right." Benevolence answered.

"I'm not bothered about that. I'd just push the cart."

"You'd be so scared that you'd pee your pants," Benevolence joked.

"You look at people through the cracks in the wall. I have done those things. One swish of a razor and the neck is bloody. You don't believe me? I've travelled to the south, to the north, to many places, so what is there I haven't gone through?" He looked at Offertory Rice again.

"Let me push the cart."

"Could you push it all the way to the village?" Benevolence asked.

"Don't be suspicious. Give me some food, please."

Turtlish Kid dealt Skedaddle a piece of corn pancake. Skedaddle pushed the cart as Turtlish Kid and Benevolence followed on behind, with their hands crossed on their backs.

In that way, Skedaddle was taken in by them.

Later on, they were met with a big tree, under which they bedded down. It was scorching hot.

XIV.

Offertory Rice didn't sleep. She sat on a stone, not far away from them, looking at something in the distance. It was awfully hot; there was a dried-out scent in the air.

Benevolence opened his eyes just in time to see Offertory Rice's taut buttocks, which apparently reminded him of something important. He turned to look at Turtlish Kid and Skedaddle, who were sleeping soundly. He then got up, went over to Offertory Rice and sat down next to her.

"Be careful of Turtlish Kid," Benevolence warned. "I found that he has wicked intentions towards you."

Offertory Rice remained still. It seemed as if she had heard nothing.

"Don't you believe it?" Benevolence asked.

Skedaddle opened his eyes and gave Turtlish Kid a kick on his body.

"Boar-fixers are a rotten bunch with no exception," Benevolence added. "Guard yourself and be sure he doesn't coax you into sleeping with him," he warned sincerely.

Hearing a wave of sound, Benevolence looked back and found Turtlish Kid standing behind him. He was overcome with embarrassment.

"Offertory Rice was smart enough to have found this cool place with a lick of breeze," Benevolence said to Turtlish Kid as he stood up. "You should have a try to see whether I am right or not if you don't believe me."

Turtlish Kid didn't move. He was tempted to give him a thick ear.

"You two should talk, you two should talk." Benevolence stopped talking and sidestepped Turtlish Kid with his body aslant.

Skedaddle was watching them from the distance. He quickly felt the money bag from Turtlish Kid's bedroll, taking out two silver dollars, slipping them into his shoe and then put it on.

In a split second, Turtlish Kid changed his mind. He no longer wanted to slap Benevolence. Instead, he wanted to spit on his face, which, in his mind, was the only way of treating people of this sort. He bowed his head, feeling that there was a lot of phlegm on the tip of his tongue. But he hadn't spat since he witnessed Skedaddle stealing the money.

"You two should talk, you two should talk," said Benevolence.

Turtlish Kid didn't spit out the phlegm.

Offertory Rice turned to look at Turtlish Kid. Her expressive eyes and her taut chest made Turtlish Kid's heart stir.

Nonetheless, Turtlish Kid turned and walked away. Offertory Rice watched his back, with her eyes drooping again. She came up to the cart, stretched her leg again and sat on it. Skedaddle walked quickly to push the cart. A fire was burning in his heart on account of those two shiny silver dollars nesting in his shoe.

"Sister, sit comfortably," he instructed Offertory Rice.

"I'll pick up speed," he anticipated, looping the rope over his shoulders and exerting more strength through his hands. The barrow really did move faster.

"What is nice? Women's thighs are what is nice."

Skedaddle overheard Benevolence making that comment to Turtlish Kid.

"Sister, do you hear me?" Skedaddle was breaking into a sweat. He looked at Offertory Rice's neck as he asked her.

Offertory Rice bumped about on the wooden-wheeled cart as it moved forward.

Skedaddle intended to do something. He had already accomplished one thing – two silver dollars were in his shoe chafing against his foot. Next, he wanted to do a good deed. Good deeds neither tire people nor cause them affliction. So people make it their intention to run into good deeds, constantly do more good deeds, and even drown in good deeds. Thinking in this way as he walked on, Skedaddle kept on looking back to see how far behind him Turtlish Kid and Benevolence were.

"I don't believe women's thighs are good," Skedaddle mused to himself.

Skedaddle reached a resolution. But the wooden-wheeled cart tipped over at the moment he made up his mind. Offertory Rice pitched down from the cart with a cry. Skedaddle ran over to her right away.

"You fell down? Let me see, let me see." He kneaded her ankles and moved his hand upwards along the leg.

"Do you feel any pain here? Here?" he inquired as he kneaded.

"Here? Here?" Skedaddle's hands were kneading down from her thigh.

"What happened? What happened?" exclaimed Benevolence.

"Upended by stones," Skedaddle answered. He pinched Offertory Rice's thigh hard.

Offertory Rice peeked at Skedaddle, who took hold of the handles ready to push again, and smiled at her.

"I have silver dollars," Skedaddle said suddenly.

"I will show you tonight," he continued, smiling again.

Turtlish Kid and Benevolence caught up with them.

"How did you manage to upturn the barrow, son of bitch?" Turtlish Kid flashed out.

Turtlish Kid dragged Skedaddle's arm and pulled him out from the barrow. Skedaddle staggered, but was complacent in his attitude.

"You pushed better than him," Offertory Rice encouraged Turtlish Kid.

Looking at the back of Benevolence's head, Skedaddle felt so unconvinced that he had the urge to teach Benevolence a few words.

"Didn't you say that women's thighs are nice?" asked Skedaddle.

"Yes?" Benevolence felt surprised.

"I don't think they are nice."

"You know nothing about women."

"I've pinched women's thighs." Skedaddle felt proud.

"You know nothing about women," Benevolence insisted.

In Benevolence's mind, Skedaddle knew little about women.

"How many women have you seen? No matter how many you have seen, you just stop at that. Have you smelt their bodies? Have you ever sat on their bellies? You know nothing," Benevolence concluded.

Unbeknownst to Benevolence, Skedaddle had opened his eyes wide and had the impulse to slap him down. Benevolence raised his head high with his hands crossed behind him.

Skedaddle didn't slap. He took a breath and exhaled. He watched Offertory Rice's back and made up his mind for the second time. He thought he must smell her body. He didn't want to ride on her belly. That was of no interest to him. At that moment, waves of pain shot through his foot. He knew this was caused by the two silver dollars under his sole. If Offertory Rice refused to let him smell her, he would tempt her with the money. She was sure to yield to the two silver dollars.

That night, they bedded down at the foot of the cliff. There was no moon in the sky. Skedaddle lay on his back for a while with his shoes as his pillow. Then he whispered to Offertory Rice: "I want to smell your body. You let me smell and I'll give you silver dollars."

Offertory Rice delivered Skedaddle a well-aimed slap square on his face. Skedaddle covered half of his face and attempted to shout but in vain. He had not expected her to whack him like that. Gently, he called out Offertory Rice's name. But

Offertory Rice didn't respond. It seemed as though nothing had happened to her and she fell asleep.

Skedaddle heard the noise of clinking metal, followed by a pair of flying shoes which landed in front of his feet. Skedaddle twisted his head to find Turtlish Kid sitting up straight, with two silver dollars clanking against each other in his hand. Skedaddle felt annoyed that Turtlish Kid was so shameless as to steal his money.

Skedaddle curbed his temper, placed that pair of shoes under his head and went to sleep. A sharp pain was probing into his heart all of the way from the sole of his foot.

At that moment, they all found it hard to fall asleep. They opened their eyes wide in the darkness. They suddenly felt something heavy approaching them.

"Mule-and-Horse Village is another fifty miles away," Turtlish Kid said to himself.

All of them heard some soil slipping down from the cliff face.

"It's going to rain," Benevolence predicted.

More and more clouds did indeed gather above them.

Offertory Rice came up to Turtlish Kid, peering at his dirty face, which made Turtlish Kid confused since he didn't know what she was going to do.

"I am ill-fated," Offertory Rice declared.

She turned over her body, sitting with half of her posterior on the cart. It was still dark, but they had to set off.

xv.

On the wild land stood a hostel, the door of which was tightly closed. Around it was nothing but wasteland.

"Mule-and-Horse Village is next to this hotel," Benevolence murmured in a very weak voice.

Actually, the bandit village itself had never crossed their minds as they went on their journey, but now they couldn't avoid thinking about it since it was their destination. On the cart they pushed was a girl and 3,000 silver dollars.

"Kill Old Eyes." That was what Grandma Six had commanded as she chewed a carrot in her mouth.

The skin on Turtlish Kid's face twitched momentarily. He observed Offertory Rice staring at him, with some expectation in her eyes. A gust of wind blew, which made the red cloth on the bamboo stick dance with a skitter. Then there came a clap of thunder, followed by a downpour. The rain crashed violently on their shoulders and on the cart, forming a rivulet on the ground.

"Turtlish Kid, you should say something, you son of a bitch," Benevolence whooped with a mouthful of rainwater.

"You go on walking if you want to," Benevolence scoffed.

Benevolence stopped at the hostel door and pushed it open.

There was nobody in the courtyard. The doors of the rooms were all closed. It was dead silent except for the sound of rainwater. Something must have happened here.

A sound drifted over to them from the kitchen. An unkempt man was propped up against the wall with his face buried in his chest, as if he had fallen asleep. The fire beneath the pot had gone out. From time to time, a thud was to be heard bursting out of the embers. An unknown substance had been boiling in the vessel.

"Hi," Benevolence shouted at the man loudly. He stepped forward to touch him but the man skewed right over. A dirty face clarted with dried blood came into view.

He was already dead.

Benevolence gave out a cry and then ran frantically around the courtyard, looking for something. He finally found a piece of stone, with which he bashed himself on his ankles a few times.

Turtlish Kid took hold of his hand tightly, pulled him up out of the mud and stared at him ferociously.

Turtlish Kid slapped him on the face.

He then slapped him a second time.

Benevolence watched Turtlish Kid, stupefied. When Turtlish Kid loosened his grip to go over into the room, Benevolence lost his balance and sank into the mud again.

"I won't go there. I'd rather die than go there," cried out Benevolence, "Old Eyes will kill us. Ah, ah…" He shielded his face in agony.

The torrential rain grew much lighter before darkness quickly descended. They stopped pressing on and bedded down there for one night in the hostel.

Offertory Rice was sitting on the *kang* in a wing room, combing her hair. Skedaddle squatted in the corner, gazing at the small dark door of the *kang*. From time to time he looked up at Offertory Rice. She made a sound while tending to her hair. A moment later, Skedaddle fell asleep, with his back leaned against the wall. Offertory Rice threw her braid to her back when it was done and stepped out of the door.

Turtlish Kid was in another room, lying on the hayrick. That was a room for storing hay. Turtlish Kid lay there. Nobody knew what he was thinking.

"Turtlish Kid." Offertory Rice called his name and entered, seeing Turtlish Kid in the hay.

"You guys won't come back alive," concluded Offertory Rice.

"I'm not a virgin girl," she confessed.

Turtlish Kid appeared not to catch her words.

"I have slept with a man," Rice said.

"With my dad. I kid you not." Offertory Rice spilled the beans.

Turtlish Kid's complexion changed dramatically in astonishment.

"Bitch!" Up jumped Turtlish Kid suddenly with a convulsion of his facial muscles. He grabbed Offertory Rice by the shoulder and opened his eyes wide. Gradually, the expression in his eyes came to be complicated and even tender.

"Offertory Rice…," cried out Turtlish Kid in a voice low enough for only her to hear it.

Offertory Rice perceived the expression from Turtlish Kid's

eyes, her breast seemed to be swelling and swelling bit by bit, which made Turtlish Kid find it too hard to control himself. He forced her body into the hay.

"Oh." Offertory Rice's exclamation was as tender as a moan of pleasure.

So was it that Turtlish Kid came to sleep with Offertory Rice. He was gasping, while Offertory Rice was moaning, with her body twisted like a snake. Later, they both found themselves weak-bodied in the hay.

"Turtlish Kid...," Offertory Rice called out.

"Offertory Rice...," Turtlish Kid called, too.

"Marry me and I will go with you." Offertory Rice promised.

Turtlish Kid lay next to Offertory Rice, unresponsive.

"I know you won't marry me." Offertory Rice resigned herself with resentment. She stood up and buttoned her blouse.

"I will never again sit on the barrow you push." She was determined.

When Offertory Rice came out of the hay room, she saw Benevolence standing outside the door. On Offertory Rice's departure, Benevolence rushed in and pounced onto Turtlish Kid. He wanted to ride on his body and beat him up. But he didn't. He was so scared and petrified by Turtlish Kid's eyes that he just held out his hand, assuming the posture of hitting.

"Stand up, Turtlish Kid," Benevolence ordered.

Turtlish Kid stood up.

"Don't move," Benevolence instructed.

Turtlish Kid didn't move.

"I'm going to hit you. Let me do it." Benevolence raised his hand.

Later, Benevolence put down his hand and walked up and down in the room. He was so stirred that he had to scold Turtlish Kid severely.

"You are just a boar-fixer," he started. "Yet daring enough to sleep with Offertory Rice, the bride-to-be. How can there be any guy as ruthless as you on the earth? Granted, she is not a virgin girl, but does that mean you have the right to sleep with her? Turtlish Kid, you put your hands on your chest to think twice, why did you have to sleep with Offertory Rice? Why not somebody else…"

XVI.

True to its name, Mule-and-Horse Village contained many stables with horses, donkeys and mules tethered up in them. The bandits made their livelihood out of gathering pack animals and selling them on. This village was their lair, where they bought animals back from Inner Mongolia, then sold them out to local buyers at the Mule-and-Horse trade fair. They transacted their cattle business in such places as Inner Mongolia, Shanxi and Gansu. It was as though they were dropping in on scattered relatives as they flitted to and fro. They were the type of gang which cherished animals' lives yet would kill people without even blinking. It was their way of life. They did so many things for the beasts: removing hair, encouraging them to mate and breed, cleaning their hooves, and seeing that they were properly shod. They knew those animals as well as they knew their own toes.

They were fellow humans and had grown up eating grain rather than grazing on meadows. Offertory Rice's dad had said as much.

On that day, they were busy as usual in the stable, cracking jokes of many kinds. Their laughter was mixed with the cries of animals, among which the donkey's voice was the most clarion. Someone was cooking in the kitchen.

The highest place in the village was Rock Mound, on which there stood many cave houses. This was where the dealers would sleep. Old Eyes lived in the cave house at the very middle. Its frontage was constructed out of wood.

A road stretched out from where the stables were and

extended to the stone parapet in the distance. Over the parapet were the foothills of the mountain.

Turtlish Kid's company approached on foot from that direction just as a colt was sidling up to a mare in the stable. The bandits who were picking clean the mare's hooves said that it was time to geld that son of a bitch. They heard the creaking noise of wooden wheels. Then they saw Turtlish Kid and his companions.

The visitors were standing by the parapet, with sunshine gleaming on their dirty faces. They were watching the bandits while in turn being watched by the bandits who were somewhat bewildered.

The bandits had thought that Turtlish Kid and his fellows were travellers who had taken a wrong turn. They got back to their own business. Contrary to their expectations, Turtlish Kid's company walked straight in the direction of the stables.

"Where is Old Eyes?" Turtlish Kid asked.

No one answered. A short bandit was chasing after a dog that was running tooth and nail. His barking was as shrill as a knife. When the bandit drew near to it, he deftly reached out his foot to step on one of the dog's hind legs.

Crack! That hind leg broke.

The dog fell down to the ground. Turning its body over, the dog yelped, sadly and shrilly, and continued running, dragging the fractured leg along the ground.

Crack! Came another sound.

A second hind leg was trodden broken.

Benevolence closed his eyes, his own legs now quivering.

The short bandit, who liked playing games, carried the dog in his hands to the kitchen. A pot with boiling water in it was prepared already. Taking up a knife, he slashed the dog's neck.

The bandit stripped off its skin and hung the pelt on the kitchen wall, with the dog's bloody head still attached. The short bandit smiled at other bandits in the stables and slipped the dog meat into the pot.

No one spoke to Turtlish Kid and his companions.

Benevolence's body was festive with fear. He opened his eyes wide and then knelt down on the ground.

"He wants to kill us!" Benevolence suddenly yelled and pointed at Turtlish Kid.

"He is going to kill us!" Benevolence cried.

Turtlish Kid seemed to have momentarily nodded off. He was roused by the bandits' laughter.

The bandits thought Benevolence was a madman.

Scared out of his wits, Benevolence slowly rose from the ground, turned around and ran away. Who knew why he behaved this way? Sometimes people just act up like this.

"He is going to kill us! He is going to kill us!"

Benevolence ran and ran, shouting all the way until he passed the parapet. No one was, in fact, chasing after him.

"Where is Old Eyes?" Turtlish Kid asked.

Skedaddle was still clutching the handles of the barrow, with Offertory Rice on top. She sensed something uncomfortable in her nose. She dug about with her pinky for a second, dislodging a piece of nasal scab. She sniffed twice and flicked the residue from her fingernails. She felt much better.

"Where is Old Eyes?" She heard Turtlish Kid ask others.

Old Eyes was drenching a horse. He was over fifty years old, wore a pair of tawny stone myopic glasses, a white gown and wide-legged trousers. He didn't look like a bandit head but like a middleman. Turtlish Kid would later learn that Old Eyes was not actually a bad guy. He was pleasant enough. Offertory Rice said as much.

The horse twisted its neck painfully, making it awkward to pour medicine into its mouth.

Skedaddle pushed the barrow straight up to Old Eyes. Offertory Rice alighted gracefully.

Turtlish Kid untied the money bag and poured out a pile of silver dollars onto the ground. Old Eyes didn't give it one look.

"It was a joke, but you people took it seriously." He finally dumped medicine into the horse's mouth and then cast a look at the face of Offertory Rice.

"It was just a joke," he repeated.

Turtlish Kid was so overwhelmed with indignation that he screamed loudly at Old Eyes.

"Fuck your mother!"

Turtlish Kid's eyes welled up with tears.

"All the people of my village have suffered because of you." Turtlish Kid felt relieved.

Old Eyes was not put out at all.

"People always make trouble out of nothing. Much ado about nothing. You've never heard people say that?" Old Eyes excused himself and gave Offertory Rice a second look.

"Go, let's go home," Skedaddle proposed.

"Hey, since you have come here you may as well take a few days rest," Old Eyes suggested.

They duly rested in the village as they had been told

XVII.

Turtlish Kid sat cross-legged on the *kang* in the stable. It had been arranged that they should sleep there, sharing the shed with a few cattle.

"This place is not so bad." Skedaddle felt satisfied with the arrangements. He peeped here and there.

Turtlish Kid was rolling a cigarette.

"Time to eat dog meat—"

They could hear the short bandit shouting. The kitchen was visible through the stable window. The short bandit lifted the lid from the pot and took a draught of the hot steam. Tempted as he was to lift out a morsel to eat, the meat was still too hot. He quickly withdrew his hand, blowing on it. Other bandits held their bowls, waiting beside the pot to see when the dog was ready to eat.

"I am gonna get some." Skedaddle stood up.

Bandits glanced at Skedaddle. Skedaddle pointed at the pot.

"Will you share some with me?" Skedaddle ventured to plead with them.

A bandit picked up a piece of meat and put it into Skedaddle's bowl.

"Eat. We eat. Fuck," Skedaddle snarled at Turtlish Kid. He slapped down the bowl heavily on the table.

Turtlish Kid didn't move. His eyes remained on Old Eyes' wooden room, which was visible from through the stable door. The short bandit was knocking on Old Eyes' wooden door, with a big bowl of choicest dog meat. He inclined his head and listened attentively, grimacing at the other bandits.

The door opened. Old Eyes came out, his body saturated with hot sweat.

"Leave the meat outside," Old Eyes demanded impatiently.

Old Eyes peed by the wooden door, then picked up the bowl and closed the door again.

"Fuck his mother," Skedaddle cursed. He felt indignant.

Skedaddle began to chew at the meat. Wrathfully he tried to flay whatever meat was left on the bone he had been served.

"What a world. Eat, we eat," Skedaddle groaned in agony.

"Fuck his mother," Skedaddle cursed a second time.

Turtlish Kid put out his roll-up cigarette. Several sparks fell from the butt. It was now dark.

The bright moon was high in the sky. The bandits had fallen asleep. Among those few rows of stables, a sprinkling of lights had not yet been put out. Occasionally the snorts of cattle and restless hooves were to be heard.

Skedaddle took off his pants, singing a couple of lines of a romantic folksong:

Undo your button first and then unbutton your arm,
Then un-belt your pants,
Let me play with you...

Old Eyes' wooden door was still shut tightly. Turtlish Kid

didn't sleep a wink the whole night, thinking about how Offertory Rice had come to sleep with Old Eyes. Skedaddle was so dog-tired that he slumbered like a log.

At dawn, Old Eyes came to see Turtlish Kid.

"Offertory Rice is not a virgin," Old Eyes concluded.

Turtlish Kid pulled a long face. He saw Offertory Rice walk out of the wooden door with an empty basin in her hand. She went to the kitchen, filled the basin with water and entered the timbered room again.

"She has slept with men," Old Eyes stated.

"Yes," Turtlish Kid admitted.

"I am afraid that you would have slept with her since you guys walked for a number of days to get here." Old Eyes surmised.

"No, no." Turtlish Kid dared not tell him the truth.

"What kind of person do you take me for?" He added, seeming to grin at Old Eyes.

"A big arse, fatty," Old Eyes scoffed.

Old Eyes took out a shovel from behind his rear end.

"Let me show you around the stables." Old Eyes changed the topic. He appeared to have forgotten about Offertory Rice's escapades with men.

"These horses were brought back from Mongolia." Old Eyes was proud as he introduced them to Turtlish Kid. He showed Turtlish Kid around a number of stables. He was very skilled at picking hooves clean. He held onto their legs and picked their hooves with two movements of his shovel. Then he put down their legs and slapped them once or twice on their rump.

"Pedigree Mongolian horses, which can make me a one hundred and fifty per cent return." Old Eyes was overcome with still greater pride.

After having been shown around, Turtlish Kid felt relieved and at ease. He even forgot the fact that Old Eyes was a bandit. He took him as a capable man. He was bewildered as to why it was that he had become a desperado. Maybe there are things in the world which happen without obeying any rules.

"Kill Old Eyes," the old woman had ordered as she chewed on her carrot.

XVIII.

That morning, Turtlish Kid paid attention to how one gang of bandits were loading packs onto the backs of animals, as if they were preparing for a long journey.

"They're going to Dingbian, a border town, to drop in at the horse fair. If you're planning on making a move back home you could go with them," Old Eyes said to Turtlish Kid.

Turtlish Kid didn't have any plan to return, nor did he speak a single word for half the morning.

"Stay a few more days if you like," Old Eyes offered, one of his hands touching a mare's belly.

"There's a pregnant foal over here," he declared.

A colt raised its hooves and cantered over to Old Eyes, its bristles tossing up and down like water.

"It's time to geld this son of bitch," Old Eyes exclaimed.

"Let me do it," Turtlish Kid chimed in.

The bandits had loaded their horses.

"This time they must go for a good price," one bandit asserted firmly.

"We should go to Mongolia on our way to Dingbian and then back from Shanxi Province," another bandit proposed. "Shanxi women have big knockers."

Offertory Rice came out from the wooden door to pour out water. She was carrying a basin, staring in the direction of the stable. She saw Skedaddle bending down to drink water from a large crock. After Skedaddle could be sure that nobody was paying any attention to him, he laid down the ladle and crept towards the wooden house.

"Offertory Rice." He peeked into the house through the window, which was on a side wall of the house.

She was sitting on the *kang*.

"How did Old Eyes treat you?" Skedaddle asked with a look of shamelessness.

Pooh! Offertory Rice spat onto Skedaddle's face through the window.

"Please let me in. I want to have a word with you."

Offertory Rice opened the door. Skedaddle stepped into the room together with the sunshine.

"Clever Offertory Rice." Skedaddle sat down on the stool, comfortably curling one of his legs. Some leftover dog meat was on the table. Skedaddle took up a piece and put it into his mouth.

"Old Eyes' place isn't bad," Skedaddle commented.

Offertory Rice was counting a stack of sheepskins. She seemed dissatisfied with them and so didn't take in Skedaddle's lament.

"Look at these three-month-old lamb fleeces." Offertory Rice invited Skedaddle to inspect them.

"Old Eyes managed to get them from Mongolia," she observed.

Skedaddle had apparently hit upon a major secret. He opened his round eyes bit by bit and made an effort to swallow the dog meat in his mouth.

"Offertory Rice, do you really want to spend the rest of your life with Old Eyes?" Skedaddle couldn't believe it.

Meanwhile, Turtlish Kid was going about gelding the colt. Old Eyes and a few other bandits had fastened it to a wooden stake. He was as skilled at fixing horses as he was pigs. He made, in that place, what appeared to be the identical type of cut he made when fixing pigs. He wiped the bloody blade once or twice on his trousers.

Skedaddle told Offertory Rice the story of how he had shaved a person dead in her home village.

"In his mind, I was giving him a shave." Skedaddle began his yarn in an enraptured way. "I slashed his neck while I was doing it. It only took one stroke of my knife to make his neck bloodied. Don't you believe me?"

"That was my dad," Offertory Rice gasped, without raising her head.

Skedaddle's eyes became as big as dinner plates.

"Your dad? You're saying he was your dad?" Skedaddle repeated.

"Was it you who slashed my dad to death?"

"You are kidding me."

"Who slashed your dad dead?" asked Old Eyes who entered the room at this very moment.

"Nobody did. Offertory Rice is joking. Hey hey, ho ho." Skedaddle appeared not to smile in the way he used to smile. He headed for the door.

"Killing your dad is killing my father-in-law," Old Eyes said as he beamed at Offertory Rice.

"Don't joke with me. Ho ho, you two stay, I'm leaving." Skedaddle treaded backwards with the bowl of leftover dog meat, and then started to run.

Skedaddle found Turtlish Kid by the edge of the cliff.

"Offertory Rice doesn't want to leave with us. She wants to stay here where there's money and plenty to eat instead," Skedaddle told Turtlish Kid.

Turtlish Kid was livid-faced in meditation. Skedaddle put that bowl of dog meat in front of Turtlish Kid.

"Eat it. I cadged it from Old Eyes' room."

"She wants to live with Old Eyes," he added.

"I didn't realize that she was that type of person," he complained.

"Bitch!" he blurted out.

Turtlish Kid made no response. His jaws bit against each other tightly and his cheeks bulged.

"What do you think we should do?" Skedaddle asked.

"Fuck! How bad it is that we come across such a thing," he moaned.

He noticed Turtlish Kid putting something into his mouth and chewing.

"Are you going to leave this big issue alone? If you think you're a man, you should do something. What's more, you've already slept with Offertory Rice." Skedaddle tried to cajole him in this way.

Finally Skedaddle saw clearly that Turtlish Kid had nothing in his mouth except for clods. Turtlish Kid was chewing at clods in no hurry. He then lifted another from the ground.

"Are you eating earth?" Skedaddle was shocked.

"Why do you eat earth?" Skedaddle asked.

Skedaddle turned away frightened, his face twisted in an ugly fashion.

"Ah ha, you're eating dirt," Skedaddle screamed. "He is eating dirt! This son of bitch is eating dirt!"

Turtlish Kid's mouth was filled with wet mud.

The bandits set out their long journey. They came out of stables, walking onto the road and passed by the parapet.

"He's eating dirt!" Skedaddle shouted.

Skedaddle went back to the stable, knelt down on the *kang* and thought of Turtlish Kid with wet mud in his mouth.

XIX.

It was still dark when Old Eyes came over to Turtlish Kid and asked him to help slice hay for the animals. Old Eyes said that as folks get older, they need to sleep less and less. Turtlish Kid replied that young people sometimes find it hard to fall asleep as well. Old Eyes concluded that this being so they should chat together as they cut the straw. Turtlish Kid agreed and put on his shoes.

There was a haystack in front of a stable. Turtlish Kid lifted and pressed the hay cutter while Old Eyes lay the hay between the two blades of the contraption. Both of them were good at cutting hay.

There came the sound of hay-cutting.

A few red rays gradually appeared on the horizon like the bloodstains scratched by jujube thorns. Offertory Rice was still asleep and so were the other bandits who stayed at home. Mule-and-Horse Village was quiet, save for the rustle of hay being sliced. Skedaddle opened his eyes to see that Turtlish Kid wasn't under his quilt. He guessed that Turtlish Kid had gone out to pee. He then closed his eyes and turned over his frame to continue sleeping.

There came the sound of hay-cutting.

The cutter chopped down forcefully while crushed hay came out and rolled to one side of the device. Every time the cutter was lifted neatly, clipped edges were to be seen. Old Eyes pressed down on the hay with his knees and handed it over to Turtlish Kid, who held the handle of the cutter, severing hay as he lifted and pressed the handle, up and down.

Turtlish Kid pressed down the cutter ruthlessly. He swept the crushed hay aside with his hand.

"You're not bad in my eyes. That's why you're being allowed to stay in our village instead of having to go back to yours," Old Eyes opined.

"There are little tricks when doing our business. When you go to Mongolia, you can borrow money from them. Don't borrow too much. You can borrow twenty bucks at first and then give them back thirty in return. They hope that people are prepared to borrow money from them. So borrow 300 the second time and go to other places to buy horses. The world is too big for them to find you! Fuck!" Old Eyes bared his heart to Turtlish Kid.

"You shouldn't be afraid when you do this business, nor should you fear death. Gutsy men are capable of doing anything. They can get whatever they want," Old Eyes instructed.

Old Eyes spoke unhurriedly, like he was telling a matter-of-fact story. No longer looking at Turtlish Kid, who he knew was listening, he buried his head.

Turtlish Kid wore a terrible look on his face. His mouth was very dry with some white chapping on the lips. Veins bulged on his temples and his eye sockets were like two soil pits.

"Kill Old Eyes." That was what Grandma Six had commanded.

"Fuck his mother," Turtlish Kid grunted in his throat. If there were anybody around to hear, they wouldn't have known who he was condemning – Grandma Six or Old Eyes.

Old Eyes failed to catch his words. Stopping passing straw to Turtlish Kid, he rather turned to take a close look at Turtlish Kid's face, without realizing that his hand was under the hay cutter.

"What?" he asked.

Turtlish Kid lopped the cutter down hard. This was followed by the sound of carpal bones splintering. Old Eyes' two hands were amputated at the wrist and fell down from the cutter onto the white crushed hay.

Old Eyes did not feel any pain. He didn't know what had happened. He opened his mouth and kept his eyes fixed on Turtlish Kid, who he thought had said something. Later, the pain hit him and his body curled into a ball and rolled about on the ground.

Turtlish Kid was dumbstruck for a while. He thought he should come up with a way of finishing the matter off. So he ran to the stable in search of something. He finally found a hoe. He picked it up and ran to the rolled-up Old Eyes who was wailing and shouting.

He pounded Old Eyes twice with the back of the hoe. It seemed that striking a human head was no different from smashing hard clods of soil. Thus he dispatched with Old Eyes, whose tawny stone myopic glasses were broken into two, with drops of pink liquid on the lenses. At that moment the sun was making every effort to emerge shred by shred from within layers of clouds. In the process of squeezing out of the clouds, a breaking sound was almost audible.

XX.

After he had made his descent down the slope outside his home village Skedaddle started to scream.

"Killed! He killed Old Eyes."

He ran hysterically onto the main street of his home village, causing chickens to flutter and dogs to yelp.

Skedaddle had never been as proud as he was that day. All the folks stampeded to greet him at the entrance of the village. They encircled him and listened as he told the most remarkable story in the world. Their eyes occasionally twinkled as they stretched wide open. Such was the degree of their spiritual hunger that they appeared to relish being made to feel profoundly astonished.

"Killed?" Tether-tight stretched his neck as limber as that of a wild goose.

"Give me some water to drink," Skedaddle ordered.

Someone handed Skedaddle a bowl of water. He tossed back that vessel. The villagers stared at his mouth, waiting for him to relate the tale.

"Cigarette," Skedaddle demanded.

Someone gave him a whole pack. He took two sharp drags.

"Killed?" Benevolence asked. He had come over, too.

Skedaddle glared at Benevolence in a despicable way.

"Human heads everywhere …" Skedaddle started.

"Ah." The village was in tumult.

"Everywhere?" People were surprised.

"Yes, everywhere…" Skedaddle repeated.

"Dead bodies piled like mountains…" Skedaddle described.

"Like mountains?"

Yes, like mountains."

"Mountains…"

"Blood gushing like rivers…" Skedaddle went on with his story.

"Like rivers?"

"Like rivers…?"

"Rivers?"

Skedaddle rabbited on like a drunkard. His story gave villagers such flushes of excitement that they didn't know what to do.

"Coming," someone shouted all of a sudden.

There was an awesome silence among people. They turned their heads around to see Turtlish Kid, standing atop the slope, the two red pieces of cloth on his neck flickering in the wind. He stood there for a while, then trod down along the slope and headed for the entrance to the village.

Turtlish Kid was right there before them.

He watched the villagers as the villagers watched him, sensing something alien. They stood there, completely unmoved. Presently, Turtlish Kid noticed that someone intended to slip away.

"You're back," Tether-tight said uneasily, his face twitching a bit.

"Hee hee." Tether-tight smiled in a friendly fashion.

"Go back to hold the baby." Benevolence kicked his wife's butt. Her belly was bulging a little.

Later on, the people peeled away one after another. Skedaddle looked around, not knowing what was wrong with them. His eyes moved rapidly.

"Hee hee." Skedaddle smiled at Turtlish Kid.

Skedaddle was gone, too.

Turtlish Kid was left alone at the entrance of the village, his face masked with dirt. Nobody knew what he was thinking at that time.

On that day, villagers braised big bowls of food for Turtlish Kid to eat, accompanied by Tether-tight, Morality Liu and a number of other neighbours. They also fried pots of seedcakes for all the villagers to eat in front of Grandma Six's house. Tether-tight swanked along the street, beating his drum as he chanted loudly: "Eat seedcakes in front of Grandma Six's house!"

"Turtlish Kid, these dishes were made especially for you,"

said Tether-tight, pointing at the bowls.

Turtlish Kid tipped a bottle of liquor down his throat, like he was pouring away dirty water.

"Eat!" Turtlish Kid invited.

Turtlish Kid forked his chopsticks and lodged them into a bowl of sliced fatty meat.

Later on, People witnessed Turtlish Kid singing as he waddled out of Grandma Six's house, with a smile on his face.

Coming, coming, coming
Coming with red and green
Coming, coming, coming
Coming into the flowery gate

They saw him totter through the earthen gate of his house. Outside the gate were many adobe bricks, which formed squares when stacked together. It occurred to them that Turtlish Kid, the boar-fixer, had pledged that he wouldn't build any more big rooms until he had a woman.

XXI.

Grandma Six's face exuded grease. It looked as though she had been applying lotion. On the cabinet cover was a pile of seedcakes, lanced together with a vertical chopstick, so they stood like a small tower. Inside her room, it was dimly lit. The people present buried their faces in the shadows.

"We can't shelter a person of this kind any longer," someone murmured.

"Of course, we can't. Who knows what disaster he will bring on us?" Benevolence echoed, squatting in the most inconspicuous corner.

"He killed Old Eyes. As a result, those bandits are sure to kill us," he surmised.

"Just you wait and see," he warned.

"He killed Old Eyes. Who knows who he will kill next?"

Benevolence spelled out the threat.

Grandma Six didn't say a word. She reached her hand over that pile of seedcakes for a carrot. With tensed muscles, yet agitated spirits, they watched the old lady. There came the inauspicious sound of chewing again, audible enough to be frightening. It was as if something were making their flesh crawl.

The moonlight that night was very bright. A hound barked somewhere several times. Many figures of men flashed out of their gates, passing through the streets and stopping in front of Turtlish Kid's earthen gate. They gave the impression of having something to discuss, but did not speak a word.

Turtlish Kid was sleeping on his *kang*. A thick red candle was burning on a wooden ledge on the wall. The emblem of his profession had been casually flung over onto the other side of his brick bed. On top of the kitchen range, connected to the *kang*, sat a big black porcelain bowl.

"Turtlish Kid," a man called in a tender tone from outside the door.

"Turtlish Kid, open up."

Turtlish Kid didn't wake up.

"Open the door!" The sound grew louder.

Turtlish Kid came to himself and had a sudden pang of thirst. He then embraced the big black porcelain bowl and drank.

The knocking sound started up again and grew louder and louder, the planks of the door vibrating violently. Turtlish Kid sensed that something was amiss. He heard the noise of the paper on the window lattice being poked. Then a finger was to be seen pressing in through a hole in the paper.

The window paper was now torn. Turtlish Kid caught sight of a number of human heads. He hadn't experienced anything of the like before, but had the urge to grasp hold of something with which to guard himself. A crowd of people flocked in through the door.

Nobody knew how Turtlish Kid met his end. That night, many people heard a baleful din emanating from his house.

But each kept to his or her own *kang*, listening attentively in silence, their eyes agape.

They didn't close the door after leaving the room where Turtlish Kid slept. A brook of blood trickled out from the threshold, like snakes creeping freely about the ground.

They rolled up their trouser legs and started to tread the earth into mud.

"Young men have more blood in their bodies than old ones," the people said with their eyes on that bloody river.

They stood in a line between the earthen gate and the room with blood flowing out, passing adobe bricks from one hand to another. Benevolence sealed up the door by laying bricks carefully within the door frame with a trowel, not leaving even the slightest crack.

He also blocked up the window.

He then daubed a layer of plaster over the adobe bricks.

Slaw, slaw – The trowel was his tool of choice. The more he smeared the smoother the layer of mud became. He didn't quit until dawn.

Slaw, slaw – He still made that slathering noise.

He raised his head and looked into the first light in the distance. His eyes happened upon the bun-like mountains which were reminiscent of his wife's breasts. He thought that his woman must still be asleep on the *kang*. There was still enough time for him to slip back and do something. He would pinch her chubby legs if she was not willing to cooperate with him. If he pinched, she was sure to cave in. When he left Turtlish Kid's house, he noticed that lines of dried blood were still laid plain to see, so he grabbed and thrust handfuls of mud to make them indistinct.

Many days later, at dawn, the sound of cantering beasts could be heard. All of the locals perceived it. The village was besieged by a gang of people who rode animals.

They were none other than the bandits from the Mule-and-Horse Village.

Notes on the Text

WEIGHTS AND MEASURES

Various traditional Chinese weights and measures are used in the course of the text:

1 *mu* = approximately 663 2/3 square metres.

1 *li* = approximately 0.5 kilometres

1 *dou* = approximately 15 kilograms

TIMEFRAME

One idiosyncrasy in Mr. Yang Zhengguang's writing style is that some of his stories are obviously set in a specific moment in history whereas others are more indeterminate. On being pressed on this issue, he has clarified:

"Dark Scenery" is the earliest tale chronologically, belonging to the lawless days of the Warlord Era (1916-28) when banditry was rife. "How Old Dan Became a Tree" and "The Billy Goat Pops In" come a decade or so after that. "Buying Wives" depicts life in the 1950s or 1960s. However, including as it does a practice that persists in remote areas to this day, so is intended to unsettle the reader. "The Road from Sandy Terrace Town" was my first effort at story-writing and was inspired by two figures I spotted in the hills of Northern Shaanxi around thirty years ago.

In "Blue Fish" there are references to three grassroots campaigns enacted under the leadership of Mao Zedong:

"Smelting Iron to Make Steel" was one of the early and shorter-lived movements begun as part of the Great Leap Forward in 1958. Under the mistaken wisdom that refined steel could be smelted by ordinary citizens (thereby kick-starting the process of industrializing the county), the government encouraged households to construct backyard furnaces, melting down any iron implements they could lay their hands on and consigning wood to the fire.

"Taking Rations Together Collectively" was the practice of all villagers eating in communal dining halls rather than cooking meals privately at home, also begun in 1958.

"The Four Clean Ups Movement" was instigated by Mao Zedong in 1963 and lasted until 1966. It aimed to root out perceived "reactionary elements" from within the Chinese Communist Party. The titular "four" in want of cleansing were politics, economy, organization, and ideology.

Although it is not mentioned by name, in "The Red Heat" Yellow Plum, her family and neighbours participate in the "Four Pests Campaign" (unofficially referred to as "The Great Sparrow Campaign" or the "Kill a Sparrow Campaign"). As part of the Great Leap Forward, the populace was exhorted to try and eradicate three species which were known carriers of disease (mosquitoes, rodents, and flies) together with the sparrows which pilfered grain and seeds. Within two years the decimation of the bird population made clear the crucial role played by sparrows in the ecosystem. They not only ate the crops, but the insects which preyed on the same vegetables and cereals. In order to save face, Chairman Mao promptly substituted bedbugs for sparrows. This would place Yellow Plum's year of birth as c. 1946.

The character would have been slightly on the older side to be playing the seventeen-year-old Iron Plum Li. *The Legend of the Red Lantern* was one of the Eight Model Operas (eventually ten more were added to the repertoire), the only form of entertainment sanctioned for the masses during the Cultural Revolution (1966-76). Mao Zedong's wife, Jiang Qing (herself a former actress), oversaw the replacement of traditional Beijing opera with these ideology-fuelled productions. The other heroines mentioned here, Jiang Shuiying, the White-Haired

Girl, Wu Qinghua (a historical figure), and Little Changbao featured in other operas in the series, namely *Song of the Dragon River*, *The White-Haired Girl*, *Red Detachment of Women*, and *Taking Tiger Mountain by Strategy*.

A handful of folk customs or popular references warrant explanation. Gallant Ren in "Blue Fish" talks of connoisseurs "chewing" tea rather than "drinking" it. In ancient times, tea was sweetmeat as opposed to a beverage, so even today tea experts talk of "eating" the brew made from the leaves. When 'Peering' Zhou in the same story observes that "'the CCP is not the KMT" he means that the Chinese Communist Party prides itself on its humane treatment of prisoners and suspects, whereas the former Nationalist (KMT) regime was said to resort to torture or duress during interrogations.

In "How Old Dan Became a Tree" Huanhuan is seconded to care for Zhao Zhen's wife during her "lying-in after giving birth." Traditionally, it was believed that a new mother should spend one month (thirty days) in confinement in the same home with her baby. This was intended to protect the health of the both. Virtuous Wang in "Dark Scenery" is furious when his wife scolds him as a "turtle egg." This insult is akin to calling someone a "bastard" since the turtle was perceived to be remiss in its parenting skills, merely burying its eggs under the sand and leaving the hatchlings to fend for, and cultivate, themselves. Old Dan's favoured put-down involving a donkey is a local Shaanxi obscenity. The insinuation is that the person's mother was raped by a donkey before giving birth and so they came out of the womb sub-humanly stupid.

Acknowledgements

The original Chinese versions of the stories were first published in the following literary journals:

"Blue Fish" in *Yanhe* (April 1994): *The Shaanxi Writers Volume*
"How Old Dan Became a Tree" in *Harvest* (February 1992)
"The Red Heat" in *Authors* (July 2000)
"The Billy Goat Pops In" in *Literary Friend* (October 1999)
"Buying Wives" in *The Novelists* (April 1995)
"The Road from Sandy Terrace Town" in *China* (September 1986)
"Dark Scenery" in *Harvest* (January 1990)

"Blue Fish" and "How Old Dan Became a Tree" were translated by Professor Hu Zongfeng (Northwest University), "The Red Heat" by Liu Xiaofeng (Civil Aviation University of China, Tianjin), "The Billy Goat Pops In" and "The Road from Sandy Terrace Town" by He Longping (Changsha Normal University), "Buying Wives" by Dr. Zhang Min (Northwest University), and "Dark Scenery" by Dr. Su Rui (Northwest University). Dr. Robin Gilbank cooperated closely in the editing and preparation of each text.

The author and translators wish to thank Jamie McGarry and Valley Press for bringing this volume to fruition. Financial support was provided by the Shenzhen Association of Literature and Art and the Centre for Chinese Literary Criticism at Northwest University. Thanks are also due to Professor Mu Tao for his role in facilitating the project and to Dr. J. Graham Jones for his assistance in proofreading.